DARK
ROAD FROM
SUNRISE

ALSO BY A.M. STRONG AND SONYA SARGENT

THE PATTERSON BLAKE THRILLER SERIES

Sister Where Are You • *Is She Really Gone*
All The Dead Girls • *Never Let Her Go*
Dark Road From Sunrise • *I Will Find Her*

PATTERSON BLAKE PREQUEL

Never Lie to Me

DARK
ROAD FROM
SUNRISE

A PATTERSON BLAKE THRILLER

A.M. STRONG
SONYA SARGENT

WEST
STREET

West Street Publishing

Cover art and interior design by Bad Dog Media, LLC.

ISBN: 978-1-942207-51-1

For Izzie and Hayden

PROLOGUE

THREE WEEKS BEFORE

THE HOUSE WAS TOO QUIET. *The silence pressed around Angel even as she tried to contain her panic. She had woken up hours ago and had been waiting ever since for Ma to unlock her door, which normally happened at 8AM sharp. It was now three-thirty in the afternoon, and she had not yet been freed or seen any sign of Ma. Unless the decades-old digital clock sitting on a nightstand next to the bed with the iron frame was wrong. But she had no way to know because there were no windows in the room. The only illumination came from an overhead ceiling light and a floor lamp with a low-wattage bulb.*

The space had not always been like that. When she first arrived, the bedroom had a window that looked out onto a yard filled with junk and enclosed by a high fence.

Within a few days, the man she knew as Carl had come home with concrete blocks and bricked the window up permanently. Now she only got to see the outside world for a few hours each day when she was allowed out of her room to perform household chores, eat at the kitchen table, or perform what Carl liked to call her nightly duties, when he would take her to his bedroom at the back of the house for an hour or two. Not that there was much to see through the home's grimy windows. Just a dusty landscape that fell to the horizon, broken only by the rusting shells of a pickup truck, at least two cars, and a couple of large barns, one of which was falling in upon itself, the roof sagging in the middle as if it had the weight of the world upon its back. She assumed this property must have once been a farm, or maybe a cattle ranch, but the land showed no sign of current usage.

"Mommy, I'm hungry," said a voice to Angel's left. She turned to see her five-year-old daughter, Cherub, sitting on a narrow bed and watching her with an exasperated look.

"I know, sweetie," she said, approaching the door and pressing an ear to the flaking painted surface.

Still no sound.

She reached down and tried the handle even though she knew it would be locked. "I'll get us both something to eat just as soon as I can, okay?"

"When?" came the reply.

"I don't know, honey. You'll have to be patient." Angel turned her attention back to the door. She gathered the nerve to call out, but then hesitated for fear of antagonizing Ma and raising the older woman's ire. Carl was away on one of his trips, and Ma always treated her worse when he left them alone together. But something wasn't right. Maybe this was just one of those slivers of mental torture—leaving her and Cherub locked in this room all day without food and water.

And maybe that was the point. Ma was sending a message. Carl might think he's in charge, but it's really me, and I choose when you eat and drink and sleep.

But Angel didn't think so. Something wasn't right.

She took a deep breath, glanced toward her daughter, and then banged a fist on the door. Consequences be damned. "Hello? Is anybody out there?"

The deed done, Angel took an instinctive step back, expecting the door to fly open and Ma to rush in, face flushed with rage. But the silence remained unbroken.

Angel hesitated for a few seconds, unsure what to do next. Was this part of Ma's plan to let her know who was in control? Make Angel and her daughter scream and beg to get the basic necessities. Maybe . . . But if it was, the woman was drawing out her cruel games longer than usual.

Angel decided that whatever Ma was up to couldn't be worse than watching her daughter go hungry. She went back to the door and pounded on it again with a clenched fist, hollering at the top of her lungs to elicit a response.

Nothing.

Ma remained stubbornly absent. The door stayed locked.

"Mommy, what are we going to do?" Cherub watched her with fearful eyes.

"I don't know." Angel went to the bed and sat down next to her daughter. She put an arm around her and held the child close. "Let's wait a bit longer, okay?"

The little girl didn't look convinced. But after a moment, she nodded mutely and laid her head against her mother's shoulder. Angel wasn't the only one who knew and feared Ma's sharp tongue. And neither of the two could be sure this wasn't some cruel trap. An excuse for Ma to vent her anger at being left alone with the pair while Carl was off doing whatever he did in the big world beyond the old house for weeks at a time.

They sat that way for another hour—mother and daughter—locked in the grip of fear fueled indecision. Then, as if an unspoken consensus had been reached, Angel looked at her daughter, stood back up, and approached the still locked door with a determination she never thought possible.

She tried the handle again, not because she expected anything to have changed, but because she needed to feel that unyielding refusal to open in order to do what must come next.

Satisfied there was no other way, Angel lowered her shoulder, still gripping the door handle with one hand, and slammed it into the door. The result was a nerve-jarring stab of pain that shot down her arm and into her chest, but did nothing to ease their captivity.

She waited, wondering if the sudden noise would bring Ma scurrying. When it didn't, Angel gritted her teeth and tried again, harder this time. All she got for her efforts was another bolt of whimper-inducing pain.

Standing back and rubbing her sore shoulder, she stared at the still locked door. Her shoulder would not do it. That was obvious. What she needed was something heavier. She looked around at the beds, and the closet which had once held clothes but now served as a makeshift bathroom with a bucket inside that she was forced to empty daily. Then her gaze came to rest on the floor lamp standing in the corner of the room. It was old and heavy, made of some unidentified metal. She unplugged it and hefted the lamp from the floor, surprised that it weighed so much.

Weight was good.

If she held it sideways, the wide end that sat on the floor would make an excellent battering ram.

Angel approached the door again and heaved the lamp backwards, then used its own weight to gain momentum as she swung it forward toward a spot between the door handle and a deadbolt that Carl had installed many years before.

Her first blow was disappointing. The door shuddered in its frame but didn't move.

The second was better.

A sharp cracking sound rewarded Angel's effort and a gap appeared between the door and the inner frame.

On the third blow, the door snapped open on its hinges in a hail of broken wood.

Angel took a step over the threshold into the dark corridor beyond. Here she paused, listening, ears straining to pick up the slightest hint of footsteps. There were none.

A small hand slipped into hers and tugged. "Mommy, you can't go out there. Ma won't like it."

Angel looked down at Cherub. "It's okay. I don't think she's coming."

"I'm scared."

"There's no need to be scared," Angel lied, gripping her daughter's hand and guiding her down the corridor.

From somewhere, she heard the faint murmur of a voice and her heart rate quickened. But then she realized it wasn't Ma or Carl. It sounded more like the TV.

She breathed a sigh of relief and pushed on, passing the bedroom where she performed her nightly duties for Carl whenever fancy took him. She glanced sideways into the room, noting the neatly made bed where Cherub had been conceived, and a shudder prickled her spine.

Across the hallway was another bedroom where Ma slept. The door was closed. Angel had only been in the room a few times and hadn't liked it. A smell hung in the air. The odor of cough syrup and disease. There were pill bottles everywhere. On her nightstand. On the window ledge. Even on top of the dresser. It was almost like Ma collected medicine. The hobby of an addict.

Angel placed a hand on the doorknob and leaned close.

"Ma. You in there?" she asked in a voice barely above a whisper because Angel wasn't sure she wanted an answer.

She didn't get one.

Angel's fingers curled over the doorknob. She turned it and let the door creak open on tired hinges.

Ma's bed was unmade, the sheets twisted and wrinkled. A head shaped dent on the pillow corresponded to a large brown sweat stain. But there was no Ma.

Angel closed the door and continued through the house.

The voices were getting louder the closer she got to the front of the building. It sounded like a talk show. One of those vapid daytime programs that always seemed to be on.

She poked her head into the living room, half expecting to see the TV playing and Ma sitting on the brown fabric sofa that had been there ever since Angel came to stay with them. But the TV was turned off, the sofa was unoccupied.

That only left the kitchen.

And now she saw the source of the chatter. A small twenty-four-inch flatscreen that Carl had mounted on the wall next to the breakfast nook so Ma could watch her shows while she cooked.

Then she saw Ma.

The old woman was sprawled on her back near the stove. She wore a pastel blue housecoat that had fallen open to reveal doughy pale skin. Her eyes were milky and dull. They stared unblinkingly at the ceiling. A purple tongue, engorged and fat, poked out between her lips.

Angel swallowed a scream.

Ma was dead. And she must have been that way for a while. Probably the night before, because a bag of popcorn sat inside the open microwave above the stove. Ma's late-night snack. If the Grim Reaper hadn't intervened, she would have plucked that bag from the microwave, sat on that brown ratty sofa in the living room, and watched the late-night talk shows until she couldn't keep her eyes open anymore and hauled her flabby junk food fattened body to bed.

Angel heard a sharp inhalation of breath, followed by a whimper. Shit. Her daughter.

"Don't look, sweetie," she said, even though she knew it was too late. "Go into the living room and stay there. Wait for mommy."

The young girl didn't move.

"Go. Now!"

When the girl still didn't move, Angel turned and physically bundled her out of the kitchen. She pushed her daughter into the living room, returned to the kitchen, and stood over Ma's corpse, wondering what to do.

She was alone in the house with her daughter. That presented an opportunity. But if she ran and Carl caught her, he would kill them both. Then he would kill Angel's family. He had made that threat often enough.

Yet if she stayed and Carl came home, he would almost certainly blame Angel for his mother's death. What would he do to her then? What would he do to her daughter?

That thought spurred Angel into action because she didn't want to find out. There was money in the house. She knew it. Carl didn't trust banks. They would need money if they were going to get away from this horrific place. But where would he hide it?

Angel ran from the kitchen, went to Carl's bedroom. She lifted the mattress and looked underneath. No money there. She went to the closet and rooted around, throwing boxes on the floor and pulling clothes out. Nothing there either. She opened the drawers of his dresser. Still nothing. Angel wanted to scream. Carl must have money stashed somewhere.

She raced back into the hallway, looked briefly into Ma's room, then decided against it. He would never keep the money there. Not with her. So where?

Then her eyes drifted up to the attic hatch in the ceiling. A string hung down. It seemed like as good a place as any to hide money. She reached up and grabbed the string, her fingers barely curling around it, and then she pulled. The hatch opened to reveal a folded attic ladder. She jumped, grabbed ahold of the bottom rung and deployed the ladder. Then she climbed into darkness, poking her head and shoulders through the oblong hole and into the space beneath the home's roof.

It was pitch black. Even after she lingered to let her eyes grow accustomed to the gloom, she could see nothing. At least until she noticed the string hanging down nearby. When she pulled it, a light snapped on.

But Carl would not make finding his money easy. It wouldn't just be sitting there, waiting for her. She would still have to search.

Angel climbed higher into the attic. She glanced around, figuring he wouldn't put it too far from the hatch, but all she saw was thick insulation between the rafters. She bent over and pulled the yellow fluffy padding back. The fibers itched against her palms, but she kept going.

And then she found it.

A metal cashbox wedged between two rafters and covered with insulation. She lifted it up, opened it, and saw six rolls of cash secured by rubber bands. Fifties and hundreds. Several thousand dollars. Enough for her and Cherub to make their escape. But there was something else, too. A sleek black pistol. Angel had only ever fired a gun once or twice, and that was a long time ago. But she wasn't leaving it behind. She pushed the money into her pockets, making them bulge, then took the gun and a box of ammo before climbing back down out of the attic. She didn't bother putting the stairs back up. What was the point?

Going to her bedroom, she gathered up what little clothes she and her daughter possessed, then went back to Carl's room and found a duffel bag. She pushed the clothes inside, along with the money, gun, and ammo. Then she slung the bag over her shoulder and raced back to the front of the house where her daughter was still waiting.

"Come on," she said, grabbing her daughter's hand again. "We're getting out of here."

"Where are we going?" Cherub asked in a small voice.

"I don't know. Anywhere." Angel rushed to the front door, snapped the deadlock back, and pulled it open.

Bright sunlight streamed in, almost blinding her.

She was about to step over the threshold and out of the house when a thought occurred to her.

"Wait here," she said to her daughter, then turned and ran back into the kitchen to a key hook near the breakfast nook. Three sets of keys hung there. She didn't know what two of them were for, but the third had a Chrysler fob attached to it. Ma's old Sebring that she hadn't driven in over a decade, but which Carl still kept running because he didn't always want to take the pickup truck.

Angel snatched the set of keys, praying there would be enough gas in the car to get them far away before they needed to stop again, and rushed back to the front door where her daughter was waiting.

Without hesitation, she grabbed her daughter's hand and stepped outside, feeling the fresh air on her face. The car was parked a few hundred feet away on a narrow driveway that ran to a distant road. Where the road went, she didn't know, but Angel didn't care, so long as it went somewhere other than here. She threw the bag in the trunk, bundled her daughter into the back, and climbed behind the wheel. The car started on the first turn. Then Angel was off with a grind of gears and a screech of tires, driving for the first time in who knew how long? And when she reached the road and turned left without bothering to use the blinker because no one was there to see it, Angel realized something. She and her daughter were free.

ONE

A WEEK in her own bed had been heavenly, Patterson Blake thought as she rode the subway from her apartment in the Queens neighborhood of Astoria to Ozone Park, and the dive of a pizza joint her father loved above all others.

Park Pizza was one of those places that had always been there, and always would. It was timeless. A fixture beloved by locals and visited with glee by the rare tourist who strayed from the bright lights of Broadway looking for the *real New York*. Even as a kid, Patterson could remember her parents taking her and Julie there for a slice of pie and a soda. It was her childhood. It was her teenage years. Now it was where she met her father six times out of ten when they got together for their bimonthly catch up dinner.

Not that she had been around for those leisurely father-daughter dates of late, which was why she had devoted her time evenly between Jonathan Grant and her dad during the week she had been home. She was making up for all the nights her father had eaten alone and perhaps gaining a few credits for those to come. Tomorrow, she would head to

LaGuardia, board a plane, and fly to Dallas. After that, she would pick up Julie's trail and follow it wherever the clues led, which right now, was Santa Fe.

The restaurant was a couple of blocks from the subway. When she entered, her father was waiting near the bar with a beer in his hand.

"Peanut!" His face broke out in a wide grin as she approached. His gaze shifted from her to the door. "I thought Jonathan might join us tonight, seeing as how you fly out tomorrow."

"He'd love to, but he can't. He's working late, as usual," Patterson replied. She had mentioned the dinner date to her boyfriend, and he'd promised to make it if he could, but something had come up. This wasn't unusual. As Assistant Special Agent in Charge of the New York field office's criminal division, he often worked late by necessity. Now, with a promotion to SAC coming down the pipe, he couldn't afford a misstep. Especially after the events of the past few weeks, which had seen Patterson framed for murder. A situation that had ensnared two employees of the Dallas field office—Marcus Bauer and Phoebe Cutler—who had stepped over the line trying to prove her innocence. "He sends his regards, though."

"That's something, at least. A shame for you, though."

"Yes. It is," Patterson agreed. With any luck, he would be waiting at the apartment when she got home later that evening. It was her last chance to see him before leaving again, and she didn't know how long she would be gone this time. She had already followed Julie's progress from Oklahoma City through Dallas and up to Amarillo. Her next stop was Santa Fe. Julie had gone there with Trent Steiger, the lead singer of the band Sunrise, who she had met in Oklahoma City and tagged along with as the band played a music festival called Tex Fest. After that, the members of Sunrise had gone their separate ways, which was how Steiger ended up playing solo gigs in a Santa Fe bar called Amy's Roadhouse. She hoped to find conclusive evidence of Julie's fate there, but if not, she would move on, going wherever the clues dictated.

"Hey," her father touched Patterson's arm. "You alright? You spaced out there for a moment."

"I'm fine." Patterson forced herself back into the present. "Just thinking about Julie. I knew when I started this that finding out what happened to her would be hard, if not downright impossible, but I wasn't expecting it to take such a toll. I needed this week away, if only to clear my head."

Her father observed her for a moment, then withdrew his hand. "I meant to talk with you about that after we eat, but since you brought it up . . . Are you sure that going back on the road searching for Julie is wise? You don't need to prove anything, and I won't be upset if you would rather stay here and return to your old life."

"Why would you say that?" Patterson asked. "Don't you want to know what happened to Julie just as much as I do?"

"Of course." Her father looked down at his drink. When he looked up again, his eyes were moist. "I've lived with the nightmare of not knowing what happened to my firstborn daughter for so long that I almost can't remember what it was like to be truly happy. But I'm not willing to sacrifice my remaining daughter's emotional well-being because of it. You looked so tired and beat down when you came back here last week. It made my heart ache. Which is why I'll tell you again, you don't need to continue on with this. You can stay here and go back to your regular duties at the FBI. We can have our weekly dinners again. You can see Jonathan whenever you want. I'll even refrain from lecturing you about the perils of dating your boss."

"I don't believe that for a second." Patterson couldn't help a smirk. "Besides, I'm not doing this out of some misguided sense of duty to you or Julie. I'm doing it to save myself because I can't afford another incident like the one that got me in this mess in the first place. Losing focus during that farm raid and getting myself suspended opened my eyes. I hadn't realized just how much baggage I'd been carrying because of Julie's disappearance. I'll never be free of that if I don't find out what happened to her, and I can't risk going to pieces in the field again."

"Well, alright then." The elder Blake nodded. "I guess you know what you're doing. Just don't take too long. It's been so nice having you back this week."

"It has," Patterson said. And she meant it. Her week back in New York had been wonderful between catching up with her dad and spending time with Jonathan. But now it was time to pick up the trail again and follow Julie wherever that led her. But not before she shared one last pizza with her father. She glanced around, noticing several customers had finished their meals, and left. There was an open table near the window. She nodded toward it. "Want to take a seat and order some food?"

"Love to." Her father picked up his beer and started toward the table. "Great." Patterson followed behind. She slipped a hand into her jacket pocket and touched the pack of photographs that lay within. Photos of Julie given to her by Mark Davis after she had proved his innocence. They showed her sister at the music festival or with Trent Steiger. There were more, too. Photos of Julie at the weird car sculpture sitting off the interstate outside Amarillo. A place their father had always talked about visiting but never had. She had sprayed the message, *for you, dad!* on one of the cars. Patterson had been itching to show them to her father all week, but had held off, saving the best for last. Now, after taking a seat, she took the bundle of photos out and slipped them across the table. "Here. You should look at these."

"What's all this?" Her father took the photos but didn't remove them from their protective paper sleeve.

"Just look at them."

Her father opened the package, the photos, and looked through them one by one. When he came to the image of Julie with the spray can standing next to the message she had written on the rusty, upended and partially buried car, his eyes grew wet for a second time. He tore his gaze away and looked at Patterson. "I don't know how you came across these . . . but thank you."

TWO

"YOU CAN KEEP THE PHOTOS," Patterson said as they walked toward the subway station at ten-thirty under a clear and starry sky. She suspected he had no intention of giving them up, anyway, since he was still clutching them like they were the most precious thing he'd ever held.

"Are you sure?" he asked, glancing briefly down at the photos. "You don't need these for your investigation?"

"No. I have copies of my own. Believe it or not, the person I got them from still had the negatives, and he let me make a couple of extra copies. I have a set for mom, too, if either of us ever see her again, that is."

"You sound so bitter. Don't be like that. It's not worth the energy."

"For you, maybe." Patterson couldn't believe her father was still trying to defend her after she walked out on them and left him heartbroken. "I choose not to forgive her. She might've lost one daughter, but she had another that she turned her back on."

"Which is true, and I can't defend that. But you must still

harbor some sliver of feeling for her, otherwise you wouldn't have made a set of photographs to give her."

"Maybe," Patterson admitted grudgingly.

"It was a thoughtful gesture." Her father looked down at the photographs again. "It's hard to believe these have been out there all this time, just waiting for you to find them." He paused and took a breath. "Just like Julie. She's out there somewhere as well, waiting for you to find her."

"I hope so." Patterson wasn't sure if he was implying that Julie was still alive, and she didn't ask. Some things were best left unspoken.

They arrived at the subway station. Before descending to the platform, Patterson turned to her father and hugged him. "Thanks for walking with me."

"Anything to share a few more minutes together." His gaze drifted toward the stairs at the sound of a passing train rumbling through the tunnels below and then back to his daughter. "Are you sure you want to continue with this?"

"We already talked about that, dad," Patterson said. "I need to finish what I started. If I don't, I'll always wonder if Julie is out there and how close I came to finding her."

Her father nodded slowly. "Don't be gone too long, and stay safe, okay?"

"I'll do my best." Patterson gave her father one more hug, then turned and descended into the station. When she reached the bottom of the stairs, she glanced back over her shoulder to see her father still standing at the top. She waved quickly and then continued on, arriving at the platform just in time to hop on a train.

Thirty minutes later, she arrived at her apartment on the second floor of a brownstone in the Queens neighborhood of Astoria. She unlocked the door and let herself in, disappointed to find that Jonathan Grant was not there waiting for her. She checked her phone and saw a text message from him.

Still at work. Minor crisis. You know how it goes. Hopefully not an over-night. Will try and call unless it gets too late.

She swallowed a flicker of disappointment and fired off a quick reply, then went to the kitchen and opened the fridge, taking out a bottle of white wine she had opened the previous evening. After pouring a glass, she went into the living room and sank onto the couch.

The apartment was silent, save for a low hum coming from the fridge, and the distant sound of traffic from the nearby interstate where it met Grand Central Parkway. The atmosphere in the room was heavy. Sorrowful. Almost as if the building shared her father's disappointment that she was leaving again. She told her smart hub to play a classic jazz station, then rested her head on the back of the sofa and closed her eyes, falling into the music. It was slow and doleful. Plaintive. It matched her mood.

Once again, her thoughts turned to Jonathan. Was this going to be her new life now that he was in line for a big promotion? Being Special Agent in Charge of the criminal division at the New York office might not seem like a huge step up from his current job as ASAC, but it came with increased responsibility and, she suspected, even longer hours. How many times would she sit at home alone while he dealt with some crisis or other? That he wasn't there with her the night before she departed to resume her search for Julie spoke volumes.

For a moment, just briefly, she considered her father's

suggestion of abandoning the quest to find her sister. It would be the easy option. But what she told her father at dinner still held true. Finding out what happened to Julie was the only way to exorcise her demons. And even if she could put her sister's ghost to rest without continuing the search, there were other considerations. Like Marilyn Khan turning Julie's case into a full-blown FBI investigation and reinstating Patterson. Something the SAC had done not to help the junior agent, but to steal some of the glory associated with putting a depraved serial killer who had been abducting women for decades behind bars.

Patterson opened her eyes, realized her glass was empty. She stood and went to the kitchen again, intending to pour another, but then changed her mind. She had to be up early in the morning to catch her flight to Dallas and she couldn't see the point in staying up and waiting for a phone call from Jonathan that might not even come despite his promise to call her later.

She rinsed the wineglass and put it in the sink, then went to the bedroom where she undressed and took a shower. Fifteen minutes later, she slipped between the covers and turned the light off after setting an early alarm on her phone. She lay in the darkness for an hour, unable to quiet the flood of thoughts that cascaded through her mind. Thoughts of Julie, the task ahead, and what she might find in Santa Fe. At some point, she fell into a fitful sleep, only to be awakened sometime later by a sense of movement in the dark bedroom.

It was Jonathan. He must have let himself in with the key she had given him. He slipped into bed next to her and mumbled an apology for not being there sooner.

"Tomorrow morning," he said as he wrapped an arm around her, "I'll drive you to the airport before going into the office."

"Tomorrow can wait. I don't care about tomorrow," Patterson said, rolling over to face him. All thought of sleep had evaporated. She pulled him close, felt the heat of his body next to hers. "You're here now, and that's what matters."

THREE

PATTERSON ARRIVED in Dallas a little after noon the next day. When she exited the arrivals lounge, she saw a familiar face waiting for her.

"Welcome back," said Marcus Bauer before embracing Patterson in a warm hug. "It hasn't been the same around here without you."

"Aw, shucks." Patterson feigned embarrassment. "You missed me."

"Actually, quite the opposite." Bauer grinned. "Life has been so peaceful. No one has shot at me or chased me. I haven't disobeyed any orders, or almost gotten fired. It's been bliss."

"Yeah. Sorry about all that. But if it makes you feel any better, I'll only be in town for a few hours. Hardly enough time to get into trouble."

"I beg to differ," Bauer said as they made their way down to the luggage carousels. "Ten minutes is all you need. There's probably a hostage crisis brewing over in short-term parking, even as we speak."

"Ouch. And yet you still volunteered to come pick me up."

"Only after promising Phoebe that I'd wear a bulletproof vest."

"Alright. That's enough." An alarm sounded, and the carousel shuddered to life. Patterson watched an assortment of luggage appear through a hole in the wall and start its looping journey around. "Jonathan told me you and Phoebe both skirted any serious punishment for aiding and abetting me when I was a fugitive."

Bauer nodded. "SAC Harris decided it was easier to say that we were working undercover on his orders, rather than reprimand us for cracking a case his task force had been working on for six months."

"A case against a sitting US senator, no less."

"Exactly. That didn't stop him from pulling us aside for a private chat and letting us know that any such actions in the future would not be so easily dismissed. Then he put me back on desk duty for another three weeks. If he could, I think he'd have barred either of us from having any further contact with you. He wasn't exactly polite in his assessment of your propensity for getting in trouble. In fact, I've never heard him pack so many swearwords into such a brief conversation."

"Double ouch." Patterson spotted her luggage and grabbed it. "I guess the Dallas field office won't be rolling out the red carpet for me, then."

"Probably not." Bauer chuckled. "But that doesn't mean he isn't grateful for your assistance in putting Senator Newport and his lapdog Detective Sergeant Ortega behind bars."

"He doesn't sound very grateful."

"SAC Harris is a complicated man." Bauer turned and

started toward the exit and the parking garage beyond. "Come on, I have something to show you."

"Really?" Patterson pulled the handle up on her rolling suitcase and hurried along behind. "What is it? Tell me."

"Not so fast. It's a surprise," Bauer said as they stepped out onto the curb. The early afternoon Texas heat was like a slap in the face after the comfortable air-conditioned airport interior.

"Not fair." Patterson grimaced and followed Bauer past a line of parked taxicabs, in front of an idling hotel shuttle, and across three lanes of slow-moving one-way traffic into the parking garage. "I hate surprises."

"Too bad." Bauer led her to his car and popped the trunk, then took her bag and heaved it inside before slamming the trunk lid. He unlocked the car and walked to the driver's side door. "Get in."

———

An hour and a half later, Patterson stood in another parking garage on the other side of the city, this one attached to the headquarters of the Dallas Police Department and stared in mute astonishment.

"Well, what do you think?" Bauer asked with a lopsided grin on his face.

"I'm not sure what to think." Patterson stepped closer to the van and placed her palm against it. The metal felt cold under her touch, the paint smooth and polished. New. It was her vehicle, for sure. The one she had purchased in cash after ditching the Toyota Corolla with faded lime green paint and oversized rims assigned to her by the FBI field office in Chicago. The van had been a means to an end. A way to survive on the run after she was accused of murder. It was old and shabby, but affordable. It had also doubled as a rolling, albeit uncomfortable, hotel room. Without the van, she would almost certainly have been apprehended, which would have made clearing her name all the more difficult, if not impossible. Now she hardly recognized it. The peeling and faded vinyl stripes along its sides were gone. The dings and rust were fixed. Its dull and oxidized white paint was now a shiny black. The old, fogged headlamps had been replaced with clear ones. The tires were new, too. Best of all, the license plates she had borrowed from a rusting old Buick sitting on a plot of land near the interstate outside of Amarillo were gone, replaced with blue US government plates. "I don't understand."

"SAC Harris figured you might like a more comfortable ride than that beater the Chicago field office foisted on you. The FBI doesn't have its own garage, but the Dallas PD motor pool does. It's where they do the maintenance on their cruisers and tactical vehicles. He called in a few favors, and they were more than happy to give your van a new lease on life. To be honest, it probably wasn't that hard a sell since you were instrumental in putting three murderers behind bars during your tenure here and clearing a good chunk of their caseload."

"I'm speechless." Patterson was overwhelmed by a swell of gratitude.

"I guess there's a first time for everything."

"Hey." Patterson punched him lightly on the arm.

"I hope you like the paint job. Dallas PD doesn't exactly have a wide choice of colors at their disposal. Black or white, unsurprisingly. We tossed a coin."

"It's perfect."

"There's more." Bauer pulled a set of keys from his pocket. "Look inside."

Patterson took the keys and unlocked the van. She pulled the side sliding door back. It moved easier now, gliding with barely any resistance. But it was the interior that took her breath away. The old threadbare seats had been reupholstered. The headliner was new. The driver's compartment gleamed. But it was the van's rear area, where Patterson had slept on a cheap memory foam mattress, that really stole the show. The rear seats had been removed to make more space. There was a wood platform across the rear topped by a new twin mattress, along with fresh sheets, a comforter, and fluffy pillows. Shelves and a cubby under the platform provided ample storage. A small cubicle had been installed behind the driver's seat. Inside was a chemical toilet and a tiny sink fed from a water tank. In front of this, on one side of the space previously occupied by the rear seats, was a narrow bench and table, complete with a power bar for her laptop and other electronics. On the other was a galley with a tiny fridge, microwave, and an overhead cupboard built between the bed and the sliding door. Four LED lights shone down, illuminating the space. The rest of the interior walls and ceiling were finished in varnished pine, while the floor was covered in dark oak vinyl planking.

Patterson's breath caught in her throat. "This is incredible. It really is like a hotel room on wheels."

"Which means no more flea-pit motel rooms off the highway," Bauer said. "Unless you prefer bedbugs, that is."

"What do you think?" Patterson grinned. Her eyes alighted on a small satellite dish fixed to the roof. "It has TV, too?"

"Nope. That's internet. You'll be connected wherever you go via satellite."

"Wow!" Patterson said. "You thought of everything."

"Speaking of that, there's one more thing I want to show

you." Bauer climbed up into the van. He went to a spot near the bed and kneeled, pressing a barely discernable button set into the floor. A square of vinyl planking popped up, opening on concealed hinges. Beneath it was a gunmetal grey panel with a keypad. He typed a code. The keypad beeped, and a second door clicked open.

"A hidden safe," Patterson said, realizing what she was looking at.

"For your guns, and any other items you don't want to leave lying around." Bauer replied, closing the panel again and locking it before swinging the section of floor back down to hide it once more. "I'll send the code to your secure email, along with instructions on how to reset it to something you'll remember."

"You guys really did all this for me?" Patterson was close to tears. But they were joyful ones.

"Anything to make finding your sister a little more comfortable." Bauer pushed his hands into his pockets. "There's a new air conditioner, and a solar panel on the roof to top up your power. They gave the engine a full tune-up as well. She'll purr like a cat. Even better, you have government plates to make life easier. You can park in all those coveted official vehicle spots. And since the van is registered to the FBI through the GSA, no one's going to pull you over for speeding. I also took the liberty of filling her up with gas, so you're all set to hit the road."

"I can't wait." Patterson wanted to climb inside and try everything out.

"Not so fast." Bauer grinned. "Tomorrow will be soon enough. I'm under strict orders to bring you back to my apartment this evening for a good home cooked meal."

"I was planning to hit the road right away," Patterson said. "It's a ten-hour drive to Santa Fe even without taking traffic into account. I figured I could make it halfway there today."

Bauer said nothing. He just raised his eyebrows and looked at her.

"Fine. I'll leave in the morning."

"That's better." Bauer looked relieved. "Phoebe wouldn't be happy if I came home without you."

"Wow." Patterson smirked.

"What?"

"Nothing." Patterson slid the van door closed and locked the vehicle.

Bauer scowled. "I'm not under her thumb, if that's what you're implying."

"Sure." Patterson started back toward Bauer's Dodge Charger with a grin on her face. "You just keep telling yourself that."

FOUR

WHEN PATTERSON WALKED into Bauer's apartment at seven o'clock that evening, Phoebe met her with a hug. "Look at us. The three musketeers, together again."

"It's only been a week," Patterson said with a grin. "And tomorrow I'll be in Santa Fe. I would have left this afternoon if Marcus hadn't given me my orders in no uncertain terms."

"As I instructed him to do," Phoebe said, finally releasing Patterson and looking over her shoulder at Bauer, who was stepping through the front door. She waited for him to close the door, then grabbed Patterson's arm. "Come on. I have a bottle of wine open on the kitchen island. Let's have a glass before dinner."

"Just the one," Patterson said, following the perky administrative assistant. "I want a clear head tomorrow for the drive."

"You know, I'm still on desk duty," Bauer said. "I could take a few days and help you follow leads up there."

Phoebe whirled on him, wine bottle in hand. "Not a

snowball's chance in hell. Every time the pair of you get together, bad things happen."

"That is not true." Bauer pulled a face. "I was only trying to be helpful."

"That's also not true." Phoebe poured the wine and handed Patterson a glass. "You're bored out of your mind on desk duty and looking for any excuse to get out of it. And it won't work, anyway. SAC Harris would never give you leave to go off on another adventure like that." Phoebe looked in Patterson's direction. "No offence."

"None taken." Patterson turned to Bauer. "Sorry, Marcus. Maybe next time." She was glad Phoebe had jumped in and barred him from going. She still remembered the kiss in the hotel room weeks before. The heat between the two of them. The last thing she wanted was a road trip with the man. It had the potential to blow up both their relationships if they weren't careful. She couldn't speak for Bauer, but she felt like her relationship with Jonathan Grant had been floundering since she started looking for Julie. Like he was pulling away. The past week had mended some of the damage, but it still felt a little off. Long distance romances were hard even when your boyfriend wasn't working a hundred hours a week and putting his job ahead of his personal life. She patted Bauer on the shoulder. "Anyway, I think your place is here with Phoebe. She needs you."

Bauer gave a wan half-smile. "It was worth a try. Back to the desk I go tomorrow."

"Oh, my." Phoebe rolled her eyes at Patterson. "He's such a drama queen for a big strong FBI agent."

"He has his moments." Patterson laughed.

"Hey." Bauer picked up his wine glass and swirled the crimson liquid before taking a sip. "I'm right here in the room."

"We know you are, dear." Phoebe grinned and turned toward the stove. "Dinner is about ready. Why don't the two of you head into the dining room and sit down."

"You need help with anything?" Patterson asked, as Phoebe took a sizzling pork roast surrounded by roasted potatoes out of the oven.

"No. Now get out of here." She shooed them toward the dining room. "And don't forget to take your wine."

———

After dinner, Patterson stood on Bauer's apartment balcony and looked out over the city. In the distance she could see downtown, with its skyscrapers reaching toward a dusky evening sky preparing to make the transition to night. She leaned on the rail and sipped her second glass of wine and wondered, like she often did, if her sister was looking up at that same sky or if her ability to admire the heavens had been cut short by some sadistic predator long ago.

"Am I intruding?" Bauer stepped out onto the balcony, wine bottle in hand.

"No. Why would you say that?"

"You looked lost in thought." Bauer reached over and topped up her wineglass. "Thought I might be interrupting some private moment."

"I was just thinking."

"Julie?"

Patterson nodded. "Whether she's dead or alive, I hope I get my answers soon. I'm not sure how much longer I can do this."

"You'll find her." Bauer leaned next to Patterson. "Speaking of which, I think you should be more careful out there from now on."

Patterson turned to Bauer, surprised at his somber tone. "Is that just random advice for a woman who gets herself into trouble at the drop of a hat, or is there some specific reason you're telling me that?"

"It's probably not a big deal, but Senator Newport walked out of jail yesterday afternoon."

"What?" Patterson could hardly believe what she was hearing. "He's a murderer. How could that happen?"

"Technically he's innocent until proven guilty. In this case, the district attorney decided there was *insufficient evidence to charge the defendant at this time*. His words, not mine. The DA also insinuated that Newport was a victim of harassment by law enforcement, notably the FBI."

"That's ridiculous. He had his crooked cop kill at least two people. He tried to send an innocent man to prison for rape and frame me for murder."

"I know. But he also has friends in high places. And I mean *high*. Like all the way to the top high. People who protect their own and don't mind looking the other way if it suits their purposes."

"More like protect their own asses. I bet he knows stuff they don't want him blabbing to prosecutors. Things that would ruin all their careers, and possibly land them next to him in a cell."

"Maybe. But it's not over. We'll get him. Until someone tells us to stop, we'll keep investigating. Building a case."

"Which means both of you need to be careful, too."

"Don't worry. We will." Bauer sipped his wine. "Chances are, he'll take his win and crawl back under whatever rock he came from. Figure that going after you—or any of us—again is too risky. But even so, you should watch your back."

"Hey. What's going on out here?"

Patterson turned to see Phoebe standing at the sliding glass doors. "Just talking shop," she said.

"Senator Newport," Bauer added.

A flash of concern crossed Phoebe's face before she regained her composure. "Let's not worry about him right now. Come on inside. Tonight is about spending time with good friends, and I don't want it ruined."

FIVE

A BLISTERING red sunset cast the headstones of Oaklawn Cemetery on the south side of Dallas in subtle hues of gold that weaved through the long shadows cast by the eponymous old-growth oak trees scattered between the graves.

The cemetery was deserted at this time of the evening, save for a solitary figure standing over a granite marker in front of which had been placed a bouquet of flowers, now starting to wilt. The figure wore a black suit and a white shirt accented by a black tie. It was a fitting wardrobe for a person surrounded by the deceased, and one might be forgiven if they mistook the dark-haired, distinguished-looking gentleman for an undertaker. But although death was his trade, cemeteries were not his office.

Behind him, walking briskly along a gravel path that ran from one of the looping roads that cut through the cemetery, was another man wearing equally somber attire. The only difference was a small United States flag pin attached to the left lapel of his jacket.

"You're late," said the man without bothering to turn around.

"No. I'm right on time," Senator Bill Newport corrected him.

The would-be undertaker slipped his shirt sleeve up to reveal a luxury Swiss watch that Newport recognized to be of such craftsmanship, rarity, and expense that most of his constituents would never give it a second look, let alone realize its value. "It's two minutes past eight."

Newport checked his own timepiece, which read seven fifty-nine. He thought about arguing, then decided against it. "Nice watch," he said.

The other man nodded thoughtfully. "Thank you. In my line of work, accurate timekeeping is important." He drew in a measured breath. "I assume you followed my instructions and left your cell phone at home."

"That goes without saying."

"And the GPS in your car?"

"I used the GPS blocker, like you said." Newport pushed his hands into his pockets. GPS blockers, small units that created an interference field around a vehicle and prevented its GPS from connecting with the global positioning satellites high in orbit, were extremely illegal. They also blocked the navigation of any emergency vehicles within range, making them also potentially dangerous. But the senator was not worried about such things. After a lifetime of shady activities, getting caught with outlawed tech was the least of his worries. "I also drove an indirect route here just in case the feds are still sniffing around. I wasn't followed."

"Good. We don't want anyone placing us together." The man in the black suit nodded toward the grave. "Cynthia Clements. 1926-2016. Ninety years old. A good run. You pick this plot for a reason? She a relative of yours?"

"Hell, no." Newport shook his head. "My parents are buried here—God rest their souls—but nowhere near this grave. I wouldn't soil their memories with what we need to discuss."

"I can understand that. In either case, we should get on with it." The black-suited man only now turned to look at Newport. "You understand that once this meeting is over, once you set me in motion, there is no going back."

"Yeah. Just like all the other times," Newport said grimly. "Don't mess this up."

"I never have before, and I don't intend to start now." The man met Newport's gaze with steely gray eyes that made him look even more like an undertaker than before. "You have the package?"

Newport shuddered, suddenly feeling like a fly being observed by a predatory spider. He reached into his jacket and pulled out an envelope, then took a moment to compose himself before handing it to the man. "Everything you need is in here."

"And the cash?"

Newport removed another envelope from the folds of his jacket, this one thicker than the first. "Ten thousand for expenses as agreed. The rest has been wired to your offshore account. Don't worry. It's untraceable. All done through shell companies and routed through friendly offshore banks. Even if anyone tracks the transaction, it'll look like I just bought a plot of land in the Seychelles."

"Some piece of land." The man chuckled. "I hope it's worth it."

"Oh, it's worth it." Now it was Newport's turn to chuckle. "Worth every dime."

SIX

PATTERSON LEFT Dallas at sunrise to beat the rush hour traffic. She had spent a wonderful evening with Bauer and Phoebe and then slept in Bauer's spare bedroom, which he insisted upon even though she was anxious to try out her newly renovated camper van. Too much wine all around, he told her sternly. And she had agreed—albeit reluctantly.

Now she was barreling along on US 287 North, a dusty divided highway with two lanes in each direction. To her left, running parallel to the southbound lanes, was a set of railroad tracks. She had already left Wichita Falls in her rearview mirror and would pass through Amarillo—a place she had no intention of stopping considering her experience the last time she was there—and would arrive in Santa Fe by early evening.

The van was a joy to drive. Before, when she was on the run, it had been clunky and slow to respond. The brakes had felt mushy. The engine lacked power. But it had also been a sanctuary and kept her safe from those who would have put her in prison for a crime she didn't commit. Now, it felt like a new vehicle. Even better, the cramped space in the rear had been transformed into an oasis of tiny-living comfort. There would be no more motels off the highway. No more unpacking all the evidence of Julie's abduction in each new location she visited. It was all there, right at her fingertips. There was even a small corkboard mounted next to the table. She had already pinned Julie's photo to it—the one taken at the buried car attraction—along with photocopies of the last two postcards her father had received way back when, and the flyer Trent Steiger had sent to Mark Davis all those years ago urging him to come out to Santa Fe and reunite with his bandmate. The originals were safely tucked inside a plastic bin within a storage area built under the bed at the back of the van, along with all the other valuable evidence she wanted to keep safe.

As she drove, Patterson's thoughts turned to her sister. The trail leading to Santa Fe was a winding one with more than one unexpected development, but she hoped that her next destination would provide a more concrete answer to what happened all those years ago. She also wondered, not for the first time, if the lead singer of *Sunrise*, the band she had traveled with, was involved in Julie's disappearance. After all, she had stayed with Trent Steiger after the band's other members went their separate ways. He was absolutely a person of interest. And if he turned out to be the reason Julie vanished, Patterson would have the answer to a question that had waited sixteen years for a resolution. That thought excited and terrified her, both at the same time.

The roar of an engine broke Patterson's chain of thought. She looked in her rearview mirror to see a black sport utility racing up behind her. It came to within ten feet of the van and flashed its lights, blinking them off and back on again twice in rapid succession. Through the windshield, Patterson could see the vague outline of a man behind the wheel, although she could not make out his features.

The sport-utility inched closer still, closing the gap between them to where she thought it would bump the van's rear end. She glanced at the instrument cluster and saw that she was doing five miles *above* the speed limit, which certainly shouldn't annoy other drivers, especially since the road—both lanes—was practically empty.

Bauer's warning was fresh in her memory.

She pressed her foot on the accelerator, watching the needle rise to ten miles above the speed limit.

The van matched her acceleration.

Patterson glanced down at her phone sitting in the van's center console. One quick call would send police units her way. But how long would they take to get to her? She reached down, touched the Glock pistol in its holster. Her service weapon. Another smaller Glock sat in a holster strapped to her left ankle. If help didn't arrive quickly enough, she had the means to defend herself. But she would rather avoid a gunfight.

Patterson reached for the cell phone, was about to dial 911, when the SUV swerved into the other lane and surged forward, engine screaming.

Patterson tensed. Dallas PD had done an excellent job of tuning her own engine, but she was no match against the much newer, more powerful vehicle that was quickly drawing parallel with her. If the occupant had bad intentions, if the passenger window slid down and a gun appeared, muzzle aimed in her direction, she was a sitting duck and would be dead long before help could arrive.

She did the only thing she could think of. Instead of coaxing the van even faster, Patterson checked her rearview mirror to make sure there were no other cars close behind her, and then slammed on the brakes.

SEVEN

THREE WEEKS BEFORE

AFTER FLEEING *the house where Carl and the now dead and slowly bloating Ma had kept her confined for longer than she cared to remember, Angel drove south with no particular destination in mind. She avoided the interstate—too fast and busy for someone who hadn't been behind the wheel in years—opting instead for backroads that cut through the vast expanse of the Coconino National Forest.*

It was getting dark now, the sun sliding below the horizon in a splashy glow of red and yellow, and she tried not to give in to the flicker of apprehension that almost made her turn around and head back to the farmhouse. Maybe it wouldn't be so bad when Carl got home, after all. Maybe he would understand that she had nothing to do with Ma's death. But Carl might be gone another week or ten days, and Ma would not be very fresh by then. The thought of living in that house with her rotting corpse sent a shiver though Angel. And she had no desire to move the woman. Not going to happen. For one thing, Carl would never believe she found Ma like that if

Angel buried her somewhere out in the fields or put her in the barn away from the house.

But she didn't turn around, because deep down, Angel knew that Carl would not be understanding. He would be the opposite. Mean and angry. Unwilling to entertain any notion that Ma could expire all on her own without help from Angel and her daughter. The woman was his rock. He idolized her with almost cult-like reverence. Finding her on the kitchen floor would wreck him, and while Angel actually smiled at that thought—about time he suffered a little—she didn't want to be a front row spectator for it.

"Mommy?" Cherub's voice drifted from the back seat. "I'm still hungry."

The words hit Angel like a wall. In her haste to escape the farmhouse, food had slipped her mind, and they had not eaten all day. Their last meal was twenty-four hours earlier at seven the previous evening. That was also the last time Angel had seen Ma, at least alive.

"We'll find food," she said, glancing quickly over her shoulder to the back seat. Cherub was sitting upright with her hands in her lap, lips pressed tightly together. She looked out of place in the rear of the car. Had she ever even been in one before? Angel couldn't remember, but probably not. Carl wasn't exactly the let's go for a drive type.

"When?" Cherub scrunched her face up.

"Soon." Angel wondered if she should have taken the interstate after all. She had skirted Flagstaff, sticking to the roads at the edge of town because she didn't want to be seen—for all she knew Carl had friends there who would recognize the car—and just kept going. Now they were in the middle of nowhere surrounded by a pristine pine-dotted landscape that might as well have been on the moon.

Frustratingly, they had passed several fast-food places as they drove out of town. Not that it mattered. She wouldn't have dared to stop at any of them for the same reason she hadn't taken the direct route through downtown. Too much of a risk. Hell, knowing her luck, Carl was already on his way back and sitting in one of those drive-thru lanes. He'd come home before with cheeseburgers and fries, or a bucket of chicken, so it wasn't beyond the realm of probability. Imagine his surprise if he saw Ma's Sebring waiting in the same line?

No, they would have to find a place to eat far from Flagstaff. Which looked like a daunting task until she saw a glow of hazy white light spilling onto the road ahead of them and realized that they had come across an outpost of civilization in the wilderness. That outpost turned out to be the Pineland Country Store and RV Camp, and it was still open.

Angel pulled off the road and found a parking spot in the small gravel lot out front. There were a good number of other vehicles there, and she couldn't help but scan the lot for a dark blue pickup with rusted front fenders and a peeling NRA sticker on the rear bumper. But if Carl was there, she didn't see him, which was a huge relief.

Angel opened her door and climbed out, then went to the rear door and unclipped Cherub's seatbelt. "Come on. Let's eat."

The kid's face lit up. "In there?"

"Yes. In there."

Cherub clapped her hands together and made an excited noise that sounded like a cross between a grunt and a squeal. She wriggled off the seat and hopped down to the ground.

Angel took her daughter's hand, was about to lead her across the lot to the country store, when a thought occurred to her. She turned and kneeled. "Listen, when we go in there, keep quiet, okay. Let me do all the talking."

"Why?" Cherub wrinkled her nose.

"Because we have to be careful now. If you do speak, don't mention your name, or mine, or where we came from. Don't mention Ma or daddy, okay?"

Cherub furrowed her brow. "What if someone asks?"

"Then you let me answer."

"Are you going to lie?"

"Maybe."

"Daddy said lying is a sin."

"Daddy isn't here, and it's to keep us safe." Angel found it ironic that Carl had instilled a sense of honesty in their daughter even though he was about as dishonest, and sinful, as a man could get. She shuddered at the thought of the sins he had inflicted upon her body over the years. But his desire to save Cherub from sin did not stem from any pious belief, but more that he wanted her to tell him the truth whenever he demanded it of her. And if she didn't . . . Angel still cried whenever she thought about the first time 'daddy' had taken off his belt and used it on his daughter. "You want to be safe, don't you?"

Cherub nodded. She remembered the belt, too.

"Good girl." Angel smiled and stood up again. Then she led her daughter toward the store, feeling lighter than she had in years.

EIGHT

THE VAN DECELERATED RAPIDLY with a screech of tires.

Something tumbled and fell to the floor with a bump in the cabin behind her.

The SUV zipped by as if it had been shot out of a cannon.

The driver leaned on his horn, giving her a long blast, and then he was ahead of her even as the van came to a shuddering halt.

Patterson steered the vehicle to the side of the road and slipped her Glock from its holster. She reached for the driver's side door, ready to throw it open and shelter behind it to defend herself if the other vehicle stopped and an assailant emerged. But the SUV was ahead of her now and still going. It slipped back into her lane fifty feet distant without indicating and sped on toward the horizon.

Patterson's shoulders slumped. She re-holstered her Glock. The SUV was not an assassin sent to exact vengeance. Just an impatient jerk, angry she was in his way. Heart still beating wildly against her chest, she took a moment to gather her nerves, then continued along the road toward Santa Fe, even as the speeding SUV shrank to nothing but a faraway black dot ahead of her.

NINE

CORBIN POPE WATCHED the fracas between Patterson Blake's van and the black sport-utility vehicle with a measure of bemusement. His own vehicle was a good quarter mile behind the pair, but the flat and featureless Texan landscape afforded him an excellent line of sight.

Pope reduced his speed and pulled over, tucking himself next to a gate behind which a dusty rutted trail led off into the hard-baked wilderness. The last thing he wanted was to come up on the van too quickly. He sat there for a moment, watching the altercation play out. Noting the reaction of the FBI agent behind the van's wheel. She had slammed on her brakes at the last moment, steered the vehicle to the side of the road even as the SUV barreled past. This provided Pope with an interesting nugget of information.

Patterson Blake was expecting trouble.

Word of Senator Newport's escape from justice had apparently traveled fast, and now she was on the defensive. That didn't bother Pope in the least. He was a master of his craft and when the time was right, she would not see him coming until it was too late. It meant he would have to be more careful, though. Patterson Blake was no ordinary target. She was Federal law enforcement. Highly trained. She wasn't like the previous jobs he had completed for the senator. That added an extra wrinkle. She was no pansy environmental activist who made it their job to stand in the way of progress and subsequently ended up as the unfortunate victim of a mugging gone wrong, or a nosy reporter digging too close to the truth, who slipped and fell from the upper deck of a parking garage. When Newport told him who his target was the previous evening in the graveyard, Pope had almost turned the job down. Not because he had any qualms about killing law enforcement—the FBI agent wouldn't be his first such assignment—but because he measured every job against an internal barometer of risk honed from experience, and this one pushed the mercury about as high as any he had ever undertaken. It was almost like a sixth sense, and his hunch had been borne out when he researched Patterson Blake later that evening. She was resourceful, cunning, and had a nasty habit of escaping deadly situations with almost preternatural ease. As if she had a guardian angel watching over her from above or something. Not that Pope believed in such things, but he wasn't foolish enough to underestimate the risk she posed.

Yet he had not turned the assignment down, because even if he guarded against hubris, he still had pride. In his entire career, Pope had only declined two jobs. The first was the assassination of an eastern bloc world leader during an overseas diplomatic trip that Pope deemed an extreme risk and almost impossible to pull off without losing his own life. He had been right. The world leader had survived, but those who plotted against him were not so fortunate. The state security services had been one step ahead, and the conspirators who weren't fortunate enough to be shot outright had spent some not-so-quality time in a Siberian Gulag before they were tortured to a slow and painful death.

The only other job he had turned down was for a different reason. He didn't kill children, even if that child was the offspring of a man much worse than Pope himself. There were better ways to warn such people that their misdeeds had consequences. Kill the man's wife, his parents, but not the kid. This one rule was as close to a set of morals as Pope had ever come, and while he realized it might be perceived as a weakness within his small community of deadly tradesmen, he wasn't willing to break it. Actually, there were two rules. Animals were also off-limits, but thankfully no one hired assassins to off Mister Tinkles, no matter how many objects the cat might have pushed from the kitchen counter onto the floor.

Up ahead, the van was moving again now. Having decided there was no immediate threat, Patterson Blake was continuing on her way. Pope waited for a big rig to thunder past, spewing diesel fumes and dust in its wake, then pulled back out and followed.

He quickly overtook the semi-truck and slipped in front of it. The FBI agent's van was barely visible through the shimmering haze of heat rising off the scorching blacktop. Pope sped up now. He couldn't afford to lose her.

After his meeting with Senator Newport ended the night before, he quickly located the FBI agent, who had flown back into Dallas earlier that day, by checking her known associates. It hadn't taken long because there were only a few such people. He discovered the van sitting outside the apartment building of another special agent by the name of Marcus Bauer.

Parking up out of sight down the street, he hurried back

to the van, intending to place a GPS tracker on it. But as he drew close something caught his eye. A security camera high on the wall of the apartments, it's cycloptic lens watching over the parking spaces. He quickly changed course and crossed the road, then returned to his car. There was no way he could install a tracker right there, under the watchful gaze of that damned camera. So instead, he settled in for the night and sat behind the wheel, eyes fixed on the van and waiting for her to move it, which she had done earlier that morning.

Pope rolled down the driver's window and rested his elbow on the sill, relishing the heat of the late summer sun. The big rig was swiftly vanishing in his rearview mirror. The FBI agent's van was still ahead of him. He reached out and turned the radio on, then twisted the tuner through a crackle of static and several distant stations that might as well have been transmissions from outer space, until he found one with a strong enough signal. It was country-radio. Old stuff like George Jones and a younger Dolly Parton. Not his favorite, but probably the best he could hope for so far out in ranch country. He settled back in his seat with one hand on the wheel, fingers tapping along with the music, and pondered upon all the ways Patterson Blake might meet with a deadly accident over the coming days.

TEN

PATTERSON ARRIVED in Santa Fe a little before eight o'clock in the evening. Her butt was sore from driving for so many hours and her legs were stiff. Pulling over on a side street north of downtown, she took a few minutes to recuperate, sliding from the driver's seat and flopping onto the bed in the rear of the van. She closed her eyes and stretched her aching muscles, happy not to be behind the wheel. She was also happy that there would be no need to find a hotel. Her bedroom on wheels was more comfortable than any off the highway accommodation, thanks to Marcus Bauer and the Dallas PD.

After a few minutes, she sat up, opened the mini fridge, and grabbed a bottle of water. She opened it and gulped down the refreshing cold liquid.

Her eyes wandered to the pin board above the small table, and the picture of Julie standing next to the half-buried cars on the highway outside of Amarillo. Next to the photo was a photocopy of the flyer for Amy's Roadhouse given to her by Mark Davis. It was a list of the bands playing each weekend.

Trent Steiger had circled his own gig hoping Davis would leave Amarillo behind and play in the band again.

Patterson narrowed her eyes. Amy's Roadhouse. It couldn't be that far away, assuming it was still in business, and she had nothing to do for the rest of the evening. She looked at the address, then checked her phone. It was still there, on US-84 outside of the city limits between Santa Fe and a dusty settlement called Pojoaque. The GPS on her phone announced it was eight miles away and a twelve-minute drive. It was also her only solid lead, although after so many years—a decade and a half—who knew if anyone would remember anything.

Still, it was better than sitting in the van all night and staring at the walls. Besides, the website for Amy's Roadhouse said they served food, and Patterson was hungry. She finished the bottle of water, threw the empty bottle into a small trashcan tucked between the fridge and the sitting area and made her way up front again. She slid behind the wheel, ignoring the protests from her tired muscles, and started the van. A minute later she was following the directions on her phone to the last place she knew Julie had been.

————

Amy's Roadhouse was exactly what it sounded like. A building made of stone and logs that sat back from the road with an unpaved parking lot out front. A wraparound porch with whirring fans to stir the humid atmosphere provided outdoor seating beneath a neon sign that also included a cowboy whose arm moved between an extended and crooked position in a jerky waving motion to lure would-be travelers inside. An adjacent dirt lot surrounded on three sides by split-rail fencing was set aside for larger vehicles. At the back, near the fence, was a row of three portable plastic restrooms. A sign at the entrance announced that overnight RV and truck parking were free. It was a smart move by Amy's Roadhouse because there was only one place to eat or drink for miles. A couple of recreational vehicles, one of them as large as a bus, and an extended cab big rig, were taking advantage of the offer.

Patterson decided to join them. She pulled through the main parking lot and entered the RV area, then found a spot not too far from the restaurant but a good enough distance from the other vehicles to afford her some privacy.

Five minutes later she was stepping inside Amy's roadhouse with the photocopy of Trent Steiger's band flyer in her hand. The interior was just about as clichéd as the drinking hole looked from the outside. A rough wood plank floor strewn with the carcasses of previously consumed peanuts cracked from their shells crunched underfoot as Patterson entered. High-top tables occupied the center of the space while booths with ripped vinyl bench seats ringed the walls beneath pendant lights with gaudy stained-glass shades in hues of red and green. A bar ran the length of one wall with enough beer taps to justify the sign hanging above that proclaimed *a hundred beers on draft*. The wall behind the bar was filled with shelves of liquor bottles glinting in more hues of red, green, and blue from multi-colored spotlights set into the cavernous, vaulted ceiling on thick wooden beams. It reminded Patterson of twinkling Christmas lights and the holidays.

Then she saw the stage at the back, beyond the tables and booths, and her nostalgia faded. This was where Trent Steiger would have performed while Julie lingered nearby, watching.

It was a Thursday, and the roadhouse was bustling, but there was no band playing tonight. Instead, country music blasted over the PA system, competing for dominance with the bar's noisy clientele. Yet Patterson could almost feel her sister's ghost walking beside her as she weaved between the tables, pushing past gathered customers wearing wide brimmed Stetson's and cowboy boots.

The bartender scurried toward her as Patterson found a space at the bar. She was a slim woman in her early thirties with dark hair pulled back into a sloppy ponytail, a barely buttoned plaid shirt tied under her ample breasts to reveal her midriff—including a belly button piercing—and shorts cut so high that the pocket linings of whatever pair of jeans had given their life for fashion poked out beneath the ragged hems on each hip. She stopped in front of Patterson, one hand holding a rag which she used to wipe down the bar and soak up the sweat from the previous customer's glass.

"What can I get you, hon?" she asked in a thick Texas drawl that somehow matched her outfit.

"Beer," Patterson said. "IPA if you have it. Something local."

The bartender nodded and went about pouring the drink. "Haven't seen you in here before. You just passing through?"

"I'll be in town for a few days. Driving cross country. Figured I'd take advantage of your free RV parking."

"Ah." The bartender placed a frothy mug of amber beer down on the counter. "Where you heading, if that's not a nosey question?"

"Not sure yet." Patterson still clutched the flyer. She found the driest spot on the bar and placed it down so the bartender could see it. The woman was too young to have been around when Trent Steiger played his gigs in the roadhouse, but maybe there were other employees who had worked there longer. "I'm looking for someone. My sister. She was dating one of the musicians on this flyer. Trent Steiger."

The bartender hunched over the sheet of paper, then looked up with surprise. "This flyer is sixteen years old. You haven't seen your sister in all that time?"

"No." Patterson swallowed a hard lump that formed in her throat. "She went missing. We don't know what happened to her or even if she's still alive."

"Wow. That's the worst. Can't imagine how you must feel. I'm real close with my sister. We do everything together."

"Make sure you cherish her," Patterson said, fighting to quell the tremble in her voice. "Is there anyone around here who would remember that far back?"

The bartender thought for a moment, then shrugged. "There's Bailey Donohoe. She's been here a while. Like forever. Probably your best bet, but I'm not sure what you hope to find out. Even if she was working here back then, I can't imagine she'd remember one particular musician. Must've been thousands of gigs here since then."

"Is Bailey working tonight?" Patterson asked.

"Naw. She's strictly a weekender. Been here the longest, so she only works Friday and Saturday. Makes enough in tips that she don't need to hustle the rest of the time and she can be home with the kids during the week while her old man works nights."

"I don't suppose you could give me her address?"

The bartender shook her head. "Can't do that."

Patterson reached down, almost slipped out her FBI credentials and asked again, then thought better of it. People tended to clam up when confronted by a federal agent. Better to play the missing sister sympathy card. "I understand. Will she be working tomorrow?"

"It's Friday, so yeah. She's pulling a double tomorrow. Noon till close. Does that most weekends. Come in early, and I'm sure she'll find time to talk."

"Thank you." Patterson relaxed and picked up her beer. She took a sip of the amber liquid and relished the tart flavor. But she wanted more than beer. The last time she had eaten was a fast-food burger almost eight hours before, and her stomach was growling. "You got a bar menu?"

"Sure thing." The bartender produced a menu and laid it in front of Patterson. "Take a look and let me know when you're ready to order."

Patterson nodded. Amy's Roadhouse served the usual bar offerings. Burgers. Hotdogs. Chicken sandwiches. Steak. All served with sides of coleslaw or fries. But she already knew what she wanted. Chicken wings, medium hot. Because as she sat there perusing the menu, it occurred to Patterson that her sister had probably ordered from a similar menu all those years ago when Trent Steiger played the roadhouse. And chicken wings were Julie's absolute favorite food. She loved them head and shoulders above everything else. More than popcorn. More than a cheeseburger and fries. More, even, than the pepperoni pizza their father put on a pedestal as if it were the food of Gods. If Julie had eaten here—and Patterson was sure she had—it would have been medium hot wings, as wet as she could get them. And in that moment, as she raised a hand to place her order, Patterson sensed her sister's presence stronger than ever. It was so clear that she almost expected to turn around and see Julie standing right behind her, a goofy smile on her face, and laughter in her eyes. But when she looked, there was no one there. Just an empty space as big as the one that had consumed her heart over the last sixteen long years.

ELEVEN

CORBIN POPE REACHED the parking lot of Amy's Roadhouse and pulled into a vacant spot between a Ford F150 and a dark green Mustang with a broken taillight and crushed rear fender. The FBI agent's van was parked in an RV lot on the other side of the restaurant.

She soon appeared and headed for the restaurant.

After waiting a long minute to make sure she wasn't going to quickly reappear, Pope climbed from his car and followed her inside.

He had been in a lot of establishments just like Amy's Roadhouse during his many years committing unsavory acts for those with enough money and discretion to make it worth his while. He liked places like this. The kind of place where a person could fade into the background—hide in plain sight—thanks to the highly transitory turnover of customers that rendered pretty much everyone just another random face in the crowd to be forgotten as soon as they stepped back outside.

The FBI agent was at the bar talking with a cute server

who obviously chose her attire to pry fat tips from the wallets of lonely truckers and traveling salesman who spent too long away from their wives. He chuckled at this, but at the same time wondered if there were even any traveling salesmen left in the world. Most everyone worked from home nowadays. They attended meetings on their laptops and iPads, the conference room reduced to a bunch of small squares on a screen. They yakked on cell phones. Sent emails and text messages. They wore a shirt and tie above boxer shorts or ripped jeans, because you never saw anyone from the waist down. Hell, most of these people probably didn't even leave their homes for days on end, having everything delivered, including their meals, which came pre-portioned and ready to cook.

Pope hated the new normal. Give him the open road any day. The freedom to roll the window down and feel the wind tussling your hair. To stop in a town you probably never even knew existed twenty-four hours ago and eat in a restaurant you might never otherwise have known about. Life was an adventure that had passed most of the country by on their way to technological subservience in the name of convenience. But not him. If he hadn't excelled in his chosen line of work, he might very well have swapped violence for a life behind the wheel of a truck.

The hot bartender was still chatting to the FBI agent. *Not gonna make any fat tips that way,* Pope thought. Better if she moved on to one of the thirsty cowboys further down the bar. He might even have been tempted to sidle up to the bar and reward her choice of easy-on-the-eyes outfit himself had it not been for the fact that he didn't want to encroach upon Patterson Blake's observational radar. She was a federal agent. As such, her spatial awareness would be heightened, and even if she wasn't looking for active threats, she would be soaking up every minute detail of her surroundings, if only on a subconscious level. The last thing Pope wanted was to trigger a sense of familiarity at some point in the future that might cause her to look more closely in his direction and get in the way of whatever he had planned.

He looked around and found a table tucked into a dark corner of the barroom that still offered an excellent view of his target. He sat down, content to cloak himself in the shadows, and ordered a whiskey sour when approached by a server who hadn't quite nailed flirty-unobtainable like the young woman behind the bar.

When his drink came, he settled back and sipped it in a leisurely manner that some might have interpreted as nursing. He liked whiskey well enough—it was his libation of choice when he wasn't working—but right now Pope only wanted the drink as a prop. A guy sitting in a bar without a drink was likely to draw unwanted attention. But put a rocks glass filled with Maker's Mark in his hand, and he might as well be invisible. Or at least, he would blend into the background to where no one would give a second look.

The whiskey was useful in other ways, too. It was easier to get close to a person if you didn't look like a threat. Feign a drunken stagger, let your jaw hang slack and your eyelids droop, and you could be right on top of a person before they even realized their mistake. Bump into them, slip a needle full of potassium cyanide between their ribs, and lurch on by before they ever even knew anything was wrong. By the time they went into cardiac arrest, you could be far enough away that no one would ever suspect a thing. Even better, if the coroner wasn't looking for poison, they would chalk the death up to natural causes. He had used that method of execution a couple of times, and although it wasn't satisfying like a high velocity round delivered from eight-hundred yards—watching a person's head disintegrate before they ever knew they were dead—it certainly got the adrenaline pumping. Not that he intended to employ that particular trick right now. In fact, he didn't even have any cyanide at hand. His goal for the short term was to observe and learn. Watch Patterson Blake and become familiar with her mannerisms. Her habits. Make sure nothing was left to chance. Only then would he decide how she was going to shuffle off this mortal coil . . . and when.

A frisson of excitement tingled Pope's spine. Most of the time, he lived in a wasteland of emotion, devoid of the sentiments most other people took for granted. He had thought long and hard about his lack of feelings over the years. His inability to feel love, joy, or even grief. And in the end, a single word came to mind that described him better than any other.

Soulless.

But on rare occasions, times like now when he was stalking his next victim, anticipating their imminent demise and how that might be achieved, he felt something akin to pleasure, albeit briefly. There was only one other circumstance when this rare emotion surfaced and he could understand a child's wonder at opening a present on Christmas morning, or the excitement of a puppy when its person came home after a long day at the office. It was the moment when the last embers of life drained, at his hands, from another human being.

TWELVE

THE CHICKEN WINGS WERE GOOD. Julie would have liked them, Patterson thought, and probably had. As she finished the last wing, sucking the hot sauce off the bone, she couldn't help but feel a sudden and strong connection to her sister, who might even have sat on the very same stool that Patterson now occupied. She glanced around, her eyes settling on the stage where Trent Steiger had played on all those years ago. Had Julie sat at one of the tables right there, watching him perform? Her throat tightened and she blinked away a tear.

At that moment, her phone rang.

It was Marcus Bauer.

"Hey. Just checking you got there in one piece," he said when she answered.

"Everything's fine. Got here a couple of hours ago and I even found a place to park the van," Patterson replied, wondering if Bauer was just checking in, or if he was worried about the senator coming after her. "I had a minor clash on the interstate with a yahoo who thought I wasn't driving fast enough but it turned out to be nothing. Just some clown in a big-ass SUV, who needs to learn some manners."

"You're sure about that?" Bauer asked.

"Yeah. I'm sure. You don't need to worry about me."

"Okay." Bauer didn't sound convinced. "You track down Trent Steiger yet?"

"I've only just arrived."

"Yeah. But I know what you're like. I bet you've already started asking questions."

Patterson couldn't help but laugh. "You got me. I'm in the bar where he played right now. They have RV parking so I'm making it my base of operations. I already have a lead. A server who was here when he was gigging, but I can't talk to her until tomorrow."

"I knew it."

"I'm not getting my hopes up. She probably won't remember him or Julie. It's been so long."

"Hey. Positive thoughts. Okay?"

"Okay."

"Have you checked in with the locals yet?"

"No." Patterson wiped a smear of buffalo sauce off the remains of her wings and licked her finger. "I'll email the field office tomorrow. Let the SAC know I'm in town. I have no intention of going there in person, though. Last time I did that I ended up stuck on an unrelated case."

"And you saved a girl's life," Bauer said.

"I'm still not going there in person." Patterson picked up her beer, draining the last of it. "Thanks for calling, Marcus. Your friendship means a lot to me."

"Me too."

"And on that note, I'm going to hang up. I'm exhausted and there's a wonderfully comfortable bed waiting in that newly renovated van." Patterson motioned for the bill.

"Fair enough. Stay safe, Patterson."

"You too, Marcus. Tell Phoebe I said hi," she said, then told him goodnight and ended the call.

While she waited for the bill to come, she glanced around, feeling suddenly vulnerable. When the bill came, she paid and climbed down from the stool, then headed for the exit, walking as quickly as she could.

THIRTEEN

CORBIN POPE WATCHED Patterson Blake pay her tab and start across the bar toward the door. He had been in the bar for over an hour and his drink was still half full. He lifted the glass and downed it in one gulp, then reached into his pocket, pulled out his wallet, and removed a twenty-dollar bill which he left underneath the empty glass. As the FBI agent reached the door, he stood, waited long enough to put some distance between them while putting away his wallet, then followed her out of the bar.

Patterson Blake was a good twenty feet ahead of him and walking across the parking lot toward the RV area. Pope's vehicle was in the other direction but positioned to give a clear view of both the roadhouse entrance and the van. Instead of pursuing her, he went to his car and climbed in, then sat in the darkened vehicle and watched as she reached the van, slid back the rear side door, and climbed inside, before pulling the door closed again.

Several minutes ticked by.

Pope waited, wondering if she would avail herself of the free overnight parking or drive back into town. He didn't know why she had left Dallas and driven all the way to Santa Fe, but he knew what motivated her. Patterson Blake was looking for her missing sister, Julie. Presumably, some clue had led her to this location. Which meant she would probably be in town for at least a few days to follow up on it. That gave him time to plan his next move. The van hadn't yet moved, and Pope could see a sliver of light in the back behind the side window, which was covered by a blind. Blake was settling down for the night. It would have been easy to wait for her to fall asleep, screw the suppressor onto his Walther P22 semi-automatic pistol, and quietly break into the van. Shoot the woman in her bed before she even knew he was there. A pair of quick shots to the head. Double tap. Easy.

But Senator Newport wanted the FBI agent's demise to look like an accident, a specialty of Pope's, because an obvious murder would draw suspicion right back to him. Newport had almost ended up in jail for life on multiple murder charges, not to mention racketeering, false imprisonment, and a slew of other crimes. He had only squeaked out of it thanks to his powerful—and nervous—colleagues who occupied positions in government where things like that could be swept under the carpet. Other people had taken the fall for his misdeeds. People without such lofty acquaintances. But a dead FBI agent—an obvious revenge killing—would be too much. No, Patterson Blake had to go out with a whisper, not a bang.

Pope reclined his seat to forty-five degrees and settled in for a long night. In other circumstances, he would have found a hotel room and re-acquired his target the next morning, but her van was basically a hotel room on wheels, and he wasn't sure enough that she would stay put to leave it unobserved. Even if she stayed overnight, she might move on to some other location early in the morning.

Which meant he needed to remain close by so that when the time came, he knew exactly where she would be. And that was fine with Pope. He had slept in worse places. As a Marine Scout Sniper in Afghanistan, he had hunkered down with his M-24 sniper rifle in abandoned buildings crawling with deadly scorpions, dug into hot desert sands outside Kandahar, and endured extremes of scorching heat and freezing cold as he waited, sometimes for days on end, to acquire his target.

Those were the good times, when he went by a different name and was given medals for his skill at killing other human beings. Not that he could complain. His current profession might be less salubrious, but it paid better. Much better. Also, he could indulge in more creative ways to complete his missions. A bullet fired from the safety of a sniper's nest lacked originality, and Pope liked to think of himself as an artist, even if his canvas was death.

The light inside the van went dark. The vehicle still didn't move. It was now almost midnight. Pope waited a while longer, just to be certain, then closed his eyes and cleared his mind. He didn't need much sleep, had trained himself over the years to operate on four or five hours a night, but he knew his limitations. Besides, he never slept deeply. That was another skill he had learned in Afghanistan, where the enemy could attack at any time of day or night. You didn't want to be off in dreamland, oblivious to the world, when a suicide bomber breached your perimeter, or a group of insurgents opened fire on your camp. Pope would sleep now, but he would still be aware on a subconscious level, his mind processing the sounds around him even as he slumbered. And if he heard the rumble of an engine from the RV parking lot, if the van moved, he would snap back awake in an instant, ready and rested.

FOURTEEN

PATTERSON FELT unsettled even after climbing into the van and closing the door. She stood there, unable to shake a vague sense of unease.

Maybe it was just Bauer's call, and his obvious concern, but she didn't think so. After the incident on the highway earlier that day with the black SUV, her sense of danger had been heightened. At first, when he had warned her that the senator was walking free and may have reprisal on his mind, she had acknowledged the risk, but dismissed the idea that he would jeopardize his ill-gotten freedom by coming after her as fanciful. But even if the SUV had nothing to do with Senator Bill Newport, it had highlighted how vulnerable she was. If the man really had revenge on his mind, she might not recognize the danger until it was too late . . . Until someone intent upon doing her harm got close enough to achieve their goal. It was hard to defend against the unknown.

In fact, Patterson had been on edge the whole time she was in the roadhouse. She knew it was ridiculous, but it was almost like she could feel the weight of eyes on her back. The gaze of a predator. She was spooked, and she knew it. Perhaps it was because of her location. She could imagine Julie feeling a similar sensation. Turning the head of someone with deadly motives and falling prey to them. And in the back of Patterson's mind, the thought that someone might really be out to get her. Those two things had come together and left her uncharacteristically perturbed.

Even as she left the bar for the relative safety of the van, her eyes swept the room, looking for threats. But if any of the bar's patrons had shown any interest in her, they were doing a good job of hiding it.

Now, she tried to shake the feeling off, but it persisted. She sat at the table for a while and went through all the evidence gathered so far in Julie's disappearance—the postcards, map with the handwritten route sketched upon it, photographs, and the old band flyer—perusing them for the hundredth, maybe even thousandth time. Yet her attention strayed.

She gathered the breadcrumbs of Julie's trip, stashed them safely back in the plastic container and returned it to storage under the bed, then turned the van's internal lights off. She went to the window, safe in the knowledge that anyone watching the van from outside would not see her, and nudged a slat of the closed blind up just enough to peer out.

The parking lot was emptier than it had been earlier. As she watched, a couple exited the roadhouse, arms around each other, and made their way to an older model pickup truck. A few moments later, the truck's headlights pierced the darkness, then swept across the parking lot as the driver turned the vehicle toward the road beyond. Soon the pickup was swallowed by the night, its journey back toward Santa Fe briefly catalogued by the receding twin red dots of its taillights, until even these faded to nothing.

Patterson stood at the window a while longer, studying

the remaining vehicles, but if anyone was returning her gaze, she could not see them. Still battling the unease that had plagued her ever since that SUV went barreling past, Patterson let the blind drop back into place and turned away from the window. She undressed in the dark, folded her clothes and placed them neatly on one of the bench seats next to the table, and placed her Glock service weapon close by and within easy reach. After that, she climbed up onto the bed and slipped between the sheets.

The last time she had slept in this vehicle was on a cheap and thin memory foam mattress that did little to hide the fact that she was lying in the back of an old panel van on a hard, unyielding floor. Her current situation was a comparative luxury compared to that, and it wasn't long before she was asleep.

FIFTEEN

POPE WAS JOLTED awake by the sound of raised voices somewhere beyond his car. His eyes snapped open, and he reached instinctively for the pistol stashed in his glove compartment. The clock on his dash read 1:24 AM. Amy's Roadhouse had emptied and was obviously closed for the evening. Its windows were dark. The only light now spilled from a pair of lanterns on the wall under the porch and a floodlight mounted on a high pole at the periphery of the property that bathed the parking lot in a pale-yellow glow. There were only a few vehicles left, not counting the overnight residents of the RV lot. He would, he realized, need to either vacate the lot until morning, or move his own vehicle somewhere less obvious in order to keep tabs on Patterson Blake and her van. Because right now, he stood out like an iceberg at high noon in an expanse of open sea.

But there was a more immediate concern. The voices that had roused him from slumber. He was finely attuned to the vibrations of danger that meant the difference between life and death in a place like Kandahar. And even if he was no longer in an active war zone, raised voices fraught with notes of distress and conflict still rang his inner alarm bells. Yet at first, he saw no obvious reason for the vociferations that had set him on edge.

Pope let his hand fall away from the glove compartment and the gun within. Maybe it was the last boozy stragglers leaving the bar and drunkenly sparring among themselves as they did so.

But then, from the corner of his eye, he caught a flash of movement accompanied by a strangled squeal from the shadowy expanse along the side wall of the bar where the floodlight barely reached. A man holding a woman tight against the wall. Pope recognized her instantly as the bartender in the *barely covering anything* cut-off jean shorts and too-tight shirt knotted to reveal her midriff, who had served the FBI agent earlier in the evening. Now, the shirt was ripped open to expose what little had previously been left to the imagination. He could see the pale swell of her bare breasts as she struggled against her attacker—a broad shouldered, muscular man in jeans and a plaid shirt, beneath a white ten-gallon hat.

From the man's stance, with one hand pressed over the woman's mouth to stifle her screams, and his victim's flailing arms as she tried to both push him away and cover her nakedness, it was obvious this was no consensual coupling. Pope could imagine how the events leading up to this situation played out. The cowboy had lingered even as the rest of the patrons finished their drinks and filed out in a shamble of alcoholic disorganization. Maybe he sat at the bar, finishing his beer a little too slowly, and chatting with the woman. Maybe he learned it was her turn to lock up, and once he couldn't linger any longer in the bar without raising eyebrows, had waited outside in the shadows as the other staff members exited the building and drove off, leaving the young woman alone and vulnerable as she locked the front doors and made her way around the side of the building to a car that he could see tucked against the back fence beyond. Then the cowboy made his move, overcome with an alcohol-fueled lust that he might or might not regret the next day, because the object of his affections wanted no part of it. Except the cowboy wasn't taking no for an answer.

Pope's hand fell again to the glove compartment. He opened it and removed the Walther, then screwed the fat metal tube of a suppressor, commonly known as a silencer, onto the barrel. He had no choice but to save this woman and deal with her attacker. Not because he felt any empathy, but for a more prosaic reason. If the bartender ended up raped, which seemed certain without his intervention, and she reported the crime, this place would be swarming with cops in a matter of hours. He didn't want that to happen, given his eventual plans for Patterson Blake. The bar surely had internal surveillance video which could place himself and the FBI agent in the same location, and even if he intended to make her death look like an accident, the coincidence of a crime against another attractive young woman on the same night they were all in the same bar might lead the police to dig deeper. Might even make him a suspect in that crime, along with every other man in the place. Especially if the good-ole-boy who was currently fumbling to get inside the bartender's shorts went too far and killed her. Then there wouldn't even be a victim left alive to describe her assailant. There was also another reason, which on its own would not have been strong enough to secure his interdiction. He loathed men who committed violence purely to satisfy their basal urges, especially when they were inept and slapdash in their execution, which the cowboy surely was. Both things together meant that Pope had good reason to get involved.

The familiar tingle of anticipation was back. He might not be able to dispatch Patterson Blake yet but come morning there would be one less thug walking the face of the earth. The only question was how to accomplish it without the victim seeing him. Pope sat there for a moment, aware that his time in which to act was growing short and contemplated his options. Then, making up his mind, he placed the Walther down on the passenger seat within easy reach, started the car, which thankfully had a quiet engine, and steered it forward, nudging the vehicle's nose to the right so he was directly facing the struggling pair. If the cowboy registered the car's presence, he made no show of it, at least until Pope switched on his high beams and flooded the darkness ahead with brilliance.

SIXTEEN

THE COWBOY JERKED BACK in alarm, obviously not expecting his crime to be so starkly illuminated. In his confusion, he relaxed his grip on the struggling woman, raised a hand to shield his eyes against the blinding glare from Pope's headlights.

The young woman took advantage of her assailant's surprise and twisted free, extricating herself from his hold against the wall. In doing so, she brought her knee up between his legs, catching him hard enough that he doubled over in pain. Then she fled, pulling her top closed as she did so, and jumped into her car parked near the back fence. A moment later, a second set of headlights speared her assailant in their glare as she peeled away, throwing up a plume of dust behind her, and barreled through the parking lot toward the road past Pope's car without paying her savior any heed.

The cowboy was still doubled over, but now realized the predicament he was in. He rose to his full height and limped toward Pope's car with clenched fists, clearly intending to inflict a measure of pain upon the person who had spoiled his fun.

That was the wrong thing to do.

Pope had already decided the cowboy could not continue breathing. There was a good chance the bartender would tell no one what happened to her, traumatic as it was, either for fear of losing her job or out of misplaced shame. He had read somewhere that eighty percent of such crimes were never reported to the police. Even if she filed a police report, he was safe since she had not seen his face. He would simply become an anonymous good samaritan. He would prefer the alternative that she stayed firmly within that eighty percent. But the cowboy was a different matter. He was angry that Pope spoiled his fun. Chances were that he was also heavily inebriated and not making the best decisions—as evidenced by his recent activities. He would not simply slink away into the darkness.

Pope glanced sideways toward the RV lot several hundred feet distant on the other side of the building, and Patterson Blake's van. Her light was still off, just like the other vehicles in the lot. The bartender hadn't made enough noise to draw attention from that quarter, mostly thanks to the cowboy's hand pressed against her mouth. The only clue of something bad happening was a heated conversation between the pair before the assault, which was too far away for anyone in the RV lot to overhear, and a lone scream when the cowboy made his move. Pope had only heard it since he was much closer and attuned to such sounds of distress.

Satisfied that Patterson Blake was still in the land of nod and oblivious to the crime that had occurred right under her nose, Pope turned his attention back to the swiftly approaching cowboy. He turned off his headlights, pulled on a pair of black gloves he always kept close by, and retrieved the pistol from the passenger seat. Then he pushed his door open and stepped out. As the cowboy drew close, he raised the Walther and issued a terse yet quiet command.

"Stop right where you are or the next step you take will be in the afterlife."

"Huh?" The cowboy faltered and hesitated, clearly understanding the gun pointed at him more than the command.

Pope rolled his eyes. "That's far enough or I shoot you in the fucking head."

This time, the cowboy understood all too well. He was angry and drunk, but not stupid. At least, not *that* stupid. He came to a halt and raised his hands. "It's all good, man. Just let me go and I'll be on my way." He nodded toward a beater of a pickup truck parked near the edge of the lot in the gloom beyond the floodlight. A truck Pope hadn't noticed before. "No need for this to get out of hand. I don't have any quarrel with you."

"Your recent behavior would indicate otherwise," Pope said in a measured voice. "And even if my gun has given you a change of heart, it's too late. You've seen my face."

"Hell, I'm so drunk, I probably won't remember in the morning."

Pope thought that might be true, but he wasn't taking any chances. Loose ends led to jail cells, or worse, the death penalty. This scumbag wasn't worth the risk. "Kneel on the ground and put your hands behind your head."

"What?"

"You heard me."

"Aw, come on, man." The cowboy glanced toward his truck, no doubt wishing he could somehow magic himself across the gap and materialize behind the wheel before a bullet found him.

Pope motioned with his gun.

The cowboy had no choice. He sank to his knees and cupped his hands behind his head. Then he watched with watery, bloodshot eyes as Pope approached him. But what he didn't see, because it happened too fast, was Pope swinging his arm sideways in a chopping motion, free hand flat like a blade, to intersect the man's neck in just the right spot to render him inert long enough for what would come next.

SEVENTEEN

THREE WEEKS BEFORE

ANGEL LED *her daughter across the parking lot of the Pineland Country Store toward the front entrance, noting the kitschy frontier vibe it exuded. A log cabin style building with a wide porch out front and a stone chimney, it had the appearance of a hangover from pioneer days, although it was too clean and straight to be anywhere near that old. Rocking chairs sat at intervals on the porch. Carved totems flanked both sides of the door. Inside was an eclectic mix of tourist trap merchandise, groceries, camping equipment, and alcohol.*

A counter ran across the side wall to Angel's left, behind which a lone employee in her forties with slack brown hair and a dead expression on her face watched mother and daughter with vague disinterest. Near the far end of the counter was a cooler cabinet within which Angel saw wrapped sandwiches and subs, salads in plastic bowls with see through lids, and slices of pie, also in their own individual plastic containers.

Her stomach growled.

"Come on." Angel steered Cherub to the cooler, grabbing a six pack of water along the way, and perused the items available. She settled on a turkey sub for herself. She looked down at her daughter. "Turkey or ham?"

Cherub thought for a moment then said, "Turkey."

Angel grabbed a second sub and two plastic knives from a tin on the counter, then went to the register and paid using some of the cash she had swiped from the farmhouse. Then her eyes drifted to a sign on the back wall—camping and RV spots available. She didn't have an RV, or a tent, but she also didn't want to keep driving aimlessly. They needed a plan. Somewhere to go. She also didn't want to go searching for a motel, which she might never find. Besides, a camping spot was probably cheaper, and she didn't know how long the money would last.

"How much for a camping spot?" she asked the cashier.

"Forty a night." The cashier chewed gum on one side of her mouth. "If you want a lake view, it's sixty."

"There's a lake?" Cherub said, wide eyed.

"Sure is, precious." The cashier looked back up at Angel. "Not that there's much water in it right now—going through a dry spell —so I wouldn't bother paying the upgrade if I were you unless you like looking at dirt."

"We'll take a regular spot," Angel said, forking over a pair of twenty-dollar bills.

"Just the one night?"

"Yes."

"Okey-doke." The cashier scooped them up, then pointed to a map on the wall behind her showing the RV park and camping spots. "Plot D1. Just follow the dirt trail around until you see the camping area. D1 is on the left."

Angel thanked the woman. She took her daughter's hand and

made for the exit. As she stepped outside, an older man in overalls was coming the other way. His gaze lingered on Angel. She shuddered and hurried past, eager to be away from him. It was only when she bundled Cherub back into the car and slammed the door against the outside world, that Angel could breathe again.

EIGHTEEN

CORBIN POPE DROVE out into the desert in the cowboy's truck with his slumbering cargo propped in the passenger seat. After incapacitating him in the roadhouse parking lot using a technique learned years before in the Marine Corps—a hand-to-hand combat maneuver known as a brachial stun that rendered a person unconscious for anywhere from a few seconds to a couple of minutes—Pope had removed a small container of the type that prescription medicine might be dispensed in from a hidden compartment in the trunk of his vehicle. But no doctor had prescribed the pills inside the container. Flunitrazepam, more commonly referred to simply as the date rape drug, was illegal for that same reason. But it also provided an easy means of keeping a person docile long enough to deal with them. In this instance, the dosage had kept the cowboy peacefully sleeping long enough for Pope to bundle him into the truck and drive miles out into the wilderness at the foothills of the Sangre de Cristo Mountains, looking for a good spot to complete his task.

And now he had found it. A sharply rising outcrop of

jagged rock close to the dark and lonely road and far enough away from civilization that the cowboy might not be found for a while.

Pope steered the truck to the side of the road and came to a stop. He sat for a moment, observing his surroundings to make sure they were alone—that no other vehicles were approaching from either direction—but the road was empty.

Satisfied, Pope swung the truck's door open and climbed out. He slammed the door and went around to the passenger side before heaving the semi-conscious and disoriented cowboy out of the cab with gloved hands. He stood for a moment, observing the cowboy to see if the drug had worn off enough for him to walk, even if he wasn't yet fully aware of his surroundings. Then he marched the drowsy man away from the road and up a barely discernible trail leading to the top of the rise. It was pitch black, and the moon had long since set, but Pope had possessed the forethought to bring a flashlight, which he now turned on and trained toward the ground. The terrain was rocky and treacherous. He wasn't worried if the cowboy slipped and fell, but Pope would rather not twist an ankle, or worse, break a leg, so far from the roadhouse given that he had no intention of driving back in the cowboy's truck. For his plan to work, the truck must remain in place.

They reached the top of the rise. The ground fell sharply away on the other side, first in a series of ledges, and then a sloping drop of at least a hundred feet.

It was perfect.

Pope nudged his prisoner, forcing him down and onto the closest ledge. Now he could breathe easier. If another vehicle did come along, they would be shielded from view. It was doubtful that even the flashlight beam would be visible from the road. But even so, there was no point in lingering. Every moment he spent out in the barren landscape miles from Patterson Blake's van was just more opportunity for something to go sideways. Right now, he was sure the FBI agent was sleeping, but he didn't like leaving anything to chance.

Pope nudged the cowboy with the barrel of his gun. "Step toward the edge, undo your pants, and go to the bathroom."

"What?" The cowboy had recovered sufficiently to recognize the unusual nature of this command. "Why?"

"Don't worry about why. Just do it."

The cowboy turned to look at Pope with wide unfocused eyes and mouth still slack from the drugs. Then his gaze dropped to the gun, and his captor's finger curled around the trigger. As if the mortal nature of his predicament had only now dawned on him, the cowboy nodded. He turned and took several shuffling steps forward toward the precipice. Reaching the edge, he unzipped his pants and proceeded to urinate, splashing his shoes with as much steaming yellow liquid as he managed to get over the edge. After he finished, the cowboy turned and started back toward Pope even as he reached down to make himself decent again.

"Leave it hanging," Pope said before the cowboy could put it away and zip himself up.

The cowboy faltered, hands at his crotch.

"Turn back around and go to the edge, then kneel down."

The cowboy hesitated, probably sensing that his life was about to be cut short even if he couldn't figure out why it had to happen with his manhood dangling and his pants unzipped. But faced with the business end of Pope's gun, he was left with no choice. After a moment, he turned back toward the edge and shuffled drunkenly forward.

Then something unexpected happened. Still unsteady on his feet, the Cowboy's boot snagged on a protruding rock, and he toppled forward, barely managing to put his hands out to break his fall before landing heavily in the dirt with a grunt.

He rolled onto his side, spitting dust from his mouth. Then he froze, eyes fixed on a serpentine form sheltering mere inches away next to the rock.

The telltale rattle that came next told Pope everything he needed to know about what the cowboy had disturbed. It was a large snake, perhaps seven feet in length, although it was hard to tell the exact size since it was coiled so tightly. But there was no doubting its identity. A Western diamondback. Extremely venomous and ill-tempered when cornered.

"Get it away from me," the cowboy screeched, suddenly finding the will to think past the drugs in his system.

The gun was heavy in Pope's hand. It would have been easy to take the snake's head clean off with one shot at such a short range, but this was a gift. He had no intention of killing the snake. In fact, he wanted it meaner. Leaning down, Pope selected a small rock.

The cowboy was still cowering in place, incapacitated by his own terror. When he saw the rock in Pope's hand, saw him toss it at the coiled serpent, he let out a startled screech.

The rock landed close to the already defensive beast's head, just as Pope intended.

Any tolerance the snake had left for the intruders in its space vanished. It shot forward, lightning fast, and buried its fangs in the cowboy's arm even as he tried to swat the creature away.

The screech became a pained wail. The cowboy clawed at the snake, which was still attached to his arm, pumping more venom into him by the second. Finally, he managed to rip the viper free and toss it over the side of the ledge, leaving one torn fang still buried in his flesh.

"It bit me." The cowboy clutched his arm, and the still embedded fang. He squirmed on the ground, face contorted into a mask of agony. "Oh God. You have to help me. I need a hospital."

Pope looked on, a half-smile creasing his lips. This was even better than he could have imagined. Now, when the cops finally discovered the cowboy's abandoned truck, and his broken body at the bottom of the outcrop, they would assume he had pulled over to empty his beer-filled bladder, climbed up onto the outcrop to pee and ran afoul of the snake. Startled and drunk, he tried to escape the angry serpent, only to slip off the edge and fall to his death. Another Corbin Pope masterpiece. But there was still one thing to do.

Pope selected another rock, larger this time, and walked over to the stricken man. He dragged him to the edge so his head was dangling in the open air and there would be no significant blood spatter on the ground to raise suspicion. Then Pope straddled the man and brought the rock down with all the strength he could muster. Once, twice, three times, until the cowboy's skull gave way with a satisfying crack.

After checking the man was dead—he didn't want any surprise resurrections coming back to haunt him later—Pope deposited the truck keys into the cowboy's jeans pocket. Now he stood and rolled the limp corpse over the side, watching it bounce and tumble all the way to the bottom a hundred feet below. Satisfied with the outcome of his efforts, Pope tossed the bloodied rock over and waited for it to land next to the corpse before picking his way back over the ridge and down the trail to the road. Then he started the long walk back to Amy's Roadhouse and his actual target. Patterson Blake.

NINETEEN

PATTERSON WALKED BACK into Amy's Roadhouse at the stroke of noon, just as soon as they opened their doors for the day, to hunt down the one person still working there who might remember Trent Steiger or Julie.

It didn't take her long to locate the woman, who looked a good deal older than her coworkers. Bailey Donohoe was in her early forties with raven-dark hair pulled tight to the back of her head in a shoulder length ponytail and a rose tattoo on her neck. She cut a willowy figure with angular cheekbones and a high forehead, and still managed to pull off the tight shorts and crop top that appeared to be the ubiquitous, if informal, uniform at Amy's.

The establishment was mostly empty, save for a few over-eager customers, most likely regulars, who had pulled into the parking lot in the moments before the roadhouse opened for the day.

Patterson strode toward the bar, heading straight for Bailey, and quickly engaged with the server. She ordered a coffee—it was much too early for alcohol—and studied a paper lunch menu for a few moments before ordering food, then got right to the point before the woman could turn her attention elsewhere. "I came in here last night looking for information about my sister. The bartender said you're the only person who's been here long enough to remember her."

"Yeah," Bailey grinned, leaning on the bar. "Call me a lifer. I've seen 'em all come and go. Some girls barely last a month. Tips are fine, but this place sure can take a toll." The grin faded. "What's the deal with your sister?"

"She's missing," Patterson replied. "This bar is the last place we know she frequented."

"She work here or something?"

Patterson shook her head. "Probably not. She wasn't twenty-one yet. Not for another six months. Couldn't serve alcohol."

"But she was hanging out in the roadhouse."

"She met a guy. He was a musician who played some gigs here."

"How long ago are we talking?"

"Sixteen years. She was on a cross-country road trip and never came back. We think something bad might have happened to her."

"Aw, hell. That's awful." A look of sympathy passed across Bailey's face. "What was your sister's name?"

"Julie," Patterson replied. "Julie Blake."

"Name doesn't ring a bell. You got a picture?"

Patterson dug into her pocket and removed a picture of Julie. One of the photographs Mark Davis had given her weeks before. It showed a smiling Julie standing next to Steiger. "This is the most up-to-date photo I have."

Bailey took the photo and stared at it for a few moments before handing it back and shaking her head. "I don't recognize either of them. Honestly, your sister could be any of ten thousand pretty girls who have walked through these doors over the last two decades. When you see as many faces as I do, it's hard to tell them apart after a while. Sorry."

"I get that," Patterson said, biting back her dismay. She returned the photo to her pocket.

"The guy in the picture. Was he the musician?"

"Yes." Patterson nodded. "Trent Steiger. He played guitar and sang."

"They all do."

"He got the gig because his cousin worked here as a bartender. You remember any employees with that surname?" Patterson asked, not expecting much. Steiger's cousin might not even share his last name depending on their relationship to each other.

Bailey shrugged. "Like I said, staff come and go all the time. Hard to remember who I worked with six months ago, let alone back then."

"What about the bar owner? There might be staff records."

"Unlikely. The original owner—that would be Amy—sold the place years ago to an out of state hospitality company called DRG Restaurant Holdings. They cleaned out her office and all the filing cabinets, took whatever they didn't just shred and toss to their corporate headquarters. I should know. I did some of the shredding along with a few of the other bartenders after hours for extra pay. Mounds of old paperwork, hopelessly out of date. Some of it went back to the fifties when Amy first opened the place. She even had old bar menus stored in a closet. Guess she didn't like to get rid of stuff."

"I see." Patterson made a mental note to look up the corporation that owned the bar and contact their HR office.

Bailey looked away as more customers entered the bar. "Sorry I can't be more helpful. Sixteen years is a long time."

"It was a long shot," Patterson said, disappointed.

"Look, I can't guarantee anything, but I still know a couple of the servers from back then. The ones that stuck around long enough to become friends. They don't work here anymore, but I'll reach out, see what they remember."

"Thank you." Patterson was grateful but suspected that their answer would be the same. Bailey was right. Sixteen years *was* a long time, especially to remember a single face in the crowd. "I appreciate the help."

"No problem. You have a photo of your sister and her friend that I can share with them?"

"I have a digital copy of the picture I showed you," Patterson said. She had made a point to digitize every image and piece of evidence she had collected regarding Julie's disappearance. "

"Great." Bailey took a pen from her pocket and wrote an email address down on a napkin, then pushed it across the bar. "You can send it here."

Patterson took out her phone and browsed through the case documents stored in a secure vault on the cloud. When she came to the picture of Julie and Steiger, she attached it to a message and sent it to the email address on the napkin. "All done."

"Perfect." Bailey checked her phone, then nodded. "Got it. You'll have to give me a few days. I'm working doubles all weekend, and I don't know how long it will take to hear back from them."

"Understood."

Bailey returned the phone to her back pocket, then she stepped away and turned her attention to other customers.

Patterson stared down into her coffee. She wasn't sure what she had expected to find at Amy's Roadhouse so long after the fact. Her sister's trail had been cold for a decade and a half, and she was lucky to have even made it this far in her search for Julie. At some point, that luck was sure to run out. If she didn't find another clue in Santa Fe, something to lead her one step closer to the truth of her sister's disappearance, Patterson would be forced to give up and accept that Julie was just another cold case that might never be solved. She wouldn't be the first, and certainly not the last. Jurisdictions all over the country had piles of cold cases that might never be satisfactorily closed. Just because she was an FBI agent didn't mean Patterson's experience would be any different. That her family would somehow get the closure others had not. It was a sobering thought, and one that left her frustrated and depressed. But if Amy's Roadhouse really was the end of the line, she would accept it, because there would be no choice.

Patterson took the photo of Julie back out and stared at it. She wished there were some way to span the gulf of years between them. To step into that image and warn her sister of the danger that lurked somewhere in her future. But the picture provided no mechanism for such an extraordinary event, and in the end, Patterson returned it to her pocket.

When her food came, she ate with little enthusiasm and eventually pushed the plate away before finishing. She wanted to get out of there, return to the van and plan her next move, whatever that would be. But before Patterson could ask for the check, Bailey reappeared, looking grim.

"Hey," she said. "I was thinking about your sister, what you said about her vanishing sixteen years ago, and I remembered something."

"About Julie?" Patterson asked hopefully.

"No. Well, maybe. I hope not because it's bad. Real bad. I don't think you're going to like it."

TWENTY

PATTERSON WAITED for the bartender to speak.

Bailey cast a nervous sideways glance down the bar, as if she were having second thoughts about approaching Patterson with the newly remembered information, and hoped some bartending emergency requiring her immediate attention would develop and save her from uttering it. Then she took a deep breath and leaned across the bar close to the FBI agent and spoke in a hushed voice. "I really hope this isn't connected to your sister, but around the time you say she disappeared, a body was found about half a mile down the road from the roadhouse on eighty-four in a ditch. A young woman, maybe early twenties. It was a big deal around here because there was some talk that she might have been right here in the bar prior to getting murdered. Maybe even left with her killer. But if that was what happened, the police never found any evidence of it, or at least, none they shared with us, but still . . ."

Patterson's blood ran cold. For a moment, she couldn't

speak. She cleared her throat and composed herself. "Did the victim have a name?"

Bailey shook her head. "Talk at the time was that she must have been a runaway, or maybe a hitchhiker. She wasn't from around here. That much I know. Someone would have reported her missing."

"None of the staff at the bar recognized her?" Patterson prayed it wasn't Julie, reasoned with herself that if her sister had been hanging around the roadhouse, someone would have identified the body. For a start, there was Trent Steiger. He was dating Julie. He certainly would have recognized her. "Maybe she was someone they served, or they saw her hanging around?"

But Bailey merely shook her head again, slower this time. "The body had been there for a while, apparently. It was in pretty bad shape from what I heard. Nothing much left for anyone to look at."

Patterson's chest tightened. "And this was sixteen years ago."

Bailey nodded.

"About what time of year?"

"It was winter. Like maybe the end of February. I remember because there were a couple inches of snow on the ground but it was starting to melt. Folk from out of state sometimes think Santa Fe is hot year-round, being New Mexico and all, but it isn't. We have a bunch of ski resorts up on the mountains that operate right through the winter until early April."

"You're sure it was in the winter?" The world around Patterson shifted out of focus. She swallowed back a wave of nausea and clutched at the bar before pulling herself together.

"Positive. We served free hot coffee and hamburgers to the cops up the road at the crime scene. They would come down here wearing their heavy coats and gloves. Come inside to warm up, especially the first evening after she was found. They were pretty much up there all night. Then they spent a couple of days searching the area. Looking for clues, I guess."

Patterson could imagine the scene. The road closed and police vehicles everywhere. The coroner's van. Forensics. She saw the officers fanning out across the landscape in her mind's eye, searching for anything out of place. A piece of clothing. Discarded cigarette butt. Even a boot print in the dusty soil. Then her mind shifted to a more unpleasant thought. Julie, alone and dead, lying in a ditch beside the road. Her sister too badly decomposed to positively identify. A cold case sitting in Santa Fe all these years while the rest of her family wondered and waited for a return that would never happen. She closed her eyes against a sudden swell of tears, turned away so Bailey wouldn't see the raw emotions washing over her, but there was no hiding it.

"Hey. I didn't mean to upset you." The bartender placed a comforting hand on Patterson's arm. "We don't even know if it was your sister."

"We don't know that it wasn't." Patterson wiped the tears away with the back of one hand. She felt foolish. Here she was, a trained and hardened FBI agent, losing it in front of a potential witness, even if that person didn't know she was a Fed. But what else could she do? After following Julie's trail from Chicago to Oklahoma City, then on to Dallas and Amarillo, the odds were increasing that she would reach the end of the road. Arrive at the place where her sister's trip took a wrong turn. Where darkness found her. Because alive or dead—and Patterson knew which of those was most likely —something awful had happened all those years ago that prevented her sister from ever coming home. Patterson breathed deeply and forced the FBI agent within her to come to the fore. "I'm sorry. I shouldn't have let my emotions get the better of me."

"Heavens, there's no need. I can't imagine how much of a mess I'd be if my sister went missing like that." Bailey squeezed Patterson's arm, then withdrew her hand. "And here you are, still looking for her. Not giving up after all these years. That takes some strength of character."

"Older or younger sister?" Patterson asked, to steer the conversation away from Julie.

"Younger by three years. She skipped town when she was eighteen. Lives in Denver now. We don't talk as often as we should. Maybe I'll give her a call later, tell her how much I love her."

"You should do that." *Because you never know when the chance will slip through your fingers like sand through an hourglass,* Patterson thought to herself.

"But not before I get you a refill of coffee," said Bailey, tapping her finger on the bar top. "There anything else you need to ask me?"

Patterson said no, then thanked the woman for her help. She watched as Bailey disappeared into the kitchen through a set of double swinging doors next to the bar. Her next step was obvious. Pay a visit to the Santa Fe Police Department and see what they could tell her about a young woman found dead in a ditch sixteen years ago. A young woman without an identity who might very well be her sister, Julie.

TWENTY-ONE

AN HOUR after finishing her meal and leaving Amy's Roadhouse, Patterson walked into the lobby of the Santa Fe Police Department's headquarters on the south side of town. It was a blocky two floor building with a side parking lot surrounded by mostly dusty landscaping dotted with weeds, bushes, and a couple of small trees that looked like they had barely survived the summer.

Patterson walked up to the front desk officer and held her FBI credentials up, then asked for a detective in the homicide division.

The officer, a heavyset woman in her thirties with rosy cheeks and curly straw-colored hair, studied the badge for a moment before picking up the phone on her side of the desk and holding a short conversation in hushed tones. After replacing the receiver, she looked up at Patterson. "Someone will be out to see you soon."

Patterson thanked the woman and put her credentials away, then stepped away from the desk. A few minutes later, a burly man in an ill-fitting charcoal colored suit appeared and made a beeline for her.

"Detective Les Anderson." He held his hand out in greeting.

Patterson introduced herself and shook the proffered hand, noting that the detective had a firm grip. She flashed her credentials again, then got right to business. "Sixteen years ago, a Jane Doe was found on US-84 a few miles south of Pojoaque. The young woman was in her late teens or early twenties. The body was too badly decomposed to be identified."

"I remember that case." The detective ran a hand through the remains of what must once have been a head of thick black hair that was now gray and thinning. "I'd just made detective. She was my first homicide. Still irks me to this day. Never could find out who she was or why someone wanted to kill her." The detective glanced sideways as the lobby door opened and an older man walked in. "How about we find somewhere more private to talk."

Patterson followed the detective to the door he had emerged through minutes before. Anderson used a key card to gain entry and held the door open for Patterson to step past him. Then he led her along a brightly lit corridor with pale white walls and a suspended ceiling that could have graced the interior of any one of a million such buildings across the country. As they walked, her shoes squeaked on the linoleum floor tiles.

"In here," Anderson said, arriving at a door marked *conference room* and ushering Patterson inside.

A rectangular cherry-colored table occupied the middle of the room, surrounded by twelve chairs. Four on each side and another at each end. A dry erase board hung on the far wall. Streaks of red and blue ink still lingered from previous meetings like faint fault lines across its surface. A projector hung from the ceiling, pointing at a rolled-up screen that could be dropped down when needed. The walls were painted the same dull white, now dinged and smudged with black marks in places where chairs had been pushed back against them.

The detective motioned for Patterson to take a seat, then sat down opposite, folded his arms, and looked at her across the table. "Care to tell me why the FBI is interested in one of our cold cases?"

"I believe it may be related to a case of my own. A young woman who went missing sixteen years ago on a road trip from Chicago to Los Angeles."

"And you think our Jane Doe might be your missing person?"

"Yes." It took all of Patterson's willpower to keep her emotions in check. The last thing she needed was to lose the veneer of professionalism in front of this homicide detective. "The subject of my investigation was last seen alive at Amy's Roadhouse. She was traveling with a musician who was playing there. After that, the trail goes cold."

"Ah. I can see why you would think our cold case and yours might intersect. What's the name of your missing woman?"

Patterson hesitated. She had hoped to avoid this question, at least until she determined if their Jane Doe even fitted her sister's description or the timeline of her disappearance. But holding out on Detective Anderson, refusing to answer, would do no good. "Julie Blake."

There was a moment of silence. Anderson raised an eyebrow. "Blake."

"Yes." Patterson knew what was coming next. The detective had surely noted the name on her credits. She doubted that FBI agents walked into the police department unannounced and asking questions very often.

"Just like you. I'm betting that's not a coincidence."

"No. It's not a coincidence. Julie was—" Patterson caught herself. "*Is* my sister."

"I assume your field office is good with you conducting an investigation into the disappearance of your own sister?" Anderson didn't look convinced. "Unless, of course, you're not here in an official capacity, in which case I'm not sure how much more we have to discuss until I get an all clear from my lieutenant."

"You don't need to worry. It's all above board," Patterson replied, slightly irked at the implication that she was running an unauthorized off-the-books investigation, even as she realized the hypocrisy, given how her search for Julie started. "You can check with Marilyn Kahn, my SAC in New York, if you like. The Special Agent In Charge of the Dallas field office will be more than happy to vouch for me, too."

"That won't be necessary." Anderson waived an apologetic hand. "Didn't mean to needle you."

"It's quite all right." Patterson swallowed her annoyance. "About your Jane Doe . . ."

"Right." Anderson stroked his chin. "She was a Caucasian female, probably in her late teens or early twenties. She'd been on the side of the road for a while when she was discovered, sitting out in the elements at the mercy of scavengers, and was partially skeletonized. Visual identification was impossible. Maybe if we'd had a clue who she might be we could have compared dental records, but . . ."

"You ran DNA?"

Anderson nodded. "Put it through the usual databases. At least, what we had available to us back then. Got no hits."

Patterson didn't want to ask the next question. Knew that she must. "How did the victim die?"

"It was a homicide. Strangulation. No doubt about it according to the coroner."

There was one more question Patterson didn't want to ask. "Was the victim . . ." she choked up. "Was she . . ."

"Raped?"

Patterson nodded.

"If memory serves, the results were inconclusive, but don't quote me on that. It's been so long. If you want more definitive answers, I'll need to pull the case file."

"Could I see that case file for myself?" Patterson asked. "Maybe get a copy of it?"

"I don't see why not. You are FBI." Anderson looked away briefly, then let his gaze settle back on Patterson with narrowed eyes. "You know, I said we couldn't match our Jane Doe's DNA sample to anyone. But if your suspicion is correct, that might not be true anymore."

"You want to take a sample of my DNA to compare against the victim." This had occurred to Patterson already, but she was waiting to bring it up. Now she didn't need to.

"It would be the easiest way to give you an answer," Anderson said. "One way or the other."

TWENTY-TWO

CORBIN POPE SAT across the road from the Santa Fe police headquarters feeling more than a little uncomfortable. He didn't like being this close to so many people with the power to put him behind bars. But at the same time, he couldn't help but chuckle. If only they knew. Corbin was probably responsible for more untimely ends in his long and bloody career since hanging up his government issued sniper rifle, than every murder the police officers in that building had investigated in all their years combined. The wolf was truly at their door, and they had no clue.

But he wasn't there to gloat at the ignorance of the men and women who had sworn to serve and protect. He was there because of one particular law enforcement officer. Special Agent Patterson Blake.

The night before, he had trudged back to Amy's Roadhouse along the dark and deserted highway after dispatching the cowboy, who now lay dead and broken at the bottom of a ridge where he would fester until some unfortunate hiker or wandering tourist found him. And when they did, the coroner would label his passing an accident. And by that time, all obvious traces of the drug Pope had administered to keep the man docile would be gone. Not that the coroner would even be looking for it. The death was an obvious enough accident that toxicology, if ordered, would be basic, and probably focus on the snake bite and associated venom. The last thing the coroner would be looking for was a date rape drug.

After killing the cowboy, it had taken over an hour for Pope to reach the roadhouse on foot and climb back behind the wheel of his vehicle. He was relieved to discover the parking lot as empty as he had left it. No police cruisers with flashing red and blue lights looking for a would-be rapist. The cute bartender hadn't reported the attempted assault, just as he suspected.

The FBI agent's van hadn't moved, probably because it was three in the morning. The windows were dark. She was sleeping. Pope reclined his seat as far back as he could without losing sightline to the van and closed his eyes, exhausted by the night's activities.

He woke at dawn, when a semi rumbled past on the highway, speeding its unknown cargo to who knew where. The first thing he did was move the car, repositioning himself on the far side of the lot close to where the unlucky bartender had parked the evening before. He didn't want Patterson Blake to spot his vehicle and wonder why it had been there all night. With the car moved, he reached into the back, to a cooler that contained an assortment of snacks he'd had the forethought to purchase the previous day and munched on a gas station ham and cheese sandwich. The bread was dry and the cheese tasteless, like eating a slice of orange plastic, but it satisfied his hunger.

A couple of hours later, the first roadhouse staff arrived.

Shortly afterward, the van's door opened, and Patterson Blake made her way across the parking lot, passing close to where Pope had been parked only hours before, and entered the establishment. She came back out an hour later and drove off, heading toward Santa Fe.

So here he was now, sitting outside the police department headquarters feeling conspicuous and watching the van, which was now parked in the visitor's lot to the side of the building.

He still had no idea how he was going to kill the FBI agent. Her death must be accomplished with more aplomb that that of the cowboy. He couldn't just overpower her, drive out into the wilderness, and throw her off some tall escarpment. That scenario just wasn't believable and invited scrutiny. A mechanical fault with her van was likewise unlikely to fool her associates at the Bureau, especially since they were aware of the senator's release and his willingness to get rid of those who crossed him.

Pope quickly considered and rejected several more tried and true methods of killing her without signs of foul play. Methods that would have worked with a less sensitive target. Staging a suicide. Accidental drowning. Drug overdose. None of them felt right.

He sighed with frustration. The answer would come to him. It always did. Maybe Patterson Blake herself would provide the means of her own demise. Just like the young sophomore senator who took an ill-advised solo rock-climbing excursion to Colorado's Eldorado Canyon several years earlier. Pope still didn't know who actually wanted the man killed, or why—the individual who hired him took great pains to keep their identity secret—but it didn't matter. The senator practically did the job on his own by free soloing a rockface too advanced for his fledgling weekend hobby.

Trying to gain purchase on a seam of friable rock too weak to hold his weight, the senator fell twenty feet onto a narrow ledge and broke his leg. The larger, deadly fall of another two hundred feet came courtesy of Pope, who simply helped him take the quick way down off the ledge. Because unlike the senator, Pope was an expert mountaineer, having completed the Assault Climber's Course while serving in the Marines. It was a skill that had served him well as a sniper, allowing Pope to find unusual vantage points from which to take his shot. At least until he was unceremoniously shown the door following a court-martial that he still thought was unfair.

But that was all in the past. The senator was a reminder that sometimes patience was rewarded. All he had to do was stick close to the FBI agent, and maybe she would create her own deadly narrative. In the meantime, he hoped she would not be much longer inside the building, because the longer he sat there and watched those cops coming and going, the jumpier he got.

TWENTY-THREE

FOR THE SECOND time in as many months, Patterson gave a DNA sample to see if her sister was a cold case murder victim. Once the deed was done, she left the Santa Fe Police Department's crime lab and met up with Detective Anderson again, who was waiting outside in the corridor with his arms folded.

He looked up at her approach. "How did it go?"

"The lab said they're going to fast track the DNA results, but it will still be a few days before they have an answer."

"Better than a few weeks. I guess being a Fed has its perks."

"I'd rather not need that perk," Patterson said, a little too sharply.

"Right." Anderson looked sheepish. "Should've put my brain in gear before I spoke."

"No." Patterson pushed her hands into her pockets and looked down at the floor. "I shouldn't have been so sensitive. You didn't mean anything by it, and I'm grateful the lab is pushing the test through so quickly."

"You're right. I didn't mean anything by it. But I should still know better." Anderson cleared his throat. "Moving on, I called over to the records department while you were in there and informed them that you will be stopping by. They'll pull copies of all the paperwork pertaining to our Jane Doe from the archives. They'll also check the relevant materials out from the evidence room so you can study the items found with the body."

"You mean like the clothes she was wearing?" Patterson asked. She wondered if finding Julie would be as simple as recognizing a favorite T-shirt or jeans.

"And the bag."

"What bag?" This was the first Patterson had heard of any additional items being found along with the murder victim.

"The girl had a backpack with her. It contained a bunch of clothes, along with some other items. That's why we theorized she must be a runaway or hitchhiker. Certainly no one from around Santa Fe. There was also an ID found in the victim's back pocket. A driver's license, but it was too badly damaged to get an ID. We were able to determine that it was out-of-state. That was the other thing that fed into the hitchhiker scenario."

"What state was it from?" Patterson's chest tightened. Julie had never switched her residence to Chicago when she left for college. If the license was issued in New York, it would be one more reason to believe that the murdered girl found out on US-84 all those years ago was her sister.

Anderson rubbed his chin with a slow thumb and forefinger. "Can't rightly remember, to be honest. It's been so long. But it was one of the northern states."

"Like New York?" Patterson asked, her mouth suddenly dry.

Anderson pursed his lips and shook his head slowly.

"Maybe. Honestly, I think you just need to look in the evidence locker. That will give you all the information you need."

The world spun around Patterson. Detective Anderson hadn't confirmed that the license came from New York, but he hadn't denied it, either. Now that she might be on the precipice of a major discovery, a part of her wanted to turn and run the other way. While Julie was still missing, while she was still out there in the great unknown, there was hope. If Patterson recognized the clothes in that backpack, confirmed the origin of the driver's license, there would be no more doubt. She would know for sure that Julie had met a tragic and terrifying end on the side of a lonely highway in New Mexico. The only thing that wouldn't yet be clear was why, and she might never get that answer.

"There's a good chance it isn't her," Anderson said, observing Patterson with blue eyes that shone coldly under the corridor's harsh fluorescent lighting, contradicting the warmth of his tone.

"I know." Patterson swallowed. Her throat felt like sandpaper. "But even if it isn't Julie, there's another family out there somewhere still wondering about their sister. Their daughter."

"That's one of the worst parts of this job," Anderson said. "It's a no-win situation. If we don't ID the victim, their loved ones spend the rest of their lives in limbo, wondering what happened and never able to put it behind them. If we get an ID, we shatter the hope, no matter how small it might be, of their loved one returning one day, safe and sound."

Patterson said nothing. Detective Anderson had summed up the Catch-22 nature of cases like this . . . of Julie's disappearance. She knew the likelihood of ever seeing her sister alive was practically nil, but hope sprung eternal, as the phrase went. Eventually realizing her silence was becoming obvious, she cleared her throat and shook the maudlin thoughts off, focusing back on what she could control. "If you don't mind, I'd like to look at the items found with the victim as soon as possible. Get those copies of the case file. Can you point me toward records?"

Anderson nodded. "For that, you'll have to drive. We have a separate records and archives building about a mile from here. By the time you get there, they should have everything you need."

"Great. Want to give me the address?"

"Sure." Anderson took his phone out. "Give me your number. I'll text it to you."

Patterson gave him her cell phone number, then waited for the message to come through before thanking the detective for his time.

Anderson nodded his acknowledgment. "If you have any more questions, or need anything else, just call me anytime."

"Actually, there is one more thing," Patterson said.

"Shoot."

Patterson told him what she needed.

Anderson listened, then nodded. "I can arrange that. Swing back by after you're finished at the records building."

"Thanks."

"No problem," Anderson said. "For what it's worth, I hope you find your sister, Special Agent Blake, and that she's not waiting for you in a cardboard box on the shelf of some evidence room."

"Me too," Patterson replied, but even as she said the words, she couldn't stifle the overwhelming sensation of dread that crept up on her. A dread that would only be resolved by finding out what waited for her a mile across town.

TWENTY-FOUR

THREE WEEKS BEFORE

ANGEL SPENT *an uncomfortable night in the front of the Sebring while Cherub slept in the back, laying across the rear seat. They had parked in the forty-dollar camping spot, which was thankfully far from prying eyes—even if it was overpriced for a patch of dirt—and ate their sandwiches. Then they settled down. The darkness encircling the car was absolute, save for the occasional pinprick of light from some other camp or RV or the yellow glow of a distant firepit. Angel didn't mind. Darkness was safety. If no one could see them, no one could tell Carl where they were.*

They left when the sun came up the next morning, continuing south. Angel drove with the driver's side window rolled down, barely able to believe that she was actually outside and in the open, and reveled in the wind whipping through her hair, clear blue sky, and sweet scent of ponderosa pine that filled the vehicle.

In the back, Cherub sat and stared quietly at the world beyond the car. She had never left the farm before, and the passing scenery fascinated her.

"Where are we going?" she asked eventually, growing bored and turning her attention from the window. She stuck her head between the front seats to look up at her mother.

"Phoenix." Angel said, knowing her daughter would not have a clue what or where that was.

On cue, she asked the question. "Who's Phoenix?" Although she pronounced more like Funonix.

"Not who . . . where. It's a city," Angel told her. A city she had decided on in the small hours as she sat awake and staring through the Sebring's windshield at the lights of a distant camper van.

They had fled the farmhouse without any plan other than escape. Get as far away from that place as possible. In fact, up until she found Ma in the kitchen, she hadn't even considered running. Even breaking out of her bedroom had been a bold move that would have earned her a beating and possibly a few days locked in the pitch black and damp cellar if anyone had been in the house to do it. As she sat in that dark car the night before she realized they needed to have a destination beyond 'anywhere but there'. And the only place she could think of, mostly because she saw signs for it back in Flagstaff and knew it wasn't too far, was Phoenix.

Something else had occurred to her, too. They needed new names. When Carl finally returned to the farm and found Ma dead and her bedroom empty, he would come after her, and she had no intention of leaving a trail for him to follow. That meant not using her birthname, either. She would need something different. Something Carl would never guess. So would her daughter. But that could wait. There were more important things. Like ditching the Sebring. It wasn't a vehicle likely to turn heads, but it was technically stolen. She doubted Carl would have the nerve to report it missing under the circumstances, but she didn't want to find out.

But Angel had a deeper worry. What would happen if they were pulled over? She had no driver's license, no ID of any kind. The car was registered to Ma, and by extension, Carl. Under the circumstances, she would have no choice but to tell the cops that she was Carl's . . . *girlfriend? Live-in lover? Common-law wife? Some variation of the above.* And in a twisted way it was accurate. She had been with him for well over a decade, had fathered his child. Lived in his house. *You're mine,* he had told her on many occasions. *All mine, and don't you forget it.* The only other option, telling the cops who she really was and returning to her life before Carl would be too dangerous for everyone involved. It wasn't an option. For all those reasons, the car had to go. And in the meantime, don't get pulled over.

Cherub squirmed on the back seat. Not used to long distance travel, she was already bored. She thought about Angel's reply for a moment, that Phoenix was a city, then asked, "Why are we going there?"

Because it's far from Carl, Angel thought. Which it was, but there was a better reason to go there. "Because they have a bus station, honey."

Cherub didn't reply.

When Angel glanced back at her, the kid was sitting with a puzzled expression on her face. "A bus is like a big car with lots and lots of seats," she explained. "We'll get on the bus, and it will take us on a far-away adventure."

"I don't like it here. I don't want to go on an adventure." Cherub folded her arms and pouted. "I want to go back."

"We can't do that, sweetie," Angel said in her most soothing voice. "We have to keep moving forward. It will get better soon, I promise."

"When?"

"How about in the next ten minutes," Angel replied, her gaze settling on a heartwarming sight.

They had been on the road for an hour and were coming into a small town with ranch-style homes at the end of dusty driveways and a small main street with an assortment of stores big and small.

110

There was even a Walmart to provide groceries and all manner of other things not just to this one outpost of civilization, but to all the other tiny hamlets and ranches in the area. And ahead of them, rising above the buildings like a beacon, something Angel hadn't seen for a very long time but brought tears of nostalgia to her eyes. A gigantic yellow M on a pole above a brick building with a red roof and a line of cars snaking around to the drive-thru. "I bet you're hungry, huh?"

Cherub nodded.

"Good," said Angel, pulling into the McDonalds parking lot and joining the drive-thru line. "Because this place has the best fries, ever. And I mean ever."

TWENTY-FIVE

WHEN PATTERSON ARRIVED at the records building, she was buzzed into the building and led straight to a secure viewing room that contained nothing but a table, four chairs, and a surveillance camera mounted high in one corner. Atop the table was a pile of paperwork in a manila folder, and two brown storage boxes with taped lids and a faded case number written on the front of each in black marker.

The employee who had met her, a mousy woman with short bobbed black hair and wire-rimmed glasses that made her look like an owl, lingered in the doorway when Patterson entered.

"I made copies of the relevant case files and crime scene photography. It's all in the folder for you to take away and study at your leisure," she said in a small voice that matched her appearance. "The physical evidence in the boxes can't leave this room."

"Thank you." Patterson started toward the desk, but the woman interrupted her.

"I'll need you to sign for chain of custody," she said,

offering Patterson a clipboard with a wad of paperwork attached.

Patterson took the clipboard and signed quickly where indicated, then handed it back. "We all good?"

The woman nodded. "Just let me know when you're finished." Then she backed out and closed the door.

Alone except for the ever-watching camera that was surely recording everything she did, Patterson approached the table. She reached out and touched the first box, noting the thick layer of dust disturbed in places by the records department staff member who retrieved it. She was loath to break the seal on the box and see what lay within. Instead, she pulled her hand away and sat down, then opened the case file, browsing through the scant information contained within.

There wasn't much to go on. The solitary witness statement was from the person who discovered the body. A man who ran out of gas further up the road and came across the grizzly scene while hiking back with a gas can to a Texaco station several miles distant. Crime scene photos showed a badly decomposed body, unrecognizable even to Patterson, who was looking for any clue that it might be Julie.

The coroner's report stated that the victim was a female Caucasian in her late teens or early twenties. Height five feet six. Long dark brown hair. Weight unknown due to severe decomposition and partial skeletonization. Undetermined eye color for the same reason. The coroner surmised the body had been exposed to the elements for up to six months. None of that provided Patterson with a definitive answer. It was as likely to be Julie as not. But there were a couple of pertinent details in the coroner's report. The victim was partially undressed, wearing only a T-shirt, which indicated a sexual nature to the crime, and that the victim probably died in the summer or early fall, since it was unlikely that she would have chosen a T-shirt to wear in the dead of winter. The police later found her jeans several feet away, along with the backpack. And there was something else, too. Her hyoid bone was fractured. Patterson knew what this meant because she had seen it in prior cases. The young woman had died from manual strangulation.

Patterson closed the case file and sat back, closing her eyes against the bright fluorescent lighting and taking a moment. An image of Julie struggling for her very life under some unknown assailant, his hands tight around her neck, pushed its way into her mind. Strangulation was an intimate act of murder. Whoever this girl was, Julie or not, Patterson was almost certain the killer had raped her. She sucked in a quick breath and opened her eyes, letting the ghastly image dispel.

The pair of boxes sat on the desk, taunting her. Daring her to open them and see what lay within. Without giving herself time to think, Patterson pushed the chair back and stood up. She pulled on a pair of latex gloves, drew the closest box toward her, and broke the seal, ripping the tape away and lifting the lid.

Inside, individually packaged with a layer of paper between each item to protect any DNA or other trace evidence that might remain, were a pair of filthy jeans covered in dirt and water stains, no doubt from their time sitting in the open and exposed to the elements through a harsh New Mexico winter. The victim's T-shirt, the one she had been wearing when she died, was in a similarly poor state of preservation inside another bag. Notable by its absence was the girl's underwear. Taken perhaps as a souvenir by her killer?

Patterson replaced the lid and turned her attention to the second box, which contained the backpack and its contents, which had been individually packaged like the layers of a cake, one atop the other. The clothes must once have been inside the backpack, but it was now empty, the zipper undone. Patterson set this aside and started removing items of clothing from the box. Another pair of jeans. Several T-shirts. A couple of light sweaters. Then an item that made her step back in horror, because she recognized it all too well. A faded and well-worn black T-shirt with a cartoon image on the front. A smiling pizza slice with arms, legs, and a pair of oversized round eyes below eyebrows that were nothing more than a pair of slanted black lines. And underneath, written in blocky white lettering:

PARK PIZZA: THE BEST SLICE OF PIE IN QUEENS!

She knew that shirt. Had seen it hundreds of times because she had one just like it. This was Julie's bag. She was sure of it. And if she needed any more proof, there was the driver's license Detective Anderson had mentioned, sealed inside a small plastic zip lock evidence bag. Exposed to the elements for months prior to discovery, it was badly damaged, just like everything else. But it was incontrovertible evidence all the same. Julie was dead. Raped, murdered, and discarded like trash on the side of a lonely highway north of Santa Fe.

TWENTY-SIX

IT WASN'T Julie's driver's license. In fact, it hadn't even been issued in New York. It was from Illinois.

The license was damaged, two-thirds of it warped, waterlogged, and unreadable after spending a winter exposed to the elements and laying in the snow on the side of a road next to the unfortunate young woman who had died there. The name was gone with most of the other information. Only the first two letters were still visible:

S T . . .

But Patterson knew what the rest of that name was, because she recognized the faded and barely discernible photograph staring back at her. It was a woman she had met mere weeks before in Chicago, although she was clearly younger on the license image. It was Julie's former best friend, Stacy.

Patterson stared at the license in disbelief. Stacy and Julie had parted ways in Oklahoma City after Justin Ferrera, a janitor at the seedy hotel where they were staying, broke into their room and stole most of their possessions including their driver's licenses and Julie's cell phone—a lifeline that might have saved her otherwise. Stacy had returned to Chicago, leaving Julie to continue the trip alone. She was still in the Windy City now, working as a public defender. How her sister had subsequently ended up in possession of the driver's license was anyone's guess, but that must have been what happened, because the murder victim was Julie. Patterson was sure of it.

She reached out and touched the Park Pizza T-shirt with a gloved hand. Picked it up and held it to her chest. A tear pushed from the corner of her eye and meandered down her cheek. The hum of an air conditioner echoing through a vent in the ceiling above the table broke the silence. A faint soundtrack to Patterson's misery that came accompanied by a steady blast of cold air. She hardly noticed.

Julie is dead and gone.

The thought rattled through Patterson's mind like an intruder in the night. Unwelcome and terrifying. This was the end she had been dreading. The one outcome she had both expected and feared. Worse, she had to break the news to her father back in New York. The elder Blake would be devastated. Her mother would need to be told, too. A woman she had not spoken to in over a decade.

When she was younger, before her mother had left for good, Patterson had clung to the hope that if Julie was found, whatever the circumstance, it would reunite her parents. Bring them together again in either joy or mourning. Now she knew better. Julie's death had no silver lining. It was nothing more than a brutal truth with the power to break her family even more than before.

A soft knock at the door intruded upon Patterson's grief. A moment later, it clicked open to reveal the mousy custodian of the Santa Fe Police Department's records division and evidence store.

"Just thought I'd check in on you," she said, her gaze alighting on the open evidence box and the T-shirt still held to Patterson's chest. A faint scowl creased her forehead at this blatant mishandling of evidence, but when she saw the look of anguish on Patterson's face, her demeanor changed. "Is there something wrong?"

"Nothing is wrong," Patterson said in a croaky voice before clearing her throat. She had no intention of sharing the horror of her discovery with the owl-like woman. "I just need a few more minutes and I'll be done."

The woman hesitated, as if unsure whether she should leave the strangely emotional FBI agent alone with the evidence, but then she gave a curt nod and retreated back into the corridor, closing the door gently behind her.

Alone again, Patterson pulled the T-shirt away from her chest. She stared at it, taking in every small detail. How the black fabric had turned a dark gray and white lettering printed upon it had cracked in a crazy spiderweb pattern like fault lines running through a thin sheet of ice. The garment was not a victim of its months spent lying out in the elements, because it had been protected by the backpack. Instead, the garment had been worn, washed, and re-worn so many times that it had taken on the comfortable patina of a favorite piece of clothing. Patterson could still see Julie wearing this T-shirt in her mind's eye. She remembered the day their parents had bought one for each of them, a couple of years before Julie left for college. Patterson had quickly grown out of her T-shirt, but Julie, who was done growing by then, had not. She had loved the T-shirt enough to take it with her when she went to Chicago. She probably wore it during long study sessions and on lazy weekends hanging around her dorm room. It had also been there at the end, when some unknown killer had placed his hands around her throat and snatched her life away.

Patterson placed the T-shirt back on the table, overcome by a sudden gut punch of grief. She leaned her elbows on the table and bowed her head into her hands. And then the single tear she had shed earlier became an uncontrollable torrent. Her sister was gone forever. Julie was dead. Closure was a bitch.

TWENTY-SEVEN

PATTERSON SAT IN THE VAN, hunched over the table, looking at all the photos and other ephemera she had gathered of Julie while chasing her sister's ghost cross-country. She kept coming back to the photo taken outside of Amarillo, near the strange car sculpture. Her sister had looked so happy. Carefree. Little did she know that death waited for her a few hundred miles down the road. Patterson wished she could warn the girl in that photo of what was to come. She would give anything just to see her sister one more time, tell Julie how much she was loved and missed. But all she had left now were memories, and a large hole in her life that would never heal.

She was exhausted. Crying could do that, and Patterson had cried enough over the last several hours to last a lifetime.

After discovering the driver's license and T-shirt in the evidence box at the Santa Fe police Department's records building, she had been overcome by an overwhelming urge to run. To get in the van and drive all the way back to New York City without looking in the rearview mirror. To put the horror of her discovery and Santa Fe thousands of miles behind her.

But the investigator within Patterson would not allow her to do that. Julie might be dead, but she still deserved justice. She would want the person who killed her to answer for their crime. And after all, wasn't that why Patterson had joined the FBI in the first place? Which was why she had pulled herself together, at least for long enough to do what was necessary. She photographed all the items in the storage boxes. Each individual piece of clothing. The driver's license. A pair of sneakers still encrusted with the dirt and grime of the last places her sister had walked.

She made sure not to miss anything, no matter how small, even going so far as photographing the individual labels inside each garment. Then she bundled everything back into the boxes, leaving it just as she had found it, and made her escape before she had time to fall apart again. Now, all that evidence was safely stored on her phone. The copies of the police files given to her by the woman who oversaw the records building sat nearby, stashed in their manila folder. She had everything necessary to continue her investigation and catch the bastard who took her sister's life. All she had to do was find his calling card among it all. Because every killer left something of themselves behind, no matter how thorough they tried to be. It all came down to whether the investigators could find it. And Patterson was determined to do that, even if it took her a lifetime.

But first, there was a more pressing matter. Breaking the news to her parents. She picked up her phone, finger hovering over her father's number. He should be the first to know. After that, she would call her mother. But she couldn't bring herself to do it. Not yet. Maybe she should start with someone easier. Like Jonathan, or even Marcus and Phoebe. A dress rehearsal for the worst phone call of her life.

But she couldn't bring herself to call anyone, because speaking it out loud, giving the words volume, made them real. And right now, while she was the only one bearing the burden of her dreadful knowledge, she could still pretend it wasn't true.

Except she knew that it was.

She was just delaying the inevitable.

"Screw it." Patterson jabbed her finger down on the phone's screen. Her father's name came up as the call connected.

The phone rang. Once, twice, a third time.

Click. It went to voicemail. Her father's baritone voice filled the speaker.

You've reached the phone of Daniel Blake. If you're selling something, I don't want it. If you're looking for money, I don't have any. If you're pushing politics, I don't care to listen. Everyone else, you know what to do at the beep.

Beep.

Patterson took a deep breath. "Hey dad, it's me. I, uh . . ."

She faltered, suddenly realizing how bad it would be to deliver the news of Julie's death in a voicemail, even if it relieved the stress of doing the deed to his face.

"I just called to see how you are," she blurted, tamping down the strain in her voice. "Love you."

Hanging up, Patterson put the phone down on the table next to the photos of Julie. Her hands were shaking. She felt like the walls were closing in around her. Smothering her.

Hours ago, after leaving the records building, she had swung back by police headquarters and picked up the item she had asked Detective Anderson to procure for her—an item not related to Julie or the girl in the ditch, but rather to her own safety—then driven back to the RV lot next to Amy's Roadhouse. She was in a state of shock and didn't know where else to go. She just wanted to park up in some out-of-the-way place and lick her wounds. Hide in the privacy of her rolling bedroom on wheels and wallow in grief.

Now she found the van's tiny rear cabin stifling. She couldn't stomach another moment looking at those photos. The police files containing the lurid details of her sister's death. She had no desire to spend the rest of the night wondering at the twists of fate that had brought her to this point in time. Julie could have gotten on that bus back to Chicago with Stacy. She could have declined the offer to ride along with Trent Steiger and his band. She could have let the musician go on his way alone after Amarillo instead of accompanying him to Santa Fe. So many opportunities to escape her fate, and yet the pieces had clicked together and sealed it, instead. If she didn't distract herself, those thoughts would roll around in the echo chamber of her head until they drove her insane.

Amy's Roadhouse was right across the parking lot, beckoning to her with the warm glow of its lights and the distant sound of a band playing on the stage. Making up her mind, she gathered together all the files and photos and stashed them safely inside the plastic container where she kept everything related to Julie. Then she unbuckled the shoulder holster containing her Glock service weapon, removed her backup weapon from around her ankle, and stashed them both in the combination floor safe installed by the Dallas Police Department for just that purpose when they renovated her van. Then she stepped outside into the balmy early evening air, and made her way toward the bar, determined to dull the pain, if only for one night.

TWENTY-EIGHT

CORBIN POPE WATCHED Patterson Blake climb out of her van and cross the parking lot before disappearing inside Amy's Roadhouse. He had been following her all day from a safe distance, first to the Santa Fe Police Department headquarters and then to a nondescript building a mile north of that location, which he soon found out was the police department's records facility. What she was doing there was anyone's guess except that he was sure it had something to do with her sister's disappearance sixteen years before. Not that he cared, except that the FBI agent's current assignment, which struck him as just a little too personal, might factor into whatever fate he ultimately decided should befall her.

After leaving the records building, Blake had driven back to the RV lot next to the roadhouse, having apparently decided that this would be her base of operations while in the city. And it suited Pope just fine. The convenience of having somewhere close by where he could eat while still keeping his target under surveillance was a godsend. Normally he ended up sustaining himself on junk purchased at gas stations and fast-food restaurants, snatching an opportunity to eat where he could. Still, he would have to be careful. He didn't want his face to become too familiar to the servers there, especially since the FBI agent appeared to have come to the same conclusion.

That raised another problem. Sitting in the parking lot of Amy's Roadhouse all day and night would make him conspicuous. It wasn't so bad during business hours, when the parking lot was full of cars and trucks that came and went at regular intervals, but night, after the bar closed, his car parked there all alone would soon come to the FBI agent's attention. The last thing he wanted was to raise her suspicions. It was common sense that a target would be easier to eliminate if they weren't aware of the danger. And anyway, Pope had no desire to spend the next three or four nights—the amount of time he figured it would take to complete his task—sleeping upright in his car with one eye open. It was uncomfortable, even if it wasn't the worst place he had ever slept.

Better to find his own base of operations somewhere out of sight and with a comfortable bed now that he was zeroing in on Patterson Blake's habits and routine. But he had no intention of leaving her completely unobserved. Luckily, he possessed the technology to make sure the federal agent was never far away, even when she was. The same tech he had tried to plant on her van the previous night.

Pope slid down in the driver's seat and watched the roadhouse door to see if Patterson Blake would quickly reemerge carrying takeout. After twenty minutes passed with no sign of her, he grabbed a baseball cap and put it on. Then, sliding from behind the wheel, he made his way toward the building, taking a wide arching route that allowed him to approach from the side rather than the more direct and obvious straight line. That way, if she stepped back outside, he could veer off before she noticed him.

Patterson was sitting at the bar when he stepped inside, head bent over a rocks glass containing an amber liquid he assumed to be whiskey. He moved closer, curiosity piqued, but stayed just far enough away not to register on her radar.

The FBI agent looked beat down, her face a picture of misery. Something had happened. He could sense it. Maybe her FBI boyfriend in New York, the one he had discovered while doing his background research on her, had broken off their relationship. Maybe it was something more serious. A death in the family?

The breath caught in Pope's throat.

Maybe she had found her sister, and it wasn't good news. If that was the case, she might not stick around Santa Fe much longer. He might have to bring the timeline up.

Pope veered back toward the door and stepped outside. He hurried to his car and opened the trunk, accessed the hidden compartment within, and took out a small black box. It was a tracker that connected directly to his cell phone. Just place it anywhere under the chassis of the FBI agent's van, and he would be alerted whenever she moved. It would only take a few minutes to attach the device to a suitable location, but now his curiosity was piqued. He had only entered the bar to get eyes on the FBI agent and make sure she was suitably distracted while he completed his task. He figured she was probably having dinner, which would buy him more time than he needed. But she appeared to be getting hammered. And she looked miserable. He wanted to find out why.

Pope lowered the trunk and hurried through the parking lot to the van. He went around to the passenger side where he would be shielded from sight by anyone exiting the roadhouse, then dropped to his knees and reached under the vehicle, looking for a suitably flat spot on the undercarriage to attach the tracker where it wouldn't easily get dislodged.

The tracker was magnetic. Once he moved close enough, it attached itself, practically leaping from his fingers and clunking against bare metal. He gave the device a quick tug to make sure it was seated properly. Satisfied that it was, he stood back up.

Glancing around to make sure he hadn't been observed, Pope circled the vehicle, arriving at the sliding side door opposite. He donned a pair of black leather gloves, then pulled a thin pick from his pocket. He went to work on the lock, disengaging it in a matter of seconds, then he slid the door back and climbed inside before closing it quickly behind him.

The van's interior surprised Pope. The vehicle was obviously an older model, even though it had received a fresh coat of paint and four new tires. But the inside was something else. It had been meticulously kitted out in a thoughtful manner that didn't waste an inch of space. Everything was bright and clean. New. He felt a twinge of envy standing there. A vehicle like this would be perfect for him, given how many nights he spent on the road each year. No more hotel rooms. No more risk that some eagle-eyed desk clerk would spot a crack in the façade of whatever identity he was using to check in.

Not that it had ever happened. Pope was an expert at creating legends—false identities with deep backgrounds and supported by documents such as a passport or driver's license. He had five such false identities he could use interchangeably as needed. He picked one identity for each job, and then burned it at the end, destroying all visible traces of that false person, so there was never a pattern between killings. Even the name he used with the senator wasn't real. Corbin Pope was a cleverly crafted alias that he reserved for clients such as Newport. Corbin was an old English name. It meant crow or raven. Two creatures closely associated with death. He thought the surname Pope made him sound trustworthy. This primary identity carried with it his reputation and enabled him to operate in the world of professional assassins. Once he accepted an assignment, he would shed it like a snake losing its skin until he needed that identity again. Only the people who hired Pope knew him by that name. To everyone else, he would be Andrew Rogers, Tim Swift, or Sean Smith. Names bland enough to be unmemorable.

From somewhere outside, he heard raucous laughter, the bang of a door. He went to the van's window and peeked out. A gaggle of twenty-somethings were staggering out of the roadhouse. Two men and two women. They had their arms wrapped around each other's shoulders as if each was trying to support the next. The group lurched toward a truck with raised suspension sitting atop wheels too wide for its body and climbed in. They probably shouldn't be driving, but it wasn't Pope's concern. If the idiots wiped out on some dark road rural highway, drove themselves headlong into a ditch, who gave crap? He let the blind fall back into place and turned to the interior of the van once more. Then he went to work.

TWENTY-NINE

PATTERSON WAS WELL on her way to skunk drunk. Three whiskeys in, she could feel the liquor burning its way through her system, dulling her senses and stripping away her better judgment. But it wasn't doing the one thing she wished it would. Purging the memories of what she had discovered in the records building from her memory long enough to let her believe Julie was still alive, if only for a few brief hours.

It was a bad idea to drink alone. She knew that. But when her phone rang, she muted it. Earlier, she had been spared the ordeal of breaking the news to her father thanks to his voicemail. Now he was calling back. The urge to hear a friendly voice was overwhelming, but she knew what would happen if she answered. She would end up breaking his heart, and she couldn't face doing that. Not yet.

Her father's caller ID disappeared from the screen. A few seconds later, a notification came through. He had left her a voicemail. She almost listened to it, decided not to. What was the point? Yet the idea of hearing a friendly voice remained.

Patterson went to her call log, found a different number, and dialed.

Marcus Bauer answered on the second ring. "Hey. Missing your old partner already?"

"Marcus." Patterson's throat tightened. All she could do was say his name.

"What's wrong?" The levity vanished from Bauer's voice.

"I found something." With her free hand, Patterson played absently with a cardboard bar coaster. "About Julie."

"Hang on. I'm putting it on speaker so that Phoebe can hear." There was a moment of rustling. "Okay. We're both here."

Phoebe's voice came over the speaker. "Hey."

"What did you find?" Bauer asked.

Patterson swallowed. She was afraid that if she tried to talk, only a sob would come out. After a moment, she composed herself. "She's dead."

Now it was Bauer's turn to remain silent while he digested what Patterson had just told him. Then he said, "How did you come to that conclusion? Tell us everything."

That was exactly what Patterson did. She told them about her conversation with Bailey, the weekend bartender. About the murdered Jane Doe left in a ditch sixteen years ago. Her conversation with Detective Anderson. And finally, her visit to the Santa Fe Police records building and what she had discovered there.

When she was done, Bauer drew in a sharp breath. "You don't know for sure the girl was Julie."

"I don't see any way it couldn't be. She had Julie's T-shirt. The one from Park Pizza back in Queens. You can't tell me that some other random woman with the same T-shirt got herself murdered in the last place Julie was seen alive."

"Until you get that DNA test back, you won't know. Until then, you should assume nothing."

"I agree," said Phoebe. "Everything you've told us is circumstantial."

"Not everything. Stacy's license was found on the body." Patterson tried to quell the tremble in her voice but failed.

"That's the friend she was traveling with?" asked Bauer.

"Yes. And even if the T-shirt is some kind of freaky coincidence, the license isn't. There's only one logical conclusion. The girl they found in that ditch is my sister. Don't ask me why or how she had Stacy's license, but she must have."

"How long did they say the DNA comparison would take?" Bauer asked.

"A couple of days. Plus, it's Saturday tomorrow and the lab won't be fully staffed. I doubt I'll hear back until at least Monday or Tuesday at the earliest."

"Patterson, I'm so sorry," Bauer said. "Have you told your family yet?"

"No. I phoned my father, but it went to voicemail. He probably hadn't finished work yet. He called me back a few minutes ago, but I didn't answer. I know it sounds crazy, but I want to preserve the illusion a few hours longer. Once I tell him there's no going back. From that moment on, Julie isn't missing anymore. She's the victim of an unsolved murder. God, I wish I could set the clock back and do that raid in upstate New York all over again. Do it right this time. Not lose it in the field and end up suspended. I should have let things be. Ignorance really is bliss."

"You don't mean that," Bauer said. "We've had this conversation before. You're better off knowing, if only so you can stop wondering."

"It doesn't feel like that right now."

"I know."

From somewhere behind Bauer, Phoebe spoke again. "Have you told Jonathan yet?"

"No." Patterson threw the coaster back on the bar. She picked up her drink and took a long swig, feeling the heat as it went down. "I probably should call him instead of you, but . . ."

"No need to explain. I get it," Bauer said. "We're easier. Less invested."

"Something like that." Patterson leaned on the bar with the phone pressed to her ear. She fought back a wave of despair. "What do I do now? How do I move on from this?"

"I think the first thing you need to do is get some sleep," Bauer said. "Where are you, anyway? It sounds loud."

"Amy's Roadhouse," Patterson admitted.

"The last place your sister was seen alive. Really?"

"It wasn't by design. They have an RV lot. I figured it was as good a place to park up as any."

"Except you're not parked up. You're sitting in the bar trying to drink away your troubles. How many have you had, anyway?"

"A few. It's not helping much, but I guess I'll sleep tonight, so there's that."

Bauer was silent for a moment. "You remember a few months back when you found me drowning my sorrows in Pioneer Jacks?"

"Sure." Patterson remembered it all too well. Pioneer Jacks was a favorite hangout of the agents at the Dallas field office. She had found Bauer in there one night in a sorry state, knocking back whiskeys like they were going out of fashion. "What of it?"

"You remember what you told me back then?"

"No," Patterson replied, even though she knew exactly where he was going.

"You're a terrible liar for an FBI agent, Patterson."

"Okay. I get what you're saying. Drinking won't solve anything." Patterson downed the rest of her drink anyway.

"Pay your tab, go back to the van, and get a good night's rest," Bauer told her. "Things will look better in the morning."

"I'm not so sure about that." Patterson ran a finger around the rim of the glass.

"Well, at least you'll be thinking straight."

"Maybe."

"Promise you'll knock it on the head?" Bauer wasn't giving in easily.

"I hear you, loud and clear." Patterson knew this was why she had called Bauer. Because she knew it was a mistake to spend all night in the bar, drinking, and wanted someone to tell her that. But now, she wasn't so sure. "I've taken up enough of your time. I'll be fine. The two of you should get back to your evening and I should get back to the van."

"That's more like it." Bauer said goodbye. In the background, Phoebe did the same. Then he ended the call.

Patterson slipped the phone back into her pocket. She looked down at the empty tumbler.

Bailey, the bartender she had spoken with earlier, noticed the empty glass and came over. She had the good sense not to ask Patterson about her day. "You looking for a refill?"

Patterson pushed the glass across the bar, almost reached for her purse to pay the tab. Then she changed her mind. "Just one more."

THIRTY

POPE SEARCHED THE VAN. He pulled out every drawer, looked in every nook of the small space, careful to leave everything exactly as he had found it so that Patterson Blake would have no idea that anyone had been there. At first, he found nothing, but then, when he looked in a compartment under the bed, he came across a plastic tub.

He lifted it out and set the tub on the table, then took the lid off. Inside was a collection of items relating to her missing sister. Postcards. A map. Photographs. Registration cards from a hotel in Oklahoma City. Even a letter inside an envelope with a damaged address. And police files. Pope removed these and looked through them. It appeared that Patterson was investigating an unidentified body found in the area sixteen years before. Presumably, she thought this might have something to do with Julie. Maybe that was why she had fled the van and was now knocking back liquor on a barstool in the roadhouse.

Something had upset her.

Pope squirreled the information away for future use. If

Patterson Blake really was in a state of distress, that might prove useful when it came time to get rid of her. He had discounted a staged suicide simply because she was an FBI agent. Coolheaded. Not prone to emotional instability. But looks can be deceptive. He decided to pay closer attention to her emotional cues in the future.

In the meantime, he didn't want to linger inside the van. He was fairly confident that she was in the middle of a maudlin drinking session, at least judging by her demeanor when he had checked her out in the bar, but who knew how long she would stay that way. She could come back at any moment and, even inebriated, would be a formidable opponent, not least because she might be armed. Also, she would force his hand. If she discovered him in the van, he would have no choice but to kill her there and then, and that would get messy.

Pope didn't like messy.

He gathered together the contents of the plastic container, which he made sure to keep in the order they had been found, and put them back, then closed the lid. He slid the container back into its cubbyhole under the bed and started for the door.

He was almost there when the toe of his shoe caught on one of the planks covering the floor and he stumbled.

He looked down, expecting to see the curled lip of a badly laid vinyl plank, but instead, Pope saw the faint outline of what he could only assume was a hidden compartment set into the floor. The trap door was almost flush with the floor, but one side was raised by perhaps a millimeter. It was pure luck his foot had snagged on it, otherwise Pope would never have noticed the compartment. A million to one chance.

Kneeling, he ran a gloved finger around the perimeter of the compartment, looking for a catch or some sort of release that would pop the door up. He found nothing. There wasn't any obvious way to open it. But when he applied pressure in a certain spot near the forward edge, he was rewarded by a soft click and the door tilted up a few inches. Beneath the panel was a floor safe with a digital combination lock.

He wondered what was inside, but breaking the combination would require more skill than he possessed. He was an assassin—Pope hated to be called a hitman—not a safe cracker. Besides, there wasn't time. A safe like that would take time, even for someone who knew what they were doing. And anyway, the likelihood was that she kept her weapons in it when she wasn't carrying them, which was what Pope would have used it for. The tools of his trade.

He pushed aside a flutter of envy. A rare flash of emotion. It was like the van had been built for him. Yet it belonged to his target. Still, it was good to know the safe was there, along with the guns he was sure were contained within. Another small piece of knowledge that might come in useful.

Closing the trap door to conceal the safe once more, Pope stood up. He crossed to the window and looked out to make sure the coast was clear, then went to the sliding door and opened it just enough to step out. A minute later, he was back in his car, and planning his next move.

THIRTY-ONE

PATTERSON RETURNED to her van a little before eleven. She walked across the parking lot, feeling slightly dizzy as she hit the fresh air. But surprisingly, she was less inebriated than she had expected. Worse, the alcohol had failed to dull the pain of her sister's death.

She climbed up into the van and flopped down on the bed, still dressed. Exhaustion pushed the edges of her mind, but so did something else. A detail she had barely noticed while looking through the boxes of evidence earlier that day.

Patterson jumped back up and reached under the bed, pulling out the plastic box containing everything she had gathered about Julie on her journey so far. She went straight to the police files and the list of items recovered with the body. There, about halfway down under the bold subheading, *Backpack Contents*, was an item she should have paid closer attention to but hadn't, because by then she was distracted by the Park Pizza T-shirt and all that it implied.

Item 14C: WBH Oregon Sweatshirt.

She pulled her phone from her pocket, browsed to the set

of photos she had taken earlier. The contents of the boxes. And there it was. The WBH Oregon sweatshirt. It was a deep red, almost burgundy. The wording was printed in a classic chunky school font. Light blue lettering with a narrow white border. She stared at the photograph, trying to reconcile everything she knew about Julie with the sweatshirt. A school in Oregon? Was it something she had picked up during her travels? Maybe from a boyfriend the rest of the family knew nothing about? It was possible, but not likely. Prior to leaving for her fatal road trip, Julie had never mentioned dating anyone who attended any school or college in Oregon, and the only romantic liaison she appeared to have had on the trip was Trent Steiger. Patterson knew for sure that he had never attended any college in Oregon. So how had her sister come into possession of the sweatshirt? It was an anomaly.

"Where did you come from?" She asked the stirring air inside the van as she looked down at the photo on her phone.

The answer remained stubbornly elusive.

Patterson removed her laptop from its bag. She pushed aside the plastic box of evidence and placed the computer on the table, then opened it. When she typed WBH Oregon into the web browser, she got a string of hits.

William Brady High School in the small city of Bend, Oregon.

Patterson browsed through the scores of hits that talked about everything from academic excellence, PTA meetings, and football games, not exactly sure what she was looking for. Giving up, she closed the laptop and sat there staring at the photo on her phone, unsure what to make of it, but convinced it meant something. William Brady High School in Oregon. It was about as far from Julie's life on the East Coast as possible. Even Chicago, where her sister had attended college, was such a distance from Bend, Oregon—over two thousand miles—that it seemed unlikely she would know anyone there, let alone be in possession of their high school sweatshirt.

So, what was going on?

The answer wasn't going to come at midnight while the room was spinning with the alcohol coursing through her system. Whatever the sweatshirt meant, it would need to wait until tomorrow.

Patterson returned the laptop to its case and slid the plastic box back under her bed. She undressed, discarding her clothing in a heap on the floor, and pulled on her nightshirt. After cleaning her teeth over the sink in the small toilet cubicle, she went to the bed and pulled the covers back. When she climbed in, the sheets were crisp and cool. It didn't take her long to fall asleep, but when she did, her sister's killer was waiting. A faceless figure with outstretched hands that chased her through the darkness in an unending game of cat and mouse.

THIRTY-TWO

CORBIN POPE WAS awake by six in the morning. He never slept late, even when he wasn't on a job, but this morning he had a particular reason for rising early. He wanted to make sure Patterson Blake's van was still parked in the RV lot at Amy's Roadhouse.

The previous evening, after breaking into the FBI agent's van he had returned to his car and waited for her to stumble out of the bar, which she did a little after ten thirty. He lingered another half hour, until he was satisfied that she wasn't going anywhere, then he drove back toward Santa Fe, and a motel he had noticed the previous day.

He checked in for five nights using one of his aliases, which was about as long as he thought the job would take even accounting for unknowns. The room was utilitarian and in dire need of an update. The TV was old—a twenty-inch flatscreen from the days when flat didn't mean thin. There were only twelve cable channels, three of which barely came in. Not that he intended to spend any time sitting in front of it. The shower stall in the ridiculously cramped bathroom had what he suspected was black mold growing in the corners. But the bed was acceptable, if a little on the hard side. Even better, he had paid cash for the room, which rarely happened anymore. Granted, he had to give the desk clerk a sob story about a nasty divorce that left his credit cards in limbo, not to mention a hefty cash deposit against damages, but it worked. Now, having seen the room, he sardonically concluded that any damage he did might just as likely be considered a renovation.

Pope picked up his cell phone from its charger on the nightstand and went to the app that connected to the tracker he had installed under the FBI agent's van. If the vehicle had moved, it should have notified him with an audible alert, but the technology wasn't infallible. The van was right where it should be, next to the roadhouse. But he suspected it wouldn't stay that way. Pope wanted to get eyes on his target, if only for his own peace of mind.

He left the room and crossed to the lobby, where he had been told a free 'deluxe' breakfast was included in the cost of his room. The food on offer was breakfast in name only. Bananas that were already turning brown. Bagels that could double as hockey pucks. Slices of stale sandwich bread on a plastic tray next to the toaster. Muffins that looked like they had sat there every morning for several days. He picked one up and put it down again, noting that it more resembled a lead weight than a bakery item. In the end, he returned to his room with a bagel, a small cup of plain cream cheese, and a paper cup of what he suspected would be barely palatable coffee.

As he stepped back into the room, the shrill ring of a phone drew his attention. It was not his handset, the one with the tracker app installed on it. This was a second handset. A burner phone activated strictly for this job that he would destroy once the FBI agent was dead. But it should not be ringing now. Once he completed his task, Pope would send a single message from that phone to the senator, confirming his success. A message that to anyone else would look like spam. The phone also doubled as an untraceable emergency contact number should something go wrong.

That it was ringing now gave Pope pause.

He put his breakfast down on a small table near the hotel room window and rummaged in his overnight bag for the phone.

When he answered, a familiar voice greeted him.

It was the senator.

"Mr. Pope, I was expecting to have heard from you by now."

"What the hell are you doing?" Pope asked, not bothering to hide his anger. He stepped into the bathroom and flicked on the overhead fan to create some white noise that he hoped would mask the sound of their conversation from prying ears. The hotel room walls were thin. The night before, he had overheard the couple in the room next door engaging in what could politely be described as an amorous romp. "Unless something has gone wrong on your end, we shouldn't be talking."

"Relax. I'm using a burner, and I know you are, too."

"That's not the point. I have rules."

"Yeah. And I'm paying you a lot of money. I want the FBI agent dead. Make it happen, sooner rather than later."

"That isn't how it works. I decide when the Fed dies, not you." If Pope were capable of angering easily, his words might have been laced with more indignation, but as it was, he merely found the Senator's reckless call irritating. "When the job's done, you'll be the first to know. Don't contact me again unless it's a genuine emergency. I'm hanging up now."

"Don't you dare hang—"

Pope ended the call. His statement to the senator hadn't been entirely accurate. Newport would not be the first to know. That honor would go to Patterson Blake, although she wouldn't be around long enough to think about it. Then he might have another situation on his hands. Senator Newport was becoming a liability. Pope had performed several 'services' for the crooked politician in the past. Getting rid of a journalist who knew too much. Disposing of a colleague who stood in the senator's way. Eliminating a rival business interest. Their professional relationship went back many years. Now, it appeared, Newport was getting too comfortable with their arrangement. Rising above his station. That wouldn't do. Arrogance led to mistakes, like the phone call he had just terminated.

Pope sighed and returned the burner phone to his bag. It was a shame, but once this job was done and his fee was in the bank, it might be time to eliminate loose ends and terminate the senator, too.

THIRTY-THREE

PATTERSON AWOKE to her phone ringing. Groggy, she fumbled around for it before her fingers closed on the handset. She sat up, wondering at first where she was before the van's interior shifted into recognition.

She answered without looking at the screen.

"It's me," said a male voice. "Bauer."

"Calling to make me feel worse than I already do?" Patterson said, wincing as a stab of pain lanced through her head. She wondered if there were any painkillers in the van.

"I take it you didn't heed my advice to stop drinking last night?"

"What do you think?" Patterson's mouth was dry and her throat fuzzy. "What time is it, anyway?"

"Ten-thirty."

"Shit. I didn't mean to sleep this late." Patterson swung her legs off the bed. Another throb of pain flared inside her skull. She opened the van's small fridge, grabbed a bottle of water, twisted the cap off, and drank half of it in one gulp. It helped, but not much. "Why are you calling, anyway? Just to gloat?"

"Actually, no. Tempting as it is to say I told you so." Bauer cleared his throat. "I have some news I think you'll be interested in."

"Go ahead." Patterson stood and let her nightshirt fall to the floor. The air inside the van raised goosebumps on her bare skin. She had left the rooftop AC running when she went to bed. The unit must have been turning on and off all night. It was a miracle that the battery wasn't dead. She would have to recharge it for sure. She went to the chemical toilet and pushed back the door, intending to empty her bladder. Bauer's answer stopped her cold.

"The Jane Doe isn't your sister."

"What? How could you possibly know that?"

"Because I phoned the Santa Fe PD forensics lab last night after we talked. Spoke to the technician working the overnight shift. Don't ask me how I did it, because I don't want to get in trouble again so soon after what happened in Amarillo, but long story short, he agreed to do the FBI a favor and test the sample you gave against your Jane Doe overnight. He just got back to me. It's not a match."

"That's impossible." Patterson forgot about her need to pee. She found a baggy sweatshirt with the FBI crest on the front and pulled it on, then went to the table and sat down. "I found my sister's tee in the evidence box, along with Stacy's driver's license. How would those be there if the victim isn't Julie?"

"I guess that's a question you'll have to answer," Bauer said. "But the test was conclusive. You are not related to the Jane Doe."

Patterson's mind flew back to the nagging discrepancy that

had bothered her the night before. The sweatshirt from a high school in Oregon. At least that made more sense now, even if a random stranger being in possession of items associated with her missing sister did not. "Can you send me the report?"

"Already have. It's waiting in your email." Bauer paused for a breath. "This is good news, Patterson."

"I know." Patterson almost slumped over onto the table with relief. She barely even noticed her headache anymore. "I was so sure it was Julie."

"I warned you last night against jumping to conclusions."

"Oh. Now you start with the I told you so's."

"Nothing of the sort. I just think you should listen to me once in a while."

"I do listen to you." Bauer spoke to someone on his end of the line. "Look, I need to go. I should have been in a threat intelligence briefing five minutes ago."

"They letting you back off desk duty?"

"No such luck. They've had me combing through dark web message boards. Riveting stuff. I'm supposed to be bringing the task force up to speed on my findings."

"Then don't let me hold you up." Patterson laughed, all the stress of the past twenty-four hours draining away. She said goodbye and hung up after promising to keep Bauer informed of her progress.

From somewhere outside came the beep of a car horn, the sound of voices. Amy's roadhouse opened at eleven on Saturdays. She went to the window, lifted the blind a few inches and peered out. There were several cars in the parking lot.

Her stomach rumbled, reminding Patterson that she hadn't eaten since lunchtime the day before. In her depressed state the previous evening, all she wanted was alcohol.

Turning back to the van's interior, she finished her

business in the bathroom, then got dressed. There were a thousand questions swirling through her mind . . . Like how her sister's belongings had ended up in the possession of some random murder victim. She also wondered why Julie had Stacy's driver's license. She was determined to call her sister's old best friend and find out. But not yet. The hangover was making her feel queasy, and putting some food in her stomach would help with that. Everything else could wait.

Leaving the van, Patterson headed across the parking lot to the roadhouse and stepped inside. Several tables were occupied already, and servers were rushing back-and-forth bringing plates loaded with corn beef hash, ham and eggs, and stacked cheeseburgers to hungry customers.

She went to the bar and found a spot, then studied the menu. When she looked up, a familiar figure was heading her way.

"Back again. You must really like this place," Bailey said, wiping the bar in front of Patterson with a cloth. "Coffee or something stronger?"

"Coffee," Patterson said quickly. The thought of another drink made her stomach churn.

"Coming right up." Bailey put a mug in front of her, then grabbed her carafe from the back of the bar. "FYI, I made some phone calls this morning before I came to work. Spoke to a couple of the servers I still keep in touch with from years ago."

"And?"

"Nothing. No one remembered your sister or her musician boyfriend. Sorry."

"That's okay. I appreciate you trying." Patterson's stomach rumbled again, and not in a good way this time. All thought of eating vanished from her mind. She felt positively queasy. Afraid she might throw up, she slid down off her stool and headed for the back of the bar.

But as she made her way down the corridor toward the women's restroom, a huge pinboard mounted on the wall caught Patterson's eye. It was positively sagging with photos of raucous evenings at the roadhouse. They were pinned one atop the other across the board's entire surface like some kind of crazy photographic collage. She stopped to examine it, pulled a pin out, and removed some of the more recent photos to discover older ones beneath.

With growing excitement, she began to remove more photos, like some sort of pinboard archaeologist uncovering the past. After five minutes, a large mound of Polaroids and glossy prints sat on the floor in a haphazard, untidy pile.

She ignored the curious looks of other customers making their way to and from the restrooms and kept going. One photo showed a smiling and obviously inebriated group gathered under a banner that read, Merry Christmas and happy new year. There was a 2008 date stamp in the corner.

Could there be even older photos further back?

Patterson picked up the pace, pulling more pictures off the board and letting them fall onto the swiftly growing stack beneath. And then she saw it. A photo with a date stamp of 2006 that sent a chill racing up her spine. There, standing between two young men, with a smile on her face, was her sister, Julie.

THIRTY-FOUR

PATTERSON SNATCHED the photo from the board and stared at it. She recognized one of the two young men with her sister as Trent Steiger. She wondered if the other was his cousin who worked at the roadhouse back then.

There was only one way to find out.

She turned and headed back across the room with the photo in her hand and put it down on the bar top in front of Bailey. She pointed to the third man in the photo. "Do you recognize this person?"

Bailey picked the photograph up and examined it. "This is from the pin board in the restroom hallway?"

Patterson nodded. "I might've made a bit of a mess back there. Don't worry. I'll put all the photos back where I found them. Do you recognize him?"

"Yes." Bailey placed the photograph back down on the bar. "His name is Treyton Cobb. But he hasn't worked here for at least ten years."

"Is he one of the people you spoke to this morning?"

Bailey shook her head. "We were never friends. Moved in

different circles. He still lives in Santa Fe, though, as far as I know. I ran into him a few years ago at a bar downtown. He works in finance I think, or something like that." She was still looking at the photo, and a smiling Julie. "Is she your sister?"

"And her boyfriend, Trent Steiger. Since they all appear to know each other, I figure it must have been him who got Trent the gig playing here. The cousin."

"Makes sense, I guess." Bailey shrugged.

"You know how I can get in contact with him?" Patterson asked. "A phone number, maybe."

"Sorry. Like I said, we weren't that friendly." She pushed the photo back toward Patterson. "Wish I could be more helpful."

"It's fine." Patterson's stomach was still giving her fits, but she ignored it.

"If you don't mind me saying, you look a smidge green around the gills." Bailey leaned on the bar. "You were knocking them back pretty quick last night. One more and I'd have been forced to cut you off."

"Guess it was lucky I stopped when I did, then." Patterson didn't need any reminders of her boozy evening. "My head's had enough as it is."

"I have just the thing."

Before Patterson could say anything, Bailey turned and disappeared into the kitchen through the double doors at the end of the bar. She came back a moment later with an egg, which she cracked into a rocks glass. She went to work, throwing several other ingredients together, then pushed the concoction toward Patterson.

"Here. Drink this. It'll work wonders."

"You sure about that?" Patterson asked. The drink looked like a murder scene with an egg yolk floating on top.

"Trust me. Ten minutes from now, you'll feel great."

Patterson picked up the glass. "What's in this?"

"You never had a prairie oyster before?"

"No, and I'm not sure I want to start now." Patterson put the glass back down. "What's in it, anyway?"

"Nothing special. Worcestershire sauce, vinegar, hot sauce, salt, black pepper, and tomato juice, all topped off with a nice raw egg. The trick is not to break the yoke." Bailey noted the glass. "Come on. It's on the house. Down in one. Don't even think about it."

Patterson picked up the glass again. She hesitated, then put it to her lips, tilted her head back, and swallowed the foul concoction in one go. She pulled a face and put the empty glass back on the bar. "Holy crap, that tastes worse than it looks."

"Give it a few minutes." Bailey grinned. "Maybe you should stick to soda tonight."

"I don't intend to be hanging around in here tonight." Patterson picked up the photograph. "You mind if I keep this?"

Bailey shrugged. "No skin off my nose. That photograph's so old I bet no one's even seen it in ten years."

"Thanks." Patterson slipped the photograph into her pocket. It was one more clue in the puzzle of her sister's disappearance. She just didn't know where it fit. She picked up the bar menu, surprised to find that her stomach actually was feeling better. Even her headache was receding. "I'll take a refill of coffee."

Bailey turned and grabbed the carafe again, then topped up Patterson's mug. "You know, I might be able to help you with Treyton Cobb, after all. One of my girlfriends who used to work here dated him several years back. They might have kept in touch. I can call her if you like."

"That would be fantastic." After her scare the day before,

thinking Julie had been murdered and dumped on the side of the road, it felt good to have hope again.

"Give me a minute." Bailey stepped away from the bar, motioning for one of her coworkers to take over her station, and disappeared into the back. A couple of minutes later, she returned with a slip of paper in her hand. There was a phone number written on it. She offered the slip of paper to Patterson. "I was right. They do still talk. This is Treyton Cobb's phone number."

Patterson took the number and studied it for a moment, then folded the piece of paper and put it into her pocket next to the photograph. She felt like reaching over the bar and hugging Bailey, but she refrained. Instead, she decided to leave a more than generous tip. One that would suitably express her gratitude. "I can't thank you enough."

"No worries." Bailey picked up the glass that contained the hangover cure and placed it in a sink under the bar. "Can I get you anything else?"

Patterson looked down at the menu. "Give me a few minutes."

Bailey nodded and stepped away. Patterson was itching to call the number on the sheet of paper. To find out what Treyton Cobb knew, if anything, about Trent Steiger and her sister. But not in the roadhouse. She wanted to do it in the privacy of the van. When Bailey came back, she ordered a BLT to go. Ten minutes later, she left Amy's Roadhouse with the wrapped sandwich in her hand and Treyton Cobb's phone number in her pocket. The one person who might shine a light on how Julie's T-shirt came to be in the possession of a murdered girl without a name.

THIRTY-FIVE

THE FIRST THING Patterson did after she got back to the van was to call Treyton Cobb. But all she got was his voicemail. She left a message identifying herself as an FBI agent and asked if he could call her back at his earliest convenience. She didn't provide any information regarding the nature of the call, figuring it would prompt him to respond more quickly.

After that, she placed another call, this time to Stacy Jensen in Chicago.

Her sister's old friend picked up on the first ring. "Special Agent Blake." There was a hint of trepidation in her voice. "Did you find Julie?"

"No. I'm still searching for her." Patterson didn't bother to mention that less than twenty-four hours before she had been distraught, thinking that Julie was the Jane Doe found dead in a ditch sixteen years ago. "I need to ask you about a piece of evidence I recently came across, though."

"I'm in court right now. You caught me during a recess,"

Stacy said. "We reconvene in fifteen minutes, but until then, I'm all yours. What is it you need to know?"

Patterson told her about following Julie's trail to Santa Fe and Amy's Roadhouse, and her discovery of the T-shirt and driver's license that had been found in the possession of a cold case murder victim with no discernible ties to her sister.

When she was finished, Stacy thought for a moment before speaking. "You're sure it was *my* driver's license found with the body?"

"There's no doubt. It's in bad condition, but the picture is still recognizable as you. And the first two letters of your name are readable."

"I don't know what to say. My license was stolen along with everything else."

"Maybe it was in one of the items of clothing found in the alley behind the hotel after the robbery." Patterson said. After her sister and Stacy had checked into the hotel in Oklahoma City, a seedy dive called the Welcome Inn, they had dropped their bags in the room and went to eat at a local restaurant. They left everything, including their purses, and took only enough cash for the food because they didn't know the neighborhood. When they got back, someone had broken into their room and stolen most of their belongings. That was what caused the argument that sent them on their separate ways—Stacy back to Chicago, and Julie continuing the trip alone. The thief subsequently discarded some of the items, including a pair of Stacy's jeans, in an alley behind the hotel. "Did you ever keep the license in a pocket?"

"All the time," Stacy answered. "I had a habit of putting it in the back pocket of my Levi's when we went out if I didn't want to carry a purse."

"Then it wouldn't be a stretch to assume that the license

was in the pocket of those jeans when they found them in the alley. That would explain how my sister came to be in possession of it."

"Still doesn't explain how it ended up next to a random Jane Doe in a ditch outside Santa Fe."

"No, it doesn't," Patterson admitted. "Maybe if I can discover the murder victim's identity, it will shed some light on that."

"If your sister and the mystery girl were both in Santa Fe around the same time, maybe she stole the stuff," said Stacy.

"Anything's possible, but it's a stretch. The same items of clothing being stolen twice by different people in as many months?"

"I never said it was plausible, just possible." Stacy chuckled. "You wouldn't believe the stuff I see as a public defender."

Yeah, I would," Patterson said. "FBI agent, remember?"

"Right. How are you going to put a name and face to your Jane Doe, if you don't mind me asking? I mean, no one has identified this girl in sixteen years."

"Honestly, for most of those years, I don't think anyone has been trying. That's the problem with cold cases. They get forgotten about, especially if there isn't a family to keep pressure on the authorities to do anything about it."

"I get that, but so much time has passed."

"And we also have tools available to us that didn't exist back then, like NamUs," Patterson said, referring to the National Missing and Unidentified Persons System. A country-wide repository of missing persons that could be used by investigators to solve cases, medical examiners to match remains with active investigations, and even members of the public to report their loved ones missing. It wasn't perfect. Only a handful of states were required to enter cases into the database by law, but it was more than they had back when the Santa Fe Jane Doe was murdered. And NamUs was just one of several such resources, including the National Crime Information Center, or NCIC, that tracked not only missing persons but also stolen vehicles, guns, suspected terrorists and more. Patterson was hopeful, especially since she had a place to start looking. "The Jane Doe's belongings also included a sweatshirt from a high school in Oregon. I'm guessing that's where she came from."

"You don't think the police would've checked that sixteen years ago?"

"I know they did because I've read the police file. There were no girls reported missing who attended that school. It was a dead end."

"Then why do you think you'll have more luck with it now?"

"Because it's the only lead I've got," Patterson replied. "And I have no choice. I need to identify that girl to uncover her connection to Julie. They must have crossed paths at some point."

"I hate to say this," Stacy said in a small voice. "But maybe whoever murdered that Jane Doe also killed Julie. Maybe they were both victims of the same serial killer."

"I know." The same thought had occurred to Patterson. She just didn't want to admit it. But she might have no choice, because it might not have been the Jane Doe who was in possession of Julie's clothing, but someone else. A killer who mixed the possessions of his victims to sow confusion. And that led to another depressing thought. Maybe the police back then couldn't find a missing girl who attended William Brady High in Oregon, because the sweatshirt wasn't hers either, any more than the driver's license or Julie's T-shirt from Park Pizza.

Patterson hoped it wasn't true, but Stacy might be right. Her sister and the girl in the ditch could very well have been killed by the same twisted person. Which meant that somewhere nearby, Julie could be lying in a ditch too, just waiting to be discovered.

THIRTY-SIX

IT WAS early afternoon and Corbin Pope was still thinking about the phone call with Senator Newport that morning. He was troubled by his client's recent arrogance. After hanging up, he had concluded that Newport might need to be eliminated once this job was over, and he still felt the same now. Unchecked, the man might become more trouble than he was worth.

But in the meantime, there was Patterson Blake to deal with. She was still holed up in her van in the RV parking lot of Amy's Roadhouse. Apart from coming out to pick up takeout food earlier that day, she hadn't moved. He wondered what kind of investigation she was conducting that didn't require her to actually do any footwork. Not that it mattered. She would be dead soon, either way. But on his timeline, not the Senator's.

Pope yawned. He hated these long stretches of doing nothing when he was surveilling a target. But he also knew that a hastily conceived plan could backfire in a myriad of unintended ways. For example, thanks to his reconnaissance the previous evening, while the FBI agent was drinking herself into a stupor, he had learned that there was a hidden gun safe under the floor of her van. That knowledge might save his life if they ever faced off head-to-head against each other. He hoped that wouldn't happen. He liked it best when his targets never even saw him coming. A deadly injection while they slept. A one-way trip off a cliff, much like the cowboy a couple of nights earlier. He even employed some of the more outlandish methods used to kill a person. The techniques Soviet era spies had used back in the Cold War, and sometimes still did. An umbrella with a poison-laced tip might sound ridiculous, but it got the job done. You could kill someone right out on the street in a milling crowd and never be noticed. One day, he thought to himself, he would use that umbrella trick. It sounded like fun.

But not on Patterson Blake.

The FBI would run toxicology on her body. They would look for foul play. There could be no suspicion of murder. More and more, he was leaning toward staging it to look like she had taken her own life. The sister angle was a gift. He had been doing some digging into Patterson Blake's past. Making some discreet inquiries through knowledgeable contacts he had cultivated over the years. The only reason she was working a case with obvious conflict of interest issues was because it hadn't started out that way. She had suffered a mild nervous breakdown, for want of a better description, while raiding the lair of a serial killer in upstate New York. By all accounts, the case had begun as a personal quest and then morphed into an official investigation when her boss found it expedient, career-wise, to do so.

The question of mental stability still hung over the FBI agent like a cloud. Even though she was technically working in an official capacity now, she would still be required to undergo a full psychological evaluation before returning to her regular duties. Even the situation with the senator that had resulted in Pope being hired to kill her played into that narrative. She had barely escaped going to prison for life, thanks to Senator Newport's efforts to frame her for a murder she didn't commit. Sure, it backfired on the senator and almost sent him to jail instead, but it would be one more nail in the coffin of her state of mind when she did the unthinkable. There would be an investigation, which would conclude that she simply couldn't cope with the enormous stress the last few months had placed upon her.

Pope smiled. He was beginning to like this idea because it fulfilled one of the basic tenets of his philosophy as an assassin. *Let your target's weaknesses work against them.* It also fulfilled the much simpler philosophy of KISS. Keep it simple, stupid.

He settled back in his seat and crossed his arms. It was still too early to make a move. He liked to study a target for at least three days, which he had found to be the optimum time to become familiar with their movements and habits. Tomorrow, he decided, would be a good time to put his plan into action, barring any unforeseen developments. He would wait until nightfall when his movements would be masked by darkness. Catch Patterson Blake by surprise and disable her before she could fight back. Then it was just a matter of finishing the job. It wouldn't be a fast death. For what he had in mind, the FBI agent would need to keep breathing for at least twelve hours after he incapacitated her. But that was fine. They could spend some quality time together, as the phrase went. And at the end of it, Patterson Blake would redecorate the van's interior with her own blood.

THIRTY-SEVEN

AS SOON AS she got off the phone with Stacy, Patterson had gone to work on her laptop searching the law enforcement databases for any clue to who the girl found in the ditch might be. She started with the obvious. The high school sweatshirt, but just as the investigators before her had discovered, there were no reports of any missing girls who attended William Brady High. And not just in the timeframe that matched when the body was found, but ever. In the entire history of the school, none of their students had vanished. At least, if they had, it wasn't in any of the databases.

After two hours, she was no closer to uncovering the identity of the Jane Doe in the ditch than she was before, and therefore no closer to uncovering a link between that girl and Julie. But when she expanded her search in NamUs to include all the caucasian women who went missing between 2004 and 2008 and had been last been seen within the vicinity of Bend, Oregon, she got two hits. The first was easily discounted. The woman was forty-eight years old when she went missing. But the second hit made Patterson's heart race. An eighteen-year-old who had gone missing in 2005.

Her name was Laura Beth Layton. She had left her parents' house after an argument about her boyfriend and never returned. It wasn't the first time she had run away. She was a troubled teen who had gone missing on three previous occasions but had always come back. This time, she didn't.

Patterson scrolled through the rest of the information, noting that her height matched that of the woman found in the ditch. The timeline matched, too. About a year before Julie went missing. It was a long time, but who knew how many months Laura Beth Layton had been out there on her own before she crossed paths with a killer. Certainly, she had traveled a long distance, either voluntarily or under duress. It was over twelve hundred miles from her hometown to Santa Fe. Assuming that she was the same person, of course. The only way to confirm that would be with a DNA test comparing a member of the missing woman's family to the girl in the ditch.

Patterson wasn't surprised that she only got two hits despite the number of people who were reported missing each year in the United States. Over six hundred thousand. Most of those were found in short order, which was one reason why they weren't in the database, but there was still a huge percentage, thousands each year, who were never seen again. But not all those people ended up in the database, especially if they had been missing for a decade or more. Unless new information came to light, most cold cases languished because of time constraints, lack of investigative personnel, or simply that they ended up forgotten about. Many Police Departments simply did not have the manpower or budget to enter all their unsolved cases into the variety of national databases at their disposal.

In this instance, the entry had only been created a couple of years before by the parents of the missing teen. That would explain why the Santa Fe Police Department had never come across it during the course of their investigation and the few occasions they had revisited the case during the ensuing years.

Patterson took down the contact details. The quickest way to find out if Laura Beth Layton was their Jane Doe would be to call and speak to them. It would certainly be quicker than waiting for DNA test results to come through. The forensics lab would give priority to current investigations over a cold case almost two decades old. If the parents confirmed that Laura Beth had a connection to William Brady High, even if she hadn't attended it, that would be good enough for Patterson. It still wouldn't answer all the questions surrounding her sister's connection to the murder victim, but she would be one step closer. She would have a name.

And a face, too. Because there were three photographs of Laura Beth Layton attached to the NamUs entry. In one, she was sitting in the bleachers at some sort of sporting event, smiling widely. In another, she was leaning against a car with her arms folded. The same smile on her face. The third and final picture was a high school yearbook photo, possibly from her senior year. They must all have been taken around the same time. She had long dark hair in all three images, except that in the yearbook photo it had been braided. Her blue eyes were radiant. They looked back at Patterson from the computer screen, so full of exuberance that it seemed incomprehensible that she might have had that life ripped away from her so savagely only months later. And that innocent smile . . . If Laura Beth Layton turned out to be the girl in the ditch, then her smile would be short-lived.

Patterson downloaded all three photographs to her

computer, then took screenshots of everything. She was eager to phone Laura Beth's family right away and confirm her suspicions but restrained herself. Protocol demanded that she appraise the lead detective on the case of her discovery. That would be Detective Les Anderson of the Santa Fe Police Department, whom she had met the day before. He would be the one to contact the family and confirm whether Laura Beth Layton and the girl in the ditch were one and the same. There was nothing more she could do.

But there was still one loose end. The man in the photograph that Patterson suspected to be Trent Steiger's cousin. He still hadn't returned her call. She took out her cell phone, phoned him again, and waited while it rang.

As before, it went to voicemail.

Patterson left another message, then hung up, swallowing her frustration. She had two good leads but could not follow up on either of them. She was at the mercy of other people. All she could do was gather up everything she had found on Laura Beth Layton, send it to Detective Anderson, and wait.

THIRTY-EIGHT

TREYTON COBB RETURNED Patterson's call late in the evening, right before she was thinking of turning in for the night. Earlier, she had sent Laura Beth Layton's NamUs file to Detective Anderson, and he had promised to look into it. Now she snatched up the phone, eager to strike another item from her list of outstanding leads.

Cobb sounded stressed when she answered. "Special Agent Patterson Blake?"

"Speaking." She sat down at the table and picked up the photo she had taken from the roadhouse pin board earlier, studying the three faces that looked back at her. Julie, Trent Steiger, and the slightly rattled man who was now on the other end of the line.

"Sorry I didn't return your call earlier. I was out of town all day and there was no cell service. I must admit, I can't imagine why the FBI is calling me." Cobb laughed nervously. "Whatever you think I've done, I assure you I haven't."

"Relax, Mr. Cobb," Patterson said quickly. "I just want to ask you a few questions about some people you might have known a long time ago when you worked at Amy's Roadhouse."

"The roadhouse. Wow! I haven't thought about that place in years. What would you like to know?"

"I found a photograph on a pin board there. You're posing with two other people. Trent Steiger and Julie Blake."

"That really must be an old photo. Trent is my cousin. We're not so close now, kind of went our separate ways, but we hung out a lot back in the day. As for the other name you mentioned, I've never heard of Julie Blake." Cobb fell silent for a few moments. "You share the same last name. Is she a relative of yours?"

"She's my sister," Patterson replied. "She's been missing for sixteen years."

"Sorry to hear that."

"And you might not remember, but you must have known her, because the three of you are in the same photograph."

"Maybe if I saw the picture, it might jog my memory, but I swear, I don't remember a Julie Blake."

"I can text you the photo," Patterson said. "I'll hang up and do it right now, then call you back in a couple of minutes."

"Sure. I'll look out for it."

Patterson ended the call and snapped a picture of the photograph with her phone camera. She attached it to a text message and selected Treyton Cobb's phone number, then hit send. After waiting a few minutes to make sure it was delivered and he had seen it, she called him back.

"Well?" she asked. "You look at the photo?"

Cobb confirmed he had, but then he said something surprising. "You're right, I know the girl in this photo, but her name wasn't Julie."

Patterson was taken aback. "You sure about that?"

"Hundred percent, although it was a similar sounding name. I just can't remember it right now. I think it began with S."

"Stacy?" Julie had been in possession of her friend's driver's license. "Was that the name you knew my sister by?"

"Yes. That's what it was. Stacy. She needed cash, got a job bartending. I was training her."

"My sister wasn't old enough to bartend. She wasn't twenty-one," Patterson said, realizing even as she spoke the words why Julie was going by her friend's name instead of her own. She had found Stacy's driver's license in a pocket of the Levi's discarded in the back alley behind the Welcome Inn after the robbery, and used it to get a job at Amy's Roadhouse because Stacy had already turned twenty-one.

"Look, I don't know anything about that. But I do remember spending a couple of days teaching her how to pour beer and mix cocktails. Not that it mattered. She didn't stick around long enough to make any money."

"What do you mean?"

"She was dating my cousin. They were pretty hot and heavy, at least when they were first in town, but then there was some sort of bust up. They argued. He told me she left town."

"They had a fight and broke up?"

"That's about the size of it. He was pretty cut up. Guess he liked her a lot, and I can see why. She was damn cute. Flirty, too. She would've made good tips had she stuck around. Honestly, I was kind of bummed she was with Trent, or I might have given it a go."

Patterson ignored Cobb's prurient comments about her sister. "You know what the fight was about?"

"Nah. I came back from my day off and she'd already gone. Trent never told me why except to say that they'd had a falling out and broken up. Never asked him exactly what went down because I didn't want to get in the middle of it. Wasn't any of my business. Still, I kind of hoped she'd show up again, keep working at the bar, but it didn't happen."

"Do you remember if she had any other friends?" Patterson asked, thinking about the girl in the ditch. "Maybe another young woman?"

"Not as I recall, but it was a long time ago, and I didn't know her for that long."

"And Trent Steiger?"

"What about him?"

"Where is he now?"

"Last I heard, he was in Vegas working as a session musician. He never really let the band thing go . . . Always thought he was going to hit it big one day with that guitar of his. And I guess he did if you call being a session musician hitting it big."

"How long ago was this?"

"I don't know, maybe a couple of months. Like I said, we don't keep in touch that much these days, but we still text back-and-forth once in a while. I can shoot him a message, ask about Stacy . . . Sorry, Julie . . . If you like."

"No. I'd rather speak to him myself if you don't mind. Do you remember where in Vegas he was working?"

"Some off-strip casino. He tried to get me out there to watch him play. He was backing up this one-hit wonder from the 80s. Can't remember the band's name. Bit before my time."

"And the name of the casino?"

"Let me check my messages. I'm sure it's in there, somewhere." There was a minute of silence while Cobb looked, then he came back on the line. "Prospector's Paradise Hotel and Casino."

"Thank you." Patterson wrote the name down on a slip of paper. It would be easy enough to confirm if Trent Steiger was still working at the casino. "Do me a favor. If you speak to your cousin, don't mention this conversation."

"Okay. Is he in trouble?"

"No. He's not in trouble." Patterson wondered if her request would have the opposite effect, and prompt Treyton Cobb to warn his cousin. She realized it might have been better not to say anything. "I want to ask him about Julie and I'd rather he didn't have time to think about it first. That's all."

"Oh. I understand."

"I appreciate that. You've been very helpful, Mr. Cobb. I don't want to keep you any longer than necessary. But if you remember anything else, no matter how insignificant it seems . . ."

"I'll call and tell you," Cobb said. "You have my word."

Patterson thanked him again and hung up. Then she opened her laptop and went to the website for the Prospector's Paradise Hotel and Casino. There was only one headliner in residence, playing six nights a week at the pretentiously named Auditorium of the Stars. A band called *The Rain*. They had been there since April. That must be who Trent Steiger was gigging with. In the morning, she would call the hotel and confirm that he was still in Vegas. Then, finally, she might get some answers about her sister from someone who was right there with her.

THIRTY-NINE

THREE WEEKS BEFORE

IT WAS *midafternoon by the time Angel arrived in Phoenix. The temperature had been steadily rising all day and now the city boiled under triple-digit heat. She was glad that Ma's car had AC, even if it didn't blow as cold as she would have liked, because if not, she and Cherub might simply have sweated to death way before they ever reached the city. She was also glad to be near the end of her journey with the car, at least once she found the bus station.*

To that end, Angel pulled into a convenience store on the outskirts of town and pulled past the gas pumps before finding a space in front of the store. Leaving the window rolled down and the engine running, she climbed out of the car. Leaning back in, she told Cherub not to move, and headed for the store.

It was cool inside the building. A faint odor hung in the air that reminded Angel of hot dogs and soda. Angel made her way to an aisle full of candy and grabbed a couple of Snickers bars, then grabbed two bottles of water from a cooler against the back wall, before going to the counter because she thought a friendly customer asking questions would be less noticeable than someone who hadn't purchased anything. When she got there, she asked the cashier—an older woman with smoker's lines around her mouth, who looked as if life had beaten her down, then kicked her some more—for directions to the bus station. It turned out to be near the airport. All she had to do was hop on I-10 and follow the signs.

Angel thanked the woman and paid for the candy bars and water, then made her way back out to the car. When she climbed in, Cherub's eyes lit up at the sight of the candy.

"Chocolate!" she exclaimed gleefully, snatching a Snickers bar from Angel's hand.

"You have to drink some water, too," Angel said, opening a bottle and passing it back to her daughter. "We don't want you to get dehydrated."

Cherub rolled her eyes but took the water, sipping it to satisfy her mother's gaze even though it was clear all she wanted was the candy.

"I guess that will have to do." Angel put the car in reverse and backed out of the space. A couple of minutes later, she joined a flow of traffic north through the city on I-10.

———

It didn't take long to find the airport. Angel exited the interstate and drove around until she found the bus station near the west side of the airport. But she didn't stop. Instead, she backtracked and followed the signposts for long-term parking. She had been wondering where to ditch the car. On the side of the road, perhaps. Or maybe in the parking lot of a supermarket or strip mall. But then she remembered that airports didn't charge for parking upon entry. The fee was always due when you returned from wherever you had flown and picked up your vehicle. Ma's car might sit for weeks or even months in long-term before anyone noticed it, especially since she parked as far from the entrance as possible.

But now she had another problem. How to get from the parking lot to the bus station. The solution presented itself in the form of a shuttle van that came trundling along just as Angel and Cherub were slogging their way across the hot pavement between the parked cars. If there was a free shuttle from the parking lot to the airport, then it stood to reason there would also be a free shuttle from the airport to the bus station.

"Come on." Angel gripped Cherub's hand and practically dragged her along toward the pickup area, so they didn't miss the shuttle. They made it in the nick of time and climbed aboard just before the driver closed the doors.

When he asked what terminal she wanted, Angel froze. She hadn't considered this because they weren't actually flying anywhere. In a panic, she blurted out the first thing that came into her head.

"Southwest." The name of an airline.

The driver nodded and closed the doors and waited for them to take their seats. There were only two left, toward the back of the shuttle. Angel sat next to the aisle, and let Cherub sit near the window.

As they pulled out of the parking lot, a huge airliner thundered overhead on its way to one of the runways. It was so low that she could see the landing gear, feel the vibration from its massive engines.

Cherub's eyes flew wide. "Is that a bus like we're going on?"

Angel couldn't help but be amused until she realized they had led such a solitary existence on the farm that her daughter had never seen an airplane before. "No, honey," she said in a voice barely above a whisper. "That's not a bus."

Cherub scrunched her face up, looking disappointed.

Angel leaned close as the shuttle weaved through the morass of traffic clogging the drop off area for departures. "A bus is just as much fun. I promise you."

"I bet it's not." Cherub dropped her head.

"Then we'll make it fun." Angel glanced out of the window to see that they were pulling up at the curb under a sign that read Southwest. Across the sidewalk was a pair of sliding doors, and she could see ticket counters beyond.

Angel stood and waited for another party ahead of them to grab their luggage from a rack behind the driver and disembark, then she steered Cherub off the shuttle and into the terminal.

Once inside, she wasted no time in looking for ground transportation. It was one level below. They took an escalator down and were soon back outside and climbing into a second shuttle that would take them out of the airport again and to the bus station. After that, thought Angel, they would hop on the first bus they came across that went anywhere in the opposite direction from Carl. And then who knew where they would end up?

FORTY

PATTERSON AWOKE EARLY the next morning eager to track down Trent Steiger in Las Vegas. But when she called Prospector's Paradise, she got nowhere. The only person who might have that information was the hotel's entertainment director, and he wouldn't be in until noon, which was still four hours away.

There were no updates on Laura Beth Layton, either. The young woman who had gone missing in Bend, Oregon, almost seventeen years before. The previous evening, Patterson had sent everything she had discovered to Detective Anderson so that he could follow up. But it was Sunday, and he wasn't working, so she wouldn't get an answer on that score for at least another twenty-four hours.

With no more leads to follow and nothing else to do, she drove into Santa Fe, which she had barely explored until now, and found a cute little restaurant in the historic district that served breakfast. Afterward, she left her van parked behind the restaurant and explored the area, finally ending up in a public square surrounded by picturesque Spanish Pueblo

Revival buildings, which appeared to be the predominant architectural style of the city.

She couldn't help but wonder if Julie had walked the same streets over a decade and a half before. Her sister had always been curious about new places and would have found the historic district, with its distinctive buildings and unusual stores that sold everything from chintzy souvenirs to fine jewelry fascinating.

A necklace sitting in the window of one particular jewelry store caught Patterson's eye. A deep golden topaz gemstone cut into a teardrop shape and hanging on a silver chain. It sparkled under the lights, calling to her. Topaz was Julie's birthstone, and for a moment, Patterson's throat closed with sorrow. She still hadn't fully recovered from thinking that the girl in the ditch was her sister. Even though she wanted closure, wanted to know what had happened to Julie and finally move on, the thought that her sister had been murdered so brutally at the hands of an unknown killer had sent her spiraling into a nightmare. She hadn't been able to think clearly until Bauer called with the news that her DNA did not match the girl in the ditch.

Patterson stared at the necklace a moment longer, then she pulled the door open and stepped into the store. Ten minutes later, she emerged again with the necklace inside a small jewelry box tucked into a brown paper bag. It was an impulsive purchase, but she couldn't bear to leave Julie's birthstone sitting there in that window. Her sister would have loved the necklace, and one day Patterson intended to give it to her, even if it was merely the symbolic gesture of laying it inside her coffin.

It was almost midday now. Patterson returned to the van and drove back to the RV parking lot next to Amy's Roadhouse. When she called the casino this time, her efforts were rewarded. She was transferred to the entertainment director, a gruff man by the name of Fred Marelli, who sounded more like a mobster than someone who booked performers for a living.

When she asked about Trent Steiger, he met her request with stubborn resistance. "Sorry, lady, but I can't give out employment information. Company policy."

A prickle of annoyance surged through Patterson at being called 'lady', but she contained her anger. Instead, she informed him that she was an FBI agent calling on official business.

"You're a Fed?" The change in Marelli's tone was obvious, even to an untrained ear.

Patterson confirmed that she was.

"Sorry. Still can't give that information out. Unless you have a warrant."

"I don't have a warrant," Patterson said, exasperated. "But it's a simple question and all I want is a yes or a no. Is there a guitarist named Trent Steiger currently employed by your hotel as a backup musician? I can't imagine what harm it would do to give me an answer."

"I'll tell you what harm it would do. If there's a Fed sniffing around one of my employees, that means trouble. What's he supposed to have done, anyway?"

"He hasn't done anything." Patterson realized she now had her answer. The entertainment director wouldn't have bothered to ask what Trent Steiger had done if he wasn't still employed by the hotel. She decided there was no point in pressing the man any further. "Thank you for your time."

"That's it?" Marelli asked, clearly surprised that Patterson had given up so easily. "We're done?"

"Were done . . . for now. Please don't discuss this conversation with anyone, and that includes Trent Steiger."

Patterson hung up. She knew where Julie's old boyfriend was now and desperately wanted to talk to him, but not over the phone.

She wanted to do it in person.

Pulling her laptop toward her, she opened it and checked for flights out of Santa Fe. It only took twenty minutes to find what she needed and book it. Then she sat back and folded her arms, contented. In less than twelve hours, she would be in Sin City.

FORTY-ONE

CORBIN POPE WATCHED Patterson Blake's van from the parking lot of Amy's Roadhouse. Earlier in the day, she had driven into town for a couple of hours where she ate breakfast and wandered the stores. Pope had kept a safe distance, never letting her out of his sight. Then she returned to the roadhouse and spent the entire afternoon hidden out of sight inside the van.

He wished he could see what she was doing.

In other circumstances, he would have installed a camera when he broke into the vehicle two nights before. That way, he could watch her at all times. But it was too risky, which was why he hadn't done it. If the FBI agent discovered a hidden camera, realized she was being surveilled, he would lose the element of surprise. Worse, it could derail the entire job. He would be forced to back off for at least a few weeks, and maybe even months, while the heat died down. The already impatient Senator Newport would not take that development well. He might even remove Pope from the job and go with another operative instead. No one had ever taken

Pope off a job, and he didn't intend to let them do it now. Which was why there was no camera in the van.

Still, at least he had the GPS tracker. Unless she crawled underneath the vehicle, or checked it with a bug sweeper, two things he was sure she wouldn't do, he would be safe. She wouldn't find it.

And he was glad of that right now, because without warning, the van was on the move again. It pulled out onto the road with the FBI agent at the wheel and headed toward Santa Fe for the second time that day.

Pope ducked down as she drove past him, then waited a few minutes for her to get a good lead, before activating the tracking app on his phone and following.

He stayed back, keeping her on a long leash and making sure that he was not visible in her rearview mirror. They headed south on eighty-four, and for a while he assumed she was heading back toward the historic district, maybe to find another restaurant for dinner. She must be getting sick of the food at Amy's Roadhouse by now.

But to his surprise, she kept going, ignoring the turn for the historic district, and heading instead toward the interstate on the south side of town.

This was a new development. Until now, there had been no sign she was wrapping up her investigation in the city— actually just the opposite—but that appeared to be what was happening. Especially when she joined I-25 south.

Pope speeded up, one eye on the road and the other on his phone screen. The GPS tracker was a handy tool, but depending on where she was going, he might lose the signal. Right now, though, it was still working perfectly. Patterson Blake's van showed up as a small red dot speeding down the highway on his phone screen.

He reached the interstate and joined the flow of traffic

south, pushing the accelerator toward the floor. There was an eighteen-wheeler struggling to pick up speed ahead of him. It belched black diesel fumes from two exhaust pipes, one on each side of the cab. Pope weaved into the middle lane and shot past it, then slipped back in front of the lumbering vehicle in time to see Patterson Blake's van taking an offramp.

Now Pope knew exactly where she was going. The airport.

He cursed under his breath. What the hell was she up to? He ran through the scenarios in his mind.

Was she picking someone up, like that ex-partner of hers, Marcus Bauer, who had helped clear her name a few weeks before? Possibly, but he didn't think so. A quick check with Siri confirmed there were no arriving flights from Dallas. Or maybe she was following a lead in her sister's disappearance, but he didn't think so. That left one other possibility. She was going there to catch a flight.

Pope swore again. He hadn't planned for this eventuality. The last thing he expected was for Patterson Blake to take flight—literally. Worse, another quick check of his phone confirmed that, although it was only a small regional airport, three flights were departing in the next two hours. One to Phoenix, another to Denver, and the last flight of the evening to Los Angeles. She could have booked a ticket on any of them, and he had no way of knowing. He also couldn't follow her and find out because he didn't have a ticket to get through security. He could buy a last-minute ticket at the check-in desk specifically for that purpose, even though it cost him a fortune, but even then, he only had a one in three chance of being right and actually being able to follow her onto the plane. Not terrible odds, but certainly not good ones.

Worse, he would have to burn an alias because he couldn't buy a ticket under the name Corbin Pope. He would also be forced to leave his car behind, and along with it, all the tools of his trade stashed in the hidden trunk compartment. Not ideal.

And he wouldn't know if any of those flights were her final destination. If she changed planes somewhere like Phoenix, the FBI agent could end up anywhere in the country.

All in all, he thought, it would be better not to react out of panic, anyway. Wherever the FBI agent went, she would be back eventually. He was a few hundred feet behind her now as she pulled into the long-term parking lot.

So, no hastily purchased tickets. No mad dash through the airport to see which gate she was at. This wasn't some perverted rom-com. Better to take some time and think it through. Analyze the situation.

Pope followed the van into the parking lot. He circled, driving slowly, and keeping his eyes on it. When the vehicle pulled into a parking space and came to a stop, he drove past and found a space of his own near the end of the row with a good view of both the van and the terminal building. At least the FBI agent's choice of departure point worked in his favor. If she had continued on to Albuquerque and its much larger international airport, only an hour further away, he would never have been able to watch her so easily and make sure she was actually taking a flight and not just meeting someone. As it was, he would lose her in short order once she entered the terminal building, which was about to happen.

Patterson was climbing from the van with a small travel bag slung over one shoulder. What was called a *go bag* in federal law enforcement parlance. He was almost certain that she also had her guns. Both her main piece and backup weapon. As an FBI agent, she was permitted to carry weapons onto the flight. In fact, it was encouraged. There weren't enough air marshals to cover every aircraft that took to the skies, and so it only made sense to use federal law enforcement officers as sky cops whenever they flew, even if they weren't technically on duty.

The FBI agent was walking straight toward him down the center of the row. It was dusk, and he had turned his lights off, so he doubted she could see into the car, but even so he slid down in his seat as she passed by. Then, less than a minute later, she crossed the road in front of the terminal, stepped around a taxi idling at the curb, and entered the building.

Pope didn't move. There was no point. If Special Agent Blake had any luggage other than her go bag, he could have simply followed her into the airport to see which bag check counter she went to. But she would already have checked in online, he was sure. Pope stared through his windshield at the quickly darkening sky and gritted his teeth. He had lost Patterson Blake. At least, for now.

FORTY-TWO

ONCE SHE WAS inside the airport, Patterson went straight to the security checkpoint. Bypassing the small line of passengers pulling their shoes off and waiting to go through the metal detectors, she headed directly to the crew line and identified herself as an FBI agent. Soon after, she was on the other side of security and heading toward the gate for her flight to Las Vegas, with a forty-minute layover in Phoenix. In four hours, she would be on the ground and taking an Uber to the Prospector's Paradise Hotel and Casino, where Trent Steiger was currently working, and a standard king room awaited her. That the hotel had vacancies at such short notice was not a surprise. It was over a mile east of The Strip and, although it had been renovated in the last couple of years, was far enough away from the tourist areas to put it firmly in the category of a casino favored by the locals. At least, if the reviews she had read online were anything to go by.

The flight was preparing to board when she arrived at the gate. Patterson made herself known to the gate agent and was quickly ushered onto the aircraft where the pilot met her.

After a brief introduction, she took her seat near the front of the plane and waited while the other passengers filed aboard and competed for much coveted overhead bin space. Twenty minutes later, they pushed back, and soon they were in the air climbing to cruising altitude.

Patterson settled in for the duration. An hour and forty-five minutes later, she was changing planes, racing through the terminal to reach her next flight, which was *conveniently* departing from a gate about as far away from where they deplaned as possible. A couple of hours after that, she stepped out of McCarran International Airport and into a stifling Nevada evening that struggled to discard the heat of the day.

A short taxi ride later, she stepped through the doors of the Prospector's Paradise Hotel and Casino. For a resort so far off the strip it was surprisingly nice. The lobby was wide and spacious with gleaming terrazzo floors and a huge chandelier comprising thousands of cut crystal pieces that hung from a high ceiling. To her right was the casino. Beyond this was a restaurant that had already closed for the night, its interior dark and empty.

She checked in and made her way up to her room on the seventh floor. It was late. Gone eleven o'clock. It was also Sunday, the only night of the week that the Auditorium of the Stars was dark. Trent Steiger and the band he was playing with would not perform until the following evening. Patterson was glad for the respite, but was curious, even so.

She left the room and took the elevator back down to the lobby, then made her way into the casino and the auditorium on the far side. Posters of the band flanked the doors leading into the theater. They looked like exactly what they were. Old rockers past their prime, trying to hold on to the vestiges of their former glory. While flying, Patterson had taken advantage of the in-cabin Wi-Fi to do some research on *The Rain*. Back in the mid-eighties, all four of the original members had sported long, silky hair that any woman would have envied. They often performed in tight shirts, showing off their muscular torsos. Only two of the founding band members now remained. The bass player had died of a drug overdose in the nineties, and the rhythm guitarist had quit to start his own band, which never even achieved the one-hit wonder status of his previous endeavor. The remaining two members looked nothing like their counterparts from almost four decades before. Their hair was mostly gone, along with their trim physiques. They looked old and tired. The other two members of the band brought in to replace the original bassist and guitar player looked younger, but not by much. There was no sign of Trent Steiger or any other backup musicians on the poster.

Patterson tried the auditorium door and found it unlocked. She poked her head inside to see a large lobby with a bar at one end and a merchandise stand. Beyond this was another set of doors. She slipped inside and crossed to them, pulling one open enough to view the interior. Rows of raked seats descended toward a wide stage that was swathed in darkness. There was a balcony above, no doubt accessed by a set of stairs on the right side of the lobby next to the bar. She guessed there was seating for at least eight hundred people but doubted it ever got anywhere near that full, at least, not in many years.

Closing the door again, she made her way back out and around the periphery of the casino floor, her gaze drawn to the large black-and-white photographs lining the walls in gold frames. They hearkened back to an era when Vegas was known as much for the mob as it was for ridiculously cheap steak dinners and the rat pack.

The hotel didn't look much different from its modern counterpart, at least on the outside, although the cars sitting under the portico, sporting large tail fins, fat chrome bumpers, and wraparound windshields, dated the images instantly.

Likewise, the interior photos displayed the height of 1950s luxury. Many of them showed famous personalities of the era lounging in the hotel bar, or standing backstage in what she assumed was the Auditorium of the Stars. Dean Martin, Frank Sinatra, and Elvis. Clearly, the property had enjoyed a higher standing back then.

Patterson soon found herself back at the elevators and rode up to the seventh floor. Back in her room, she went to the window intending to draw the curtains, but then hesitated, awed by the view. There, in a gap between two tall metal and glass condo buildings, the Las Vegas Strip glittered like a jewel in the night. Even though her mind was on Trent Steiger and what he knew about Julie, even though she wasn't in the city for pleasure, Patterson couldn't help but feel a swell of excitement when she looked at that sparkling oasis of excess.

Shaking the sentiment off, she closed the curtains and turned back into the room, intending to take a much-needed shower and get ready for bed. But at that moment, there was a sharp knock at the door.

FORTY-THREE

CORBIN POPE HURRIED toward Patterson Blake's van in the long-term parking lot of the Santa Fe Regional Airport. It had been two hours since the FBI agent had disappeared inside the terminal building, and by now she would be well on her way to wherever she was going. In fact, all the flights scheduled to depart should have left already. That was why he had waited so long before climbing out of his car and approaching the van. He wanted to make sure there was no one around to see him break into it for the second time that week.

He had also wanted to scope out the location of any surveillance cameras that might be watching the parking lot, but he needn't have worried. The only cameras were trained on the lot's entrance and exit. There were no cameras covering the interior of the fenced off compound.

When he reached the van, Pope pulled on a pair of black leather gloves, removed the lock pick from his pocket, and had the door open in under five seconds. He climbed up into the vehicle and looked around. The bed was made—the covers pulled up over the pillows. Everything was neat and in its place, except for a slip of paper lying on the small table. A piece of paper that Patterson Blake had jotted something down on in blue ink.

Prospector's Paradise Hotel and Casino, Las Vegas.

So that was where she was going.

Pope sat at the table and stared at the handwritten note. What possible business could the FBI agent have in Sin City? More to the point, how long would she be gone? He hated the thought of sitting around in Santa Fe for days on end, waiting for Patterson Blake to return. Maybe it would be better if he flew out there and tracked her down. And it wouldn't be hard. Unless he was misreading the situation, he knew exactly where she would be. At least, according to that slip of paper.

But there was one problem. The next flight, with a layover in Phoenix, wouldn't depart until seven fifteen the following evening. Not that he wanted to fly there, anyway.

Pope checked his phone.

It was a nine-hour drive from Santa Fe to Las Vegas, not counting rest stops, food, or traffic along the way. Eleven hours was probably a more reasonable assumption. That meant that if he left right away, he could be in Las Vegas by eight the next morning, Pacific time. It meant driving through the night, and Pope was tired. He would also have to return to the motel first and collect his belongings. But it was doable, especially if he made use of the amphetamines stashed in the trunk of his car for situations just like this. He had first used them toward the end of his time as a Marine sniper, and while they wouldn't be his first choice for a stimulant, a couple cups of coffee just wouldn't cut it. Not in a situation like this.

Now all he needed was accommodation. Checking his phone again, Pope found plenty of rooms available at the Prospector's Paradise. He booked one for five nights, figuring that would give him enough time regardless of what the FBI agent was up to. He sincerely doubted she would still be alive after two.

He used another of his fake identities to make the booking. Walter Davenport, a different name to the one under which he had checked into the motel on the outskirts of Santa Fe.

He used a credit card associated with that identity to pay for the room, entering the card number and expiration date from memory because he only ever carried personally identifiable items for whatever identity he was currently inhabiting. By the time he arrived in Vegas, his wallet would contain Walter Davenport's driver's license, two credit cards, and a wholesale club membership card. Right now, they were all hidden in the secret compartment concealed inside his car's trunk, along with the background items for every other identity he wasn't currently using.

Satisfied with his plan, Pope got up from the table. He looked around, making sure that everything was exactly as Patterson Blake had left it, then he climbed out of the van. But instead of returning to his car, he went around to the backside of the vehicle. There was one last thing he needed to do, because he didn't intend for the FBI agent to make it back to Santa Fe. Remove the tracking device he had installed a couple of days earlier. The last thing he wanted was for the FBI to discover it attached to the underside of her vehicle after the FBI agent's untimely death.

It only took a few seconds to retrieve it. GPS tracker in hand, Pope climbed back into his car. He exited the parking lot, paying the fee in cash, then drove to the motel. Forty-five minutes later, after popping a couple of small white pills that would make sure he didn't fall asleep at the wheel, he was heading southwest on the interstate toward Albuquerque, where he would connect with I-40. After that, it was just a question of pointing his vehicle west until morning.

FORTY-FOUR

PATTERSON FROZE, her hand instinctively reaching for the Glock pistol in its shoulder holster. There was no reason for anyone to be at her hotel room door so late in the evening.

"Who's there?" she asked, approaching the door and standing to one side without opening it.

"My name's Jason Lund. I'm the security director here at the Prospector's Paradise." came the reply. "Please open the door, Special Agent Blake."

"I've only got your word for that." Patterson had no intention of opening the door to a stranger, even if he did claim to be hotel security.

"Special Agent Blake, we need to talk." There was a slight huff from the other side of the door. A sigh of exasperation. "How about this. Call down to the front desk. They'll confirm my identity."

Patterson didn't respond. Instead, she went to the room phone and did as the man on the other side of the door suggested. There really was a man named Jason Lund working for the resort as security director. And when the front desk checked with his office, they told her that he really had gone up to see a guest on the seventh floor.

Patterson hung up and returned to the door. She slipped the gun back into her shoulder holster and opened it, keeping the security bar engaged. When she peered through the gap, she saw two men in the corridor, both wearing dark suits with white shirts. The only difference in their attire was their neck ties. One was red, the other a dark blue.

The closer of the pair held up his ID on a lanyard to confirm that he was indeed the head of security. "Please open up, Special Agent Blake. I'd rather not talk through this gap."

Patterson closed the door, pulled back the security bar, and opened it again. She made no move to hide the gun in its shoulder holster slung over her shirt. "How can I help you, gentlemen?"

Lund jerked a thumb toward the man standing a few paces behind him in the corridor. "This is our entertainment director, Fred Marelli. He informed me about your call earlier and I flagged your name to alert me if you popped up on any of our reservation or floor systems. And here you are."

"Is there a problem with that?" Patterson asked.

"I don't know, you tell me." Lund glanced past Patterson toward the interior of the hotel room. "Perhaps we could have this conversation somewhere other than in the corridor."

Patterson stepped aside and let the two men enter. She closed the door. "Now, care to tell me what this is about?"

"May I see your credentials?" Lund asked.

Patterson went to her jacket, which she had placed over a chair upon entering the room and withdrew the slim wallet containing her FBI badge and identification. She held it up for Lund to see, then snapped the wallet closed and returned it to the jacket pocket. "Well?"

"You were inquiring about one of our staff members earlier," Lund said, his gaze flicking quickly to the Glock in Patterson's shoulder holster. "A man named Trent Steiger."

"That's right."

"Mr. Marelli informed you he couldn't give out information about employees over the phone, not even to law enforcement unless you had a warrant."

Marelli shifted from one foot to the other. "It's hotel policy. The same is true for guests."

Lund continued. "Now, less than eight hours later, you're checking into our hotel."

"I need to speak with Mr. Steiger," Patterson said, deciding there was no point in beating around the bush. "I'm working a missing persons case. He might have relevant information."

"I see." Lund cleared his throat. "The hotel is always happy to cooperate with law enforcement, of course, but any request to interview an employee on resort property needs to be made through official channels. I'm curious why you didn't feel it was necessary to do that."

"Mr. Steiger is not part of any criminal investigation," Patterson replied. "I want to ask him some questions about a young woman he briefly dated sixteen years ago. I'm happy to do that somewhere else, like at his apartment. All you need to do is give me his address."

"Mr. Steiger doesn't have an address." Lund folded his arms. "At least, not off property. All our performers live on the premises for the duration of their contract."

"We prefer it that way," Marelli added. "Makes it easier for rehearsals, and our talent doesn't have to fight through Las Vegas traffic to get here every day."

"So you see," Lund said. "It's quite impossible for you to speak to him somewhere else."

"Mr. Lund, we're on the same side," Patterson said. "I'm not here to cause trouble, and my business with Trent Steiger has nothing to do with the hotel, nor will it reflect badly upon your establishment. All I want is half an hour with him and then I'll be out of your hair."

"That won't be possible, I'm afraid." Lund shook his head.

"How about you let Trent Steiger make that decision."

"I don't need to." A tight smile lifted the edges of the security director's lips. "All our employees sign contracts that specifically state when and how they can interact with law enforcement on hotel property."

"I'm sure he leaves the building sometimes," Patterson said, exasperated. "I'll simply approach him somewhere else, not on your property."

"You have that right, of course, should he choose to speak with you," Lund said. "But I will be advising Mr. Steiger of this conversation and making sure he understands that he is not required to answer any of your questions."

"I'm sure you will." Patterson suspected that the head of security would go one step further. He would make sure Trent Steiger's lips remained firmly closed, regardless. "Will there be anything else, gentlemen? It's late and I'm tired."

Lund observed her for a moment with narrowed eyes. Then he shook his head. "I think we're done here. However, a word of caution. You're free to enjoy the world-class facilities at the Prospector's Paradise Hotel and Casino, of course, just like any other guest. But if I discover that you have approached Trent Steiger, or any other member of our staff, in the furtherance of your investigation without my permission, I will have you escorted from the premises. Do we have an understanding?"

Patterson remained silent. She clenched her jaw and

refrained from telling the combative security director exactly what she thought.

Lund nodded. "I'll take that as a yes."

Patterson went to the door and held it open for the two men to leave. "If you don't mind?"

Lund hesitated a moment, then stepped through it with the entertainment director at his heel. In the corridor, he turned back to her. "One more thing. Your weapon. Our standard policy is not to allow guests to bring guns onto the premises, but I'll make an exception for you as a professional courtesy, since you *are* a federal law enforcement officer. But please make sure you keep it either in the room safe or concealed at all times when in the resort's public areas."

"Naturally." Patterson closed the door in his face before the security director could say anything else. She engaged the deadlock and swung the security bar across. Only then did she allow her frustration to escape as a single curse word. A brief concession to her annoyance. Then she shook the moment off and got right back to business, because there were bigger issues at play than the petty minded and obstructive security director.

She grabbed her laptop and went to the two-seater couch on the wall opposite the bed. She spent the next ten minutes with the laptop open and balanced on her knees, all her attention on the screen, before closing it again and picking up her phone.

She made a call and waited for an answer. Then she dove right in. "Hey, it's me. Sorry for calling so late, but you were right. It's happening. When can you get here?"

FORTY-FIVE

POPE DROVE THROUGH THE NIGHT, the pills he had swallowed back in Santa Fe keeping him awake and alert. When they began to wear off, he pulled off the interstate and into a twenty-four-hour gas station where he swallowed two more, washing them down with a couple of swigs from a bottle of water that had been nice and cold when he purchased it in a convenience store before leaving Santa Fe, but which had since lost its chill.

After topping up with gas, he hit the road again, barreling west toward the Silver State, going as fast as he dared without risking the attention of any bored highway patrol cops looking to pad their statistics for the month.

Traffic was light, even around Albuquerque, thanks to a combination of it being Sunday, and the late hour. He was making better time than expected. At this rate, he would arrive in Las Vegas ahead of schedule and be able to check into the hotel and crawl into bed for a few hours before tracking down Patterson Blake and figuring out his next move. He might even have time to play a few hands of poker and clean out some unsuspecting tourist who thought that one weekend a year in Sin City made them a card shark.

Pope actually was good at the game, although mostly because he possessed the kind of mathematical mind that allowed him to beat the odds and predict with a fair level of accuracy which cards remained in the deck. He called it skill. The casinos called it counting cards, and they were aggressive in making sure that those who engaged in it were kept far away from the gaming floor. But they hadn't caught Pope. For one, he never used the same alias twice when he was in the city. Second, he always made sure to keep his wins believable —even deliberately losing once in a while—to avoid attracting unwanted attention. His job had brought him to Las Vegas more than once, and he couldn't afford to end up in anyone's facial tracking database.

In fact, that was why he had started playing cards. In a city synonymous with gambling, the best way to blend in was to gamble.

As he drove, Pope occupied his mind by running through different scenarios for getting rid of the FBI agent, but he kept coming back to the same conclusion. Her instabilities stemming from the loss of her sister were too good an opportunity not to use, and Vegas was as good a place as any for Patterson Blake's life to end. By the time he crossed the state line into Arizona, he had come full circle and decided that his original plan was still the best.

After almost six hours of driving, Pope was nearing Flagstaff. He was also getting hungry. He stopped at a Denny's on the west side of town and took a break from driving. Forty-five minutes later, he was back on the road. At the dry and dusty town of Kingman, perched on the edge of the Mojave Desert, he left the interstate behind and started northwest toward Boulder City, and the Hoover Dam. A couple of hours later, just as the first rays of dawn sun were burning up the eastern horizon, the glittering lights of Vegas came into view in the distance. By the time he was driving back in the other direction, Corbin Pope mused to himself, Patterson Blake would be dead, and then he just had to deal with the senator, who would not be far behind.

FORTY-SIX

PATTERSON WOKE EARLY the next morning. She had laid awake the night before thinking about Trent Steiger, and the hotel's strangely unhelpful attitude. She wasn't going to be speaking with him anytime soon and unless she made the request official. That much was clear. Which meant placing a call to the New York field office, and the one person she knew could set things quickly in motion.

Jonathan Grant.

She hadn't spoken to him since he showed up at her apartment the night before she flew back to Dallas, crawling into bed next to her in the early hours and waking her up. She had been pleased to see him, but when they made love, it felt different. Like something had changed. When he drove her to the airport the next morning, their conversation was stilted. It was as if neither one of them knew how to get past recent events. Gone was the easy camaraderie they had enjoyed for most of the previous week, when it had felt like old times.

Now, several days later, she was going to call him not because of their relationship, but because she needed him in a professional capacity. The fact that she hadn't tried to call before that spoke volumes about the state of their lives. Sure, she had texted him a few times to say good night and received a similarly worded text in return. When this was over, she told herself, they would need to have a serious talk.

But not right now.

It was 7 AM in Vegas, which meant 10 AM on the East Coast. And it was Monday. She dialed his number, hoping he wasn't entrenched in some hours long meeting.

When he answered, she could hear the frustration in his voice. "It's about time you called, although now isn't the best time. I'm about to step into a terrorism response briefing, and then I have a one o'clock with Marilyn Kahn."

"I should've called you before. I'm sorry." Patterson felt a surge of longing for the way they used to be. "I've just been so tied up in this investigation since I got back. I haven't had time."

"That busy, huh?" The incredulity in Grant's voice was hard to miss. "Couldn't even find ten minutes at the end of the day."

You could have called me, too, Patterson thought to herself, but she didn't repeat it out loud. Now was not the time to get into a huge argument. Instead, she took the high road. "I know. I'm sorry."

"You've already said that." Grant sighed. "Look, I don't have a lot of time. Is this a social call, or do you need something from me?"

"I need your help," Patterson admitted, grimacing. She could imagine what Grant was thinking. She only called when she had a problem. No wonder there were cracks in their relationship. "I tracked down Trent Steiger to a casino hotel in Las Vegas. But I can't get close to him. The management is being stubborn, and he has some kind of weird clause in his contract about speaking to law enforcement. I need you to make the request official. Get me some face time with him."

"Shouldn't be too hard to do." Grant was silent for a few seconds. "Are you actually *in* Las Vegas?"

"Yes. I flew here last night from Santa Fe. Butted heads with the security director of the hotel before I even managed to unpack my toothbrush. I don't know what the guy's problem is, but he doesn't seem to like cops."

"Okay. Give me until this afternoon, and I'll see what I can do. What's the name of the hotel?"

Patterson told him. "Thank you for this. I appreciate it."

"Don't mention it."

"Jonathan . . ." Patterson was overcome by a sudden sense of dread. What if their relationship couldn't survive her search for Julie? What if it couldn't survive Grant's promotion to Special Agent in Charge? What if they were already going their separate ways and didn't even realize it?

"Yes?"

"We're going to be okay, right? The two of us."

"Patterson, this isn't the time or the place." There was background noise behind Grant. The sound of a door opening and closing. Voices locked in hushed conversation. He had stepped into the briefing. "I'll take care of your issue with the casino, but I have to go now."

"Oh. Okay." Patterson's throat tightened. "Love you."

"Yeah. I'll call you later." The line went dead.

Patterson stared at the phone in disbelief. He hadn't bothered to return the sentiment. Maybe it was worse than she thought. But there was nothing she could do about it from thousands of miles away on the other side of the country. The best she could hope was that they made it through long enough to patch things up when she got back to New York.

With nothing else to do until Grant called back, she went to the bathroom and turned on the shower. After a visit from Jason Lund, the hotel's head of security, the previous night, she had shucked off her clothes, pulled on her nightshirt, and fallen into bed without bothering to even wash her face. She had been exhausted.

She turned to the mirror, noting the dark rings around her eyes and the way her shoulders slumped. She looked about as bad as she felt. Patterson needed caffeine. But not before freshening up.

Letting the nightshirt fall to the floor, Patterson climbed into the shower and stood under the hot jet of water. She stayed that way for ten minutes after she finished soaping up, relishing the way the water played over her body, soothing her sore muscles, and sending a prickle up her spine.

She stepped out and dried herself, then got dressed. By the time she reached the lobby and went in search of coffee, her mood had lightened. But it quickly soured again when she noticed a uniformed security guard trailing her from a discreet distance. Apparently, Jason Lund didn't trust her not to pursue Trent Steiger on hotel property. He was keeping tabs.

Well, if that was how it had to be, so be it. Grant would take care of the situation, she was sure, and then the hotel's security director would be put in his place. In the meantime, all Patterson could do was contain her frustration and avoid giving Lund the pleasure of thinking he had gotten under her skin.

FORTY-SEVEN

THREE WEEKS BEFORE

THE BUS TRUNDLED *through the inky night on its way to San Diego. Sitting near the back, Angel could hardly keep her eyes open. Cherub sat beside her, staring out the window even as she suppressed a yawn. Back in Phoenix, Ma's car sat in a long-term parking lot outside of the airport. It would be weeks before anyone gave the car a second glance, but even so, Angel was glad to have left the car behind. It was her last link to Carl and that dreadful farmhouse that she had occupied with him for so long. She relaxed back into her seat and stroked Cherub's hair, smiling when the girl turned to look at her. She felt lighter than she had in years. Even if Carl did somehow track the car, he wouldn't have a clue where she had gone next. He was more likely to assume she and Cherub had boarded a flight to some far-flung place than hop on a bus to the West Coast. And even if he figured out that she had left Phoenix by road, there was no way he could find her destination. She didn't even have a place in mind until she checked the departures board at* the bus station and saw that the next departure—San Diego—was in forty minutes.

So here they were, riding through the darkness and putting more miles between themselves and Carl with every passing moment. At her feet, pushed under the seat in front, was the duffel bag containing all their worldly possessions, including the money she had taken from the farmhouse, and Carl's pistol, along with the accompanying ammunition. The cash amounted to several thousand dollars, which she hoped would support them for a while when they reached the city. It would certainly secure temporary accommodation. She hoped there would never be a need to use the gun but felt better for having it.

"Cute kid."

Angel was pulled from her musings by a voice to her left. She looked around to see an older woman with graying hair and bright green eyes staring at her.

When Angel said nothing, the woman flashed an apologetic smile. "Sorry. Didn't mean to intrude upon your privacy, but these bus journeys get mighty lonely. I've done this trip enough times to know that the hours pass quicker if you have someone to talk to." The smile faded. "I'm Helene, by the way."

Angel hesitated a moment. She had intended to come up with fake names for herself and Cherub but hadn't yet gotten around to it. Now she said the first ones that came into her head. "I'm Mandy," she said, plucking the name of a high school friend out of thin air. "And my daughter here is Rosie."

"Rosie. Such a beautiful name." Now the woman smiled again.

"Thank you." Angel hoped the woman would settle back into her seat and leave them alone.

No such luck. Helene shifted sideways so her legs were off the side of the seat and in the aisle. She was now facing Angel and Cherub almost head-on. "You got a man waiting in San Diego? A husband maybe?"

"No," Angel replied without elaborating. She didn't want to discuss her private life with this stranger, even if what she told the woman would be lies.

"I know. I'm prying." Helene appeared to sense her unease. "But you'll have to forgive me. I find it fascinating why folk put themselves through the hassle of a long and uncomfortable bus journey like this. Me, I have a daughter there. Grandkids. Boy and a girl. I try to see them at least once a year, although I'm not sure how much longer I'll be able to make this trip. These seats play havoc with my arthritis."

"I'm sorry to hear that." Angel turned her attention frontward again, hoping Helene would take the hint.

"Not much of a talker, are you?"

"Just tired. It's been a long day." Angel sensed Cherub pressing against her. When she looked down, the child was sleeping, lulled into slumber by the rhythmic thrum of the bus's wheels on the blacktop.

Helene's gaze shifted from Angel to Cherub, then she turned away wordlessly and settled back into her seat. If she had anything else to say, she obviously thought better of it.

Angel leaned her head back and closed her eyes. They wouldn't arrive in San Diego until morning, stopping first in Yuma, Calexico, and El Centro, two places Angel had never been. She had briefly considered disembarking at one of these waypoints because her money might go further there, but decided both were too close to Phoenix and the abandoned car. Besides, San Diego was on the coast. There were beaches. Cherub had never seen a beach, let alone played on one. So, San Diego it was. But before then, Angel wanted to get some much-needed rest. She had barely slept the night before, sitting upright behind the wheel of Ma's Sebring in the camping area the night before and she could feel the exhaustion flitting around the edges of her consciousness.

She opened her eyes briefly and looked down at Cherub to make *sure her daughter was comfortable. Then Angel let the exhaustion win and succumbed to a deep but troubled sleep. And when she did, Carl was waiting in her dreams, leather belt dangling from one hand ready to lay it across her naked back and exposed rump again and again until the skin turned red with welts, just like he would in real life if they ever let him find them.*

FORTY-EIGHT

AFTER CHECKING into the hotel using an alias that he would quickly discard at the end of this job, Corbin Pope went straight to his room on the tenth floor, kicked his shoes off, and dropped onto the bed without even bothering to get undressed. After following Patterson Blake for most of the previous day and then driving through the night in a mad dash to reach Las Vegas, he was exhausted.

He was also ticked off.

Pope didn't like surprises. They had a habit of ruining his carefully laid plans. And Patterson Blake taking a flight to Vegas without warning was certainly a surprise. If it wasn't for that, he would be back in Santa Fe preparing to finish his assignment and collect the remainder of his payment from Senator Newport. Instead, he was two states away from where he expected to be and feeling the effects of the ten-hour drive now that the drugs he had used to stay awake were wearing off. Still, he thought to himself, there was no reason why Patterson Blake couldn't be quickly dispatched just as soon as he found out which room she occupied.

If he had been more naïve, Pope would simply have asked at the check-in desk and made up some story about being an old school friend, or perhaps a work colleague. But he knew they wouldn't divulge that information without first phoning her room and seeking permission. Gone were the days when people trusted each other. Nowadays, a strange man asking for the room number of an attractive woman was more likely to end in tragedy than a heartfelt reunion. In this case, it certainly would have. At least for Patterson Blake.

And even if he could have convinced the desk clerk to give him the FBI agent's room number, he wouldn't have done it. An unknown visitor calling on her right before she was found dead would surely raise suspicion. After that, all the hotel would need to do was pull an image of his face from the front desk security camera and he would be suspect number one. Better to keep a low profile and get the information he wanted another way. And he knew how to do it.

But not right now.

Pope needed sleep. He was, after all, still human, even if he didn't possess the empathy almost everyone else on the planet seemed to be cursed with. He also wanted a clear mind when it came time to kill the FBI agent.

He closed his eyes and tried to silence his chattering mind. That was one of the worst things about always staying alert. The mind never stopped working. He was constantly on guard.

In a place like Kandahar, that was a good thing. It could save your life. But here, in a quiet Las Vegas hotel room where the biggest threat was some jerk slamming a door too loud when they stumbled back to their accommodation in an alcoholic stupor after wasting obscene amounts of money in the casino, it was irritating.

But despite the constant deluge of sensory data that refused to quit pouring into his brain, Pope finally succumbed to his exhaustion and fell into a deep and dreamless sleep.

FORTY-NINE

PATTERSON'S PHONE rang at noon. She had spent the last three hours pacing her room, unable to focus, and anxiously waiting for Grant to take care of the hotel and casino's obstructive head of security. She felt useless, sidelined, and at the mercy of others. Now she picked up the phone, except it wasn't her boyfriend come boss in New York calling. It was Detective Anderson.

"I've got some news for you," he said when she answered. "Your hunch about the girl found in the ditch panned out. We're almost certain that our Jane Doe and the teenager who went missing in Bend, Oregon, are one and the same."

"Laura Beth Layton."

"Yup. We won't know for sure until we get the results of a DNA comparison with a sample her mother is going to provide, but I'm expecting it to come back as a match."

"How can you be so sure?" Patterson asked, although she was elated that at least one strand of her investigation was resolving itself.

"The high school sweatshirt. Turns out she had a boyfriend who attended William Brady High. He gave her his sweatshirt about a year before she went missing as kind of a commitment thing. It was one of her favorite pieces of clothing. Her mother confirmed that she never saw the sweatshirt again after her daughter went missing. We still need to track down the old boyfriend and ask him if the sweatshirt we have in our evidence room matches the one he gave to Laura Beth Layton, but I'd say it's pretty much a foregone conclusion that it will."

"Anything else would be way too much of a coincidence," Patterson said.

"Exactly. Now all we have to do is figure out what she was doing so far from home, and who killed her."

"I might be able to help with that," Patterson said, thinking about her sister's T-shirt and Stacy's driver's license that were both in the possession of the dead girl. "There must be a link to my sister there, somewhere. I'm in Vegas right now to interview the last person we know that she was traveling with. A man named Trent Steiger, who was romantically involved with her."

"You're in Vegas?" Anderson sounded surprised. "When did that happen?"

"Yesterday. A lead I was following came together. I booked a last-minute evening flight out of Santa Fe. I should be back in a couple of days if all goes well."

"Must be nice. Furthest they ever sent me is the courthouse in Albuquerque, and that only happens when I have to give evidence in some state case."

"Don't worry, you're not missing much. I've spent most of my time in the room so far."

"Not much of a gambler, huh?"

"On a federal agent's salary?" Patterson suppressed a snort. "Maybe if they promote me to ASAC one day."

"I haven't known you very long, Special Agent Blake, and maybe I'm way off base, but you strike me as a little too . . ." Anderson was clearly struggling to find the right word. "Independent to get that promotion."

"You mean opinionated," Patterson said with a mirthless laugh.

"That's not quite how I would have put it," Anderson replied. "But yeah, pretty much."

"Meh. You're probably right. Honestly, I'm not sure I want a desk job, anyway. I like fieldwork."

"Birds of a feather." Anderson chuckled. "You really think that lead of yours in Vegas might have information about our Jane Doe? That there might be a connection to your sister?"

"She's not a Jane Doe anymore, remember?"

"Right. Laura Beth Layton. I'd sure love to close this one."

"If I ever actually talk to him, I'll let you know."

"Having some issues with an uncooperative witness?"

"More like issues with his boss. I have my field office on it. Hopefully, they'll come through. If not, I'll find another way."

"I have no doubt about that. Good luck out there, Special Agent Blake."

"Thanks. I'll need it."

"And please, keep me in the loop."

"Goes without saying." Patterson told him goodbye and hung up. She opened the document folder on her phone and found the photos of Laura Beth Layton she had downloaded from the NamUs database a couple of days before. She stared at them for a long while, wondering what secrets the long dead girl had taken to her grave.

The Jane Doe in Santa Fe now had a name and face, but she still didn't have a background. How had she ended up so far from home? What was she doing with Julie's T-shirt and Stacy's driver's license in her possession? Had Julie met her at some point? Were they friends? These were questions that might never have answers, but if they did, Trent Steiger might just hold them. It was now doubly important that she speak to him.

FIFTY

AN HOUR after Detective Anderson told her about Laura Beth Layton, Patterson sat at the desk in her hotel room with her laptop open. A video was playing on the screen. It was the second time she had watched it, the first being the previous evening before she climbed into bed. She studied every detail now, making sure she hadn't missed anything. When it was over, she played it again and smiled to herself. It was only a matter of time now.

She picked up her phone and fired off a quick text message to Marcus Bauer. His reply came less than a minute later. She read it, smiled again, then went to slip the phone back into her pocket.

At that moment, it rang.

Jonathan Grant's name lit up on the screen.

"All done," he said when she answered. "You won't be having any more trouble with the hotel. They've agreed to cooperate fully with your investigation."

"Thank you." A flood of relief washed over Patterson. Without access to Trent Steiger, she would never find out what had happened to Julie in Santa Fe or discover the connection between her sister and Laura Beth Layton.

"You're welcome. Although it's no surprise that you got push back from that security director. You managed to pick the one casino that might as well still be stuck in the fifties mob era."

"What do you mean?" Patterson asked.

"Two words. Oscar Rossi."

"Am I supposed to know that name?"

"No. But I bet the Las Vegas field office knows it all too well. Rossi's a smalltime hood with big aspirations. Both his father and grandfather had ties to the Las Vegas mob going all the way back to Bugsy Siegel. In fact, Oscar Rossi's grandfather worked for Siegel at the Flamingo back in the mid-forties."

"I'm not sure what any of this has to do with Trent Steiger," Patterson said.

"Because Rossi owns the Prospector's Paradise. Has done ever since the last owner, a man named Harlan Biggs, and his general manager, Wagner Mitchell, both met an untimely end out in the desert. The Vegas field office can't prove anything, but apparently Biggs borrowed money from Rossi to renovate the hotel, which had become so dilapidated that no one wanted to stay there. The loan wasn't exactly aboveboard, and the interest rate was so high there was never a chance he would pay it back. When the renovations took longer than expected and the hotel couldn't reopen on time, it sealed the deal. Biggs was unable to make his payments, and Rossi, who had made sure to be listed as a business partner in the hotel venture as collateral against the loan, called in the debt."

"You mean he took over the hotel."

"Right. But not before driving Harlan Biggs and Wagner Mitchell out into the desert and teaching them a deadly and rather gruesome lesson. At least, that's the theory, although there isn't a shred of evidence linking Rossi to either death."

"I guess that explains why they don't want their employees talking to the police," Patterson said.

"Exactly. Even if it has nothing to do with Oscar Rossi's dubious business activities. Men like Rossi tend to be paranoid. That's how they survive."

"After hearing that, I'm surprised they were willing to cooperate at all."

"It took some persuading," Grant said. "But in the end, the hotel's security director realized it would be in his employer's best interest not to stand in your way."

"Do I want to know what you threatened him with?" Patterson was impressed.

"I just pointed out that right now he was dealing with us on an informal basis, but that if we were to get a warrant, we might come across other activities that justified investigation in the natural course of enforcing it."

"You blackmailed him."

"I'm the ASAC at the New York field office, Patterson. I don't blackmail people. I just point out the wisdom of their cooperation, and what might happen if they don't. All in the interest of complete candor."

"Right." Patterson laughed. "We'll go with that."

"You need anything else?"

"No." Patterson was anxious to hunt down Trent Steiger now that she had been given the go-ahead. "You've done more than enough. Thank you."

"You're welcome." Grant hesitated. "Look, I'm sure I don't need to tell you this, but be careful out there."

"I'm always careful. Besides, I have no interest in kicking Oscar Rossi's hornet's nest. Once I find out what Steiger knows about Julie, I'm out of here and back to Santa Fe."

"I wasn't talking about Rossi. He isn't stupid enough to harm an FBI agent. Especially one who's staying in his hotel. I'm more concerned with Senator Newport."

"I've got that under control," Patterson said. "It's all good."

"That's what worries me. Please, promise me you'll be careful?"

"I already did, didn't I?"

"I suppose."

"Hey." Patterson hated to think of Grant all the way on the other side of the country worrying about her needlessly. "I'll be fine. I can take care of myself."

"I know you can. Just watch your back." There was a moment of silence punctuated only by a slight exhalation of breath. "I love you."

"I know," Patterson replied, relieved that he had finally said it. "I love you, too."

She hung up and went to the room safe. Unlocking it, she took her guns out, both her service weapon and the backup Glock that sat in an ankle holster. After looking in the mirror and making sure no one could see them about her person, she went to the hotel room door, drew back the deadbolt, and stepped out into the corridor. As she was heading for the elevators, her phone buzzed. She took it out to find a text message waiting for her.

'I'm here.'

There was also a room number.

Patterson acknowledged the text and returned the phone to her pocket. Then she went in search of Jason Lund, the hotel and casino's disagreeable security director.

FIFTY-ONE

POPE WOKE up refreshed and ready to take care of Patterson Blake. He climbed off the bed and took his laptop out, placing it on the desk. After grabbing a bottle of water from the minibar and twisting the top off, he settled in front of the laptop.

The computer looked like any other run-of-the-mill notebook PC, but in reality, it was a highly secure unit with NSA level encryption, multiple layers of security, and software that ensured the laptop was undetectable even when joining an open network like the one provided by the hotel. In short, Pope's laptop was about as impenetrable as any machine carried by a top-level spook.

It also contained all the tools needed to sniff out a computer system's vulnerabilities and hack into it. Which was what Pope intended to do right now with the reservations system at the Prospector's Paradise Hotel and Casino.

It only took him a few minutes to find an unpatched security vulnerability in the hotel's production network and jump from the guest Wi-Fi into the secure intranet used by employees. In theory, everything he needed would be connected to this network. But now he encountered his first hurdle. The intranet's firewall was sturdier than he expected, possibly because he was dealing with a Las Vegas casino and not some budget hotel chain using off-the-shelf software. But it was no match for the tools on his laptop, and soon Pope was masquerading as a trusted device inside the resort's internal systems and accessing their reservations database.

The first thing he did was find Patterson's room and then check the rooms on each side. As he hoped, one of them was adjoining. If the hotel received a booking for two rooms, the occupants of each could move between them without having to step into the corridor thanks to a pair of back-to-back connecting doors. If the rooms were rented separately, those doors would remain locked, barring access to the other space. Most of the rooms at the Prospector's Paradise were set up in this fashion. Even the suites on the fourteenth and fifteenth floors could be connected to their neighbor, making even larger suites if required.

Pope relaxed. If Patterson Blake's room wasn't adjoining, it would have been much harder for him to gain access and finish his task because even if he made a copy of her key, the deadbolt and security latch would be difficult to bypass without making enough noise to draw attention.

But there was a problem. The adjoining room was occupied for the next three nights. The simple solution would be to just kill the occupants, but that wasn't practical or tidy.

But all was not lost. Actually, far from it.

It only took a few seconds for Pope to find a vacant luxury suite on the fifteenth floor and reassign it to the couple occupying the seventh-floor room adjacent to the FBI agent. Next, he programmed the door lock to accept the key cards they already had. After that, he created a fake booking for their original room so he could come and go as he pleased.

Now there was only one more step.

Pope reached into his bag and pulled out a headset with earphones and a mic, much like those used by reservation services and dictation professionals. He put it on and adjusted the mic so that it sat in front of his mouth. Then, turning his attention from the hotel's reservation system to a VOIP calling app that had the ability to seamlessly connect with the hotel's own internal telephone system through the same security vulnerability, he placed a call to the room.

"Hello?" The voice that answered was female.

Good. They were in their room. "Mrs. McElroy, this is the front desk. I know this is a major inconvenience, but we have to move you to another room. There's nothing to be alarmed about, I assure you. It's a maintenance issue."

"What?" Mrs. McElroy's voice rose in pitch. From behind her, a male voice asked what was going on. "Why? We only checked in yesterday evening and there's nothing wrong with our room."

"I'm aware of that." Pope thought she sounded pretty, even with a note of stress in her voice, but there was no way to tell. "It's actually the room above you that has an issue. A broken pipe under the toilet. It's unlikely to affect you, but we don't want to take a chance, so we're moving you as a courtesy."

The man must have stepped close to the receiver, because Pope heard him mumble something about how inconveniencing guests was not courteous.

Pope had expected this. "I'm aware that it's an inconvenience, which is why we've upgraded you to a luxury suite on the fifteenth floor. It's very nice. Has a view of the Strip."

"Really?" The woman's voice had dropped back to its original pitch now that she realized they might actually be benefiting from the situation. "A luxury suite, you say?"

"Yes. It's only one bedroom," Pope said, referencing the details of the suite on the reservation system. "But it has a separate lounge area with a 75-inch TV, and a jetted tub big enough for two. As an additional courtesy, we'll also load five hundred dollars in credit onto your players club cards. Two hundred and fifty on each one. Feel free to take in a show, enjoy one of our world-class restaurants, or simply try your luck on the gaming floor. I do hope that's acceptable to both of you."

"Yes," Mrs. McElroy said without waiting for her husband to confirm it. "It's more than acceptable. When will the new room be ready?"

"It's ready for you right now," Pope said. "The suite number is 1502. The key you already have will unlock the door. I've gone ahead and transferred them. Those same keys will also work to access your current room for the next hour so you can transfer your belongings. Is that enough time?"

"More than enough," Mrs. McElroy said, sounding excited.

"Excellent. If you need anything else, please don't hesitate to call down and let us know."

The woman assured Pope that she would, then hung up, no doubt eager to take her husband and check out their new luxury digs. He had given them an hour but suspected it would take them half that time. He also didn't think they would call the front desk for fear that the hotel might decide the upgrade was too generous and rescind the offer. But just to be sure, he placed a command in the hotel's system, rerouting any calls they made to the front desk from either the seventh-floor room or the luxury suite straight to his laptop. Then he made good on his promise and loaded two hundred and fifty dollars in credit onto each of their players club cards.

Finally, he removed another device from his bag. A handheld key card programmer. It was a useful piece of equipment which was easy to come by if you knew where to look. It had come in useful on more than one assignment.

He connected it to the laptop, withdrew a pair of blank cards from the bag, and made duplicate keys—known in security circles as ghost cards—for both Patterson Blake's room, and the soon-to-be vacated adjoining room.

Everything was coming together nicely. But for his plan to work, he still needed one more thing. For the FBI agent to leave her room long enough for him to slip in using the duplicate key card and disengage the deadbolt on the connecting door between her accommodation and the neighboring one, an act which would probably go unnoticed. After that, he would have unfettered access to her room through the adjoining door without ever having to use a key.

Entering late at night while she was sleeping, he would inject the sleeping woman with a sedative before she even knew he was there. A sedative just strong enough to keep her docile. Then he would force her to swallow enough pills to make her death look believable. More pills would be sprinkled on the bed, along with the empty pillbox. If he was lucky, he might even get her to pen a note saying how much her sister's disappearance had weighed on her over the years and how she couldn't go on any longer, although he thought that might take more persuasion than he was willing to apply.

But it didn't matter. She was sure to have a picture of her sister somewhere in the room. Perhaps more than one. Place that in her hand, make it look right, and the deadly tableau would speak for itself.

When he was done, it would be a simple matter of retreating back through the adjoining room, locking the deadbolt on that side of the connecting door, and vanishing into the night. By the time someone discovered her body, likely a member of the housekeeping staff, he would be hundreds of miles away and speeding back toward Dallas, eager to collect his money from Senator Newport and tie up one last loose end.

FIFTY-TWO

PATTERSON SAT across the desk from the hotel's security director and endured his withering gaze. It was clear that he was not a fan either of Patterson or her methods of getting what she wanted.

"I have been instructed to cooperate with your investigation," he said in a stiff voice. "At least so far as it pertains to Trent Steiger. I'll inform him of your request and let him know it has been cleared through upper management. Obviously, it will still be his choice whether he speaks with you, at the end of the day."

"I understand," Patterson said. "Please impress upon him that he's not in any trouble. I just need to know what happened between him and the subject of my investigation sixteen years ago when they were in Santa Fe."

"Does the subject of that investigation have a name?" Lund asked, raising an eyebrow.

Patterson had been waiting for this question. In other circumstances, she would have declined to answer, but in this instance, it just might convince Trent Steiger to speak with her. At least, if he had ever had any true feelings for her sister. "Her name is Julie Blake."

"Blake." Lund spoke the word more of a statement than a question, but his surprise was obvious. "The same as you."

"Yes." Patterson shifted in her seat as the security director's eyes bore into her.

"That's some kind of coincidence." Lund rubbed his chin with his thumb and forefinger. "Who would have thought?"

Patterson figured she might as well tell the truth. "It is not coincidence. Julie Blake is my sister. She went missing sixteen years ago on a cross-country road trip, and I'm trying to find out what happened to her."

"I see." Lund pulled the hand away from his face. He folded his arms. "When you say she went missing, I'm assuming you don't mean voluntarily."

"No. I believe someone took her," Patterson replied. "She never would have broken off contact with her family and vanished like that of her own free will."

"And Trent Steiger is involved in this, somehow."

"He was her boyfriend back then. They had traveled together from Dallas, then to Amarillo, and finally Santa Fe where he was playing gigs in a local bar. For all I know, he was the last person to see her alive."

"And yet you say he's not in trouble."

"Not at the moment." Patterson could imagine the cogs turning in Lund's head. Girls missing for that long mostly ended up dead. He was surely wondering if there was a murderer in his employ. "I have no reason to believe that Trent Steiger did anything to my sister, but of course I can't rule that possibility out."

"Of course." Lund's previous combativeness was gone. Now he looked uneasy.

And no wonder, thought Patterson. If it came out that

Trent Steiger was indeed involved in the disappearance of a young woman, it would draw unnecessary scrutiny upon the hotel, if only by association. There might be questions about whether other young women had gone missing over the years, potentially even while he was working at the Prospector's Paradise Hotel and Casino. Given that the hotel was owned by a low-level mobster who was suspected in the deaths of the previous owner and general manager, any such interest by the FBI would be unwelcome. She decided to smooth the waters just in case Oscar Rossi had a change of heart and decided to play hardball until he was presented with a warrant.

"Just so you know, I don't believe Trent Steiger had anything to do with my sister's disappearance," Patterson said quickly. "I've already spoken to his cousin, who said that they had a falling out, and she left. If Trent Steiger's version of events corroborates that scenario, which I'm sure it will, then he has nothing to worry about."

"I'm pleased to hear that."

"But he still might have information that could lead me to her. Once I get that information, I'll be out of your hair."

"The sooner the better," Lund replied, his face now an unreadable block of stone. "Leave it with me, and I'll let you know."

"Thank you." Patterson suspected that she would be talking to Trent Steiger sooner rather than later. Lund would do everything in his power to get rid of her soon as possible, because her presence in the hotel no doubt made his boss jittery. "There is one more thing that I need."

"Which is?"

"I'd like to look at the last twelve hours of security footage from the check-in desk."

"I'm not sure what that has to do with Trent Steiger."

"It doesn't have anything to do with him, at least not directly. I'm looking for a face in the crowd."

"You're pushing your luck, Special Agent Blake."

"And you've been told to cooperate with me," Patterson countered.

"It wasn't a blanket order. I was told to let you speak with Trent Steiger if he agreed to it."

Patterson leaned forward and rested her elbows on her knees. She met Lund's gaze. "Should I make another call back to my field office?"

"That won't be necessary. I'm sure we can work something out. Just so long as it has nothing to do with any investigation into the hotel and casino, or its personnel, including Mr. Rossi."

"It doesn't. You have my word."

"Good." Lund glanced sideways and up toward a small camera mounted in the top corner of his office. A red blinking dot under the lens indicated that it was operational. "If that turns out not to be true, I have a recording of your assurances. When would you like to look at the footage?"

"There's no time like the present."

"Very well." Lund pushed his chair back and stood up. "I'll show you the registration desk footage for the last twelve hours. But nothing else. Understood?"

"Understood." Patterson rose to her feet and followed the security director out into the corridor. She was one step closer to speaking with Trent Steiger. Now she needed to confirm whether he was the only person she should be worried about.

FIFTY-THREE

THE SURVEILLANCE ROOM at the Prospector's Paradise was hidden beneath the hotel on a sub-level, accessible only by a staff elevator. Patterson hadn't known what to expect but wasn't prepared for just how large the room actually was. It rivaled that of surveillance rooms in places like CIA headquarters in Langley, Virginia, or maybe the NSA's digs in Fort Meade, Maryland, although she had never visited the latter.

But where the comparisons ended was the number of staff. When Patterson had visited CIA headquarters a couple of years before, she had found it teaming with operatives, their eyes glued to the screens as if their lives depended on it. Here, there were only three staff members staring up, bleary-eyed, at the hundreds of small screens that covered an entire wall of the enormous and dimly lit room. Most of them, Patterson noted, were focused on the casino floor, and especially the gaming tables. Blackjack. Poker. Craps.

"I know what you're thinking," Lund said as they

approached the wall of monitors. "How can three employees possibly watch everything that's going on inside the casino?"

"The thought had crossed my mind," Patterson replied.

"The answer is that they don't. It would take an army of staff to watch every single monitor twenty-four hours a day."

"But still, three people?" Which really meant two people at times during the day, Patterson thought, when restroom breaks, lunches, and shift changes were accounted for.

"Truth is, we don't need to monitor everything in real time," Lund said. "That would be a huge task in a hundred thousand square-foot casino, not to mention all the other public areas like the lobby, shops, restaurants, and bars. We record everything, obviously. If there's an issue, we can always rewind and take a look. And computers have taken on a lot of the workload over the past few years. AI is getting better all the time. We already have facial recognition that can pinpoint bad actors before they ever get near a gaming table. We can even flag suspicious activity as it happens for review by a human operative. State-of-the-art stuff."

"I see." Patterson wondered how much of this was just the security chief bragging. The equipment looked old and certainly not the cutting-edge tech he boasted about. "What about the check in desk footage? Can I see that now?"

"Sure, sure." Lund steered her toward the closest of the three operatives. "This is Franklin. He can pull up the footage you need."

Franklin looked up and flashed a toothy, white smile. "Just give me a time period and a camera. I'll do the rest."

"The registration desk," Patterson answered. She made a quick mental calculation in her head. "How about we start with the period from 6 AM through noon."

"We've got five cameras focusing on the registration

desk," Franklin said. "But only one of them shows a long view of the entire registration area. What exactly are you looking for?"

"I need to know if a certain individual checked into the hotel." Patterson took her phone out and opened an email containing a screenshot she had taken on her laptop the evening before. It was a cropped image of a man's face in profile. The lighting wasn't good, but there was enough detail to discern his features. She showed the image to the surveillance room operative. "Can you do anything with this?"

Franklin studied the photo for a few moments before nodding. "It's a bit grainy but I can work with that. And you'll be pleased to hear that we don't need to sift through goodness knows how many hours of footage until we go cross-eyed. There's an easier way."

"The facial recognition software I told you about," Lund said from over Patterson's shoulder.

"Right." Franklin nodded. "Just send me a copy of that photo and I'll do the rest. If all you're looking for is a simple yes or no on whether this individual checked into the hotel, you don't even need to hang around while I do it."

"How long will that take?" Patterson asked.

"No more than an hour. I'll expand the search to run from midnight all the way up to the present, just to be sure we don't miss anything. Will that work?"

"There's no way he would've checked in before midnight last night," Patterson said. "But if it's all the same with you, I'll stay here while you run the comparison."

Franklin shrugged. "Suit yourself. You can send the photo to me at the security desk email address."

"And that would be?"

Franklin told her the address, then made a showing motion with one hand. "Now, if you don't mind, I hate people looking over my shoulder while I work. There are plenty of seats around here and fresh coffee in the breakroom. Feel free to make use of both. I'll have your answer shortly."

Patterson sent the photo, then stepped back.

Lund mumbled something about needing to take a load off and found a vacant chair at a desk in the center of the room, upon which sat a bulky computer system. He clearly intended to wait, probably to escort Patterson back up to the public areas once they were done.

Coffee sounded good.

Beyond a door on the other side of the room, Patterson saw a vending machine and what looked like a small kitchen area. The breakroom. She asked Lund if he wanted a cup, but he declined.

When she returned with a coffee and took a seat next to him, Lund glanced sideways at her. "Your sister. She's been missing for sixteen years?"

"Yes." Patterson set the coffee down. It didn't taste fresh.

"Damn. Must be tough. Spending all that time not knowing where your loved one is. I can't imagine."

"It hasn't been easy."

"I bet. That why you became a Fed?"

"Not only because of that," Patterson said. "But I guess it had a lot to do with it."

"I thought about becoming an FBI agent at one time many moons ago." Lund made a sound that almost came out as a laugh, but not quite.

"What happened?" Patterson asked.

The security director stared off into the corner of the room. "I went to the dark side instead. It pays more."

Patterson lapsed into silence. She drank her coffee, staring down into the tepid liquid.

Forty-five minutes later, Franklin waved a hand in the air. "Special Agent Blake? I've gone through all the footage."

Patterson jumped up and joined him at the monitors. "Anything?"

Franklin shook his head "No. There were several individuals that came up blank against the image you provided because we couldn't get a clear view of their faces, either because they looked down the whole time, or someone else blocked our view of them. Just blind luck."

"Could someone avoid the cameras deliberately?"

Franklin nodded. "I guess. If they were really careful, but that would be much harder. They would have to calculate each camera's field of view and then make sure to either put themselves in a blind spot, which can't be done if they're right there, checking in, or angle themselves in such a way that their face is unreadable. It would take some skill."

"What about other cameras in the lobby?"

Lund cleared his throat. "Anyone who could avoid showing up on our registration desk surveillance likely wouldn't be stupid enough to show themselves elsewhere in the lobby. We could run a check against the recordings from every camera in the hotel and on the casino floor since last night, but it would be a while. There's just so much footage."

"And if your man doesn't step foot into the casino, where the bulk of our surveillance is located, he could conceivably get to his room without being caught on any cameras."

"How could that be?" Patterson asked. "Don't you have full coverage of all the public areas?"

"We do. On the ground floor." Lund shuffled, obviously uncomfortable. "But not all the cameras actually work. We've been meaning to replace them, but, well . . ."

"And there are no cameras in the hotel's corridors or elevators," Franklin said.

"I see." Patterson sighed. For all she knew, a dangerous individual was in the hotel even as they spoke, and she had no way to confirm it. Which meant trusting her gut, and her gut was telling her to run.

FIFTY-FOUR

WITH HIS LAPTOP bag slung over his shoulder, Corbin Pope took the elevator to the hotel's seventh floor. There was no one around. The custodial staff had already finished cleaning the rooms and the occupants of those rooms were either down in the casino frittering their money away or on the Strip gazing wide-eyed at all the shiny things.

He came to a stop outside room 7046, formerly occupied by Mr. and Mrs. McElroy, who were now enjoying their much larger accommodation on the fifteenth floor. A *do not disturb* sign still hung on the handle, no doubt forgotten in their haste to switch rooms.

Pope left it there and used the ghost key he had created earlier to let himself in, turning the knob with a tissue in his palm to avoid leaving fingerprints. As the door clicked closed behind him, he took a pair of leather gloves from his pocket and pulled them on before touching anything else. He would have done so in the corridor, but a gloved man inside a Vegas hotel when it was a hundred degrees outside would stick in the memory of anyone he encountered.

The room still bore the signs of its previous occupation. The bed was unmade, the covers pushed back. There was trash in the garbage can. Chocolate wrappers. A couple of soda cans. An empty bottle of cheap champagne and a condom wrapper. The McElroy's had obviously gotten straight to business when they arrived the day before, making full use of their room. He could only imagine the fun they would have in the suite he had so generously assigned to them.

Moving on, Pope went to the desk and took his laptop out. For the second time that day, he connected to the hotel's internal computer system and placed a call to the phone in the room next door, spoofing the front desk. When the FBI agent didn't pick up, he waited ten minutes, then called again.

Still no answer.

In all likelihood the room was empty. He closed the laptop and slipped it back in his bag, then went to the connecting door between the rooms. He pressed his ear against it, listening for any sound coming from the other side.

There was nothing but silence.

Now for the riskiest part of his plan. He could not be a hundred percent sure that Patterson Blake was not in the room, either sleeping or in the bathroom. But if he wanted to complete the mission, he had no choice but to go through with this next step.

The first part was easy. He turned the deadbolt, unlocking the connecting door on his side. After checking that it opened, he went back to the front of the room and stepped out into the corridor, glancing left and right to make sure there was still no one around.

He was alone.

Pope went to the FBI agent's room and used the second

ghost key. This room also had a *do not disturb* sign hanging on the handle. Ignoring it, he opened the door a couple of inches. So far so good. The deadbolt wasn't engaged.

Neither was the swing latch. Now he was sure that Patterson Blake was not there. She would be too security conscious not to lock her door from the inside when she was present.

Stepping inside, Pope closed the door gently behind him. He couldn't afford to linger too long inside the room in case the FBI agent returned. The first thing he did was unlock the connecting door. There was a small chance she would see that the latch was turned the wrong way, but only if she had bothered to take note of it in the first place. Now, when he returned later that night, he would be able to enter through the adjoining room.

Pope turned and scanned the rest of the room. He pulled back the closet door and stuck his head inside. There was a jacket and a couple pairs of pants hanging up. The wall safe door hung open, which meant she was armed, because she would never leave her guns unsecured. That was even more reason not to linger. If she came back and found a gloved man who obviously didn't work for the hotel waiting in her room, the chances were that she would shoot first and ask questions later.

Pope closed the closet door and stepped into the main area. The bed in this room was also unmade, but she had pulled the covers up and rearranged them into a semblance of neatness.

The go bag he had seen her carrying the night before sat on a luggage rack. He unzipped it and looked inside, careful not to disturb anything. The bag was mostly filled with clothes, but there was also a manila folder tucked into a side compartment. He pulled it out and checked the contents, which appeared to be the same items he had discovered in a plastic tub under the bed in the van. Photos of the FBI agent's sister. An old map. A letter, and some discolored registration cards from a hotel in Oklahoma City. She obviously didn't trust leaving the evidence of her sister's road trip locked in her van at the airport in Santa Fe. This was good. He could stage those items, maybe even rip a picture of Julie Blake in half to make it look like the FBI agent had lost hope. Fallen into a deadly depression. Even without a suicide note, Patterson Blake's intentions would be obvious to all but the most suspicious of investigators.

Smiling, Pope returned everything to its place, zipped up the bag, and made for the connecting door. A couple of seconds later, he was on the other side in the room that had recently been occupied by the McElroy's but was now registered for the next five nights to a nonexistent couple by the names of Pat and Jack Carlton.

Making sure both connecting doors were shut tight, and engaging the deadbolt on his side, Pope went to the hotel room door, stepped back out into the corridor, and slipped off his gloves. Then he hurried back toward the elevators, satisfied that everything was in place for what he was going to do later that night.

FIFTY-FIVE

THREE WEEKS BEFORE

THREE HUNDRED AND *twenty miles southwest of the house where Ma was staring up sightlessly at her kitchen ceiling, the Greyhound bus carrying Angel and her daughter pulled up at the curb next to a dilapidated bus stop in Yuma, Arizona, with an angry hiss of air brakes. The sound, and the accompanying lurch as the bus came to a halt, were enough to pull Angel from a fitful sleep. The dream she was having, in which Carl dragged her into his bedroom by her hair, threw her on the bed, and proceeded to punish her with his belt for some unspecified transgression that she may or may not have committed, evaporated like morning mist.*

"Fifteen-minute rest stop," the driver announced over the PA system. "Stretch your legs, but don't wander too far from the bus. If you get left behind, it's a long walk to San Diego."

Angel looked down at her daughter, who was only now emerging groggy and bleary-eyed from sleep.

"Are we there yet?" the child asked, turning to look out of the window.

"No, not even close." Angel watched several passengers ahead of her rise from their seats and start down the aisle. She stood and took Cherub's hand. "Let's get off for a few minutes."

"I don't want to. I'm tired."

"You'll feel better once you get some fresh air." Angel tugged at her daughter's hand, but Cherub resisted, pulling back the other way. Angel sighed with exasperation. The passengers ahead of her had cleared the aisle now, and people further back in the bus were filing past, eager to take advantage of the brief respite from the road.

"I can watch her for a few minutes," said a voice from across the aisle. It was Helene, the woman she had spoken to earlier who was traveling to see her grandchildren.

"That's very kind of you," Angel said, hesitant to leave her daughter with a stranger. "But it's not necessary. I don't want to impose."

"Heavens. It's no trouble. And you have no need to worry. I've been looking after children on and off for fifty of my seventy years. She will be fine, and we'll both be right here on the bus when you get back."

"I don't know . . ." Angel wasn't so much worried about the woman doing something nefarious, stealing her child—after all where could she go without disembarking from the bus in plain view —as much as leaving Cherub on her own with a stranger to say something she shouldn't. But when she looked back down, her daughter was sleeping again, head resting on the window.

"Go stretch your legs," Helene said. "I'll keep an eye on her. I bet she'll just sleep right through, anyway."

Angel wavered a moment longer, then decided that it would be fine so long as she wasn't gone too long. She thanked the woman and stepped into the aisle, then made her way to the front of the bus and disembarked.

It was warmer than she expected outside. Even under the cloak of night, the air still clung to the heat it had gathered throughout the day. The bus sat next to a dilapidated building that looked like it hadn't been used in years, perhaps even decades. At one time, it had been a hotel, as evidenced by the rusting sign that still hung on one corner of the building. It must have been swanky in its time, constructed in a Spanish Colonial style with arches framing a breezeway that ran the length of the building and two floors with balconies, the higher of which mirrored the ground-floor arches.

Angel walked the length of the bus, following the sidewalk, and stepped around scattered passengers who stood with cigarettes pressed to their lips, eager for their fix of nicotine before the bus started on the next leg of its journey. The smell of cigarette smoke combined with diesel fumes from the idling bus made her queasy, and she was glad to step away and breathe the fresher air further along the sidewalk.

Only a few passengers had ventured this far, most having gone only the required distance to light up. She met the gaze of another young woman who stood cradling a baby in her arms. When the woman smiled, she returned the gesture and kept going until she reached the corner. This was about as far as she dared to wander. The blocks beyond were dark and unwelcoming. A railroad track on a raised embankment sat across the road beyond a thin sliver of vacant land interspersed here and there with scraggly shrubs. A freight train with more cars than she could count sat stationary upon the rails like a temporary wall blocking the rest of the city from her view.

Angel stood for a couple of minutes, happy to be away from the confines of the bus. The back of her legs ached where she had sat in the same position for so long, and there was a crick in her neck. She stretched and lifted her eyes briefly upwards toward the vast expanse of stars scattered across the heavens. When she looked down again, a figure was emerging from the dark breezeway under the hotel's shabby arches. A man with wavy black hair and stubble on *his chin. He moved from the shadows; face briefly illuminated by the headlights of a passing car.*

The breath caught in Angel's throat.

Because in that instant, as the light played across his features, she recognized him. It was Carl.

FIFTY-SIX

IN THE CORRIDOR outside the video surveillance room, Jason Lund pulled Patterson to one side. "Is there something I should know about, Special Agent Blake?"

Patterson had been waiting for this question ever since the hotel's facial recognition software had failed to find a match with the image on her phone. She shook her head. "It's nothing you need to worry yourself with."

"I'm not so sure about that." Lund turned to block her path, apparently thinking she might continue on without adequately addressing his concerns. "I have a responsibility to keep this property safe. I can't see for the life of me what the man you were looking for in there has to do with you interviewing Trent Steiger. I don't like being kept in the dark about events in my own hotel. If there's going to be trouble, now is the time to tell me about it."

"I can assure you I have everything under control," Patterson said, even though it might not be true. The man in the photo on her phone was dangerous, but she had no proof he had followed her from Santa Fe. Just a gut feeling. And she had learned to listen to her gut.

Lund observed her with narrowed eyes. "If I find out that you're holding back on me—"

"I'm not holding back on you."

"So you say."

"Look, once I speak with Trent Steiger, I'll be out of your hair. With regard to the man that I was looking for in there, the chances are he isn't even in the hotel. Your employee said it himself. It would be almost impossible for someone to avoid the cameras in your lobby on purpose." *They would have to be a skilled covert operative*, she thought. Exactly the kind of person that Senator Newport might send after her. Just because the hotel surveillance system hadn't come up with a facial match, didn't mean she was safe in the hotel. Which was why she had called in backup. And that was where she intended to go next, just as soon as she got rid of the hotel's security director. "Do you have any other concerns, Mr. Lund?"

"Yes, but I don't think I'm going to get anywhere with them." Lund started back along the corridor toward the elevator. "Just promise me that if anything changes, if you think of anything I need to know, you will inform me right away."

"Naturally," Patterson said as they reached the elevator. "And as for Trent Steiger . . ."

"I'll be in touch."

"I'll look forward to it," Patterson said, then stepped into the elevator. They rode back up and soon she was striding across the lobby floor toward another set of elevators that went to the guestrooms in the tower above the casino. She hit the button for the eighth floor. A few minutes later, she was standing outside of a room that wasn't her own.

She knocked.

There was a scuffle of movement from the other side of the door. When it opened, Marcus Bauer was on the other side with a big grin on his face. "Do you think the Bureau's per diem stretches to the blackjack tables?"

Patterson stepped past him and into the room. "I doubt it, but I'd love to see you try."

FIFTY-SEVEN

"THANKS FOR COMING at such short notice," Patterson said after Bauer closed the hotel room door.

"You're welcome," he replied. "Although some groveling might be in order to Phoebe when this is all over. She was not impressed with me dropping everything and jetting out here to help you."

"Yeah. Sorry about that. Didn't mean to put you in a bad position there."

"She'll come around." Bauer went to the window and stared out over the Las Vegas skyline. "It's my job, after all. I was more concerned with SAC Harris since I'm technically still in his bad books. Every time I help you, trouble ensues, and my desk duty gets extended. The way I'm going, I may never get back to real fieldwork. The only cases I'll get will be when you come calling."

"I wouldn't complain about that," Patterson said. She and Bauer hadn't exactly had the best of starts, but now she trusted him with her life. "And I'm glad you've got my back."

"Always," Bauer said. "Are you sure he's here in Vegas?"

"No. I don't have any proof, but my gut tells me he is." Patterson joined Bauer at the window. "Why else would he follow me to the airport?"

"That was some quick thinking on your part, putting a concealed camera inside the van. If it wasn't for that, you might not even have seen him coming."

"I suspected someone was following me even before the camera." Patterson still remembered her first night in the RV parking next to Amy's Roadhouse. How she couldn't shake the feeling of being watched. She had gone to the window and looked out over the parking lot, and at the time had noticed nothing particularly unusual. But then, the next day, a car from the night before was still there. The driver had moved it and probably thought she wouldn't notice, but she did. Under normal circumstances, she wouldn't have given it much thought, but with Senator Newport walking free and possibly harboring a grudge, she was on high alert. That was why she asked Detective Anderson to procure a surveillance camera for her. One that she could check via the internet. And it had paid off when she got an alert that someone was in her van at the airport. Someone who shouldn't have been there. But she was one step ahead.

"And you're sure Newport is behind it?"

"Who else could it be?" Patterson responded. "Strange men don't follow me, break into my van, for no reason. He's a hired gun."

"Okay. I believe you," Bauer said. "That's why I'm here. I can't believe you set a trap for the guy. That was pretty smart."

"I was pretty much convinced I had a tail by the time I got to the airport. That's why I left that slip of paper with the hotel name written on it in plain view inside the van. If somebody was out to get me, they wouldn't be able to resist breaking in to look for a clue regarding my destination, then they would reveal themselves."

"And come here," Bauer said.

"Right. And now that he's taken the bait I intend to take him down."

"Assuming he actually took the bait," Bauer said. "We still don't know for sure that he's in the hotel."

"He's here. I can feel it, and I'm sure he won't wait much longer to make his move."

"Which means you *really* have to watch your back now." Bauer said.

"I know," Patterson said. "That's where you come in."

"Tell me more," Bauer said.

Patterson was about to reply, but at that moment, her phone rang. It was the hotel's security director, Jason Lund.

"I talked to Trent Steiger, and he agreed to speak with you," he said. "Come down to the Auditorium of the Stars. The band is in the middle of a sound check before their performance tonight, but he'll find a few minutes when they take a break."

"Great." Patterson turned away from the window. "I'll be right down."

Bauer glanced her way as Patterson hung up the phone. "Trent Steiger?"

Patterson nodded. "I have to go. I'd invite you along, but I don't want to spook him."

"No worries. I'm going to take a walk. Make sure I know the layout of the hotel." Bauer stepped away from the window. If our mystery guy makes a move tonight, I want to be ready."

"Good idea." Patterson went to the door, stepped out into the corridor, and started toward the elevators. A couple of minutes later, she was striding into the Auditorium of the Stars.

FIFTY-EIGHT

PATTERSON PAUSED a moment before entering the Auditorium of the Stars to collect her thoughts. She had a feeling that her time with Trent Steiger would be short, and she didn't want to miss anything.

She stepped inside and crossed the lobby, pulling one of the auditorium doors open.

The band was on stage, running through a song Patterson didn't recognize. There were six of them in total. The four regular band members, and two session musicians, one of which she assumed to be Trent Steiger. The music was loud and echoed back upon itself in the empty auditorium, giving it an almost tinny quality.

Before she could take another step, a man in black pants and a polo shirt with the word *crew* printed on it hurried toward her from the direction of a sound desk at the back of the auditorium.

He waved his arms. "Excuse me, miss, you can't be in here. Show doesn't start until eight."

"I'm not here for the show," Patterson replied, turning

toward the man. "I'm here to see a member of the band. Trent Steiger."

"You still can't be here. There will be a meet-and-greet in the lobby after the performance. I'm sure the band will be happy to sign autographs."

"No, you don't understand," Patterson said, reaching for her credentials. "I'm not here for autographs. I'm an FBI agent—"

"It's all right, Ollie. You can go back to the sound check," said a voice to her left. "I gave Special Agent Blake permission to be here."

Patterson turned to see Jason Lund hurrying toward her, a sheen of sweat on his forehead.

He drew close and came to a halt, breathing heavily. "Sorry about that. The band might not have scored a hit in almost forty years, but we still get crazy fans trying to sneak in sometimes. We normally keep the doors locked before showtime, but I opened them so you could get in."

Patterson returned the credentials wallet to her pocket. "No problem."

"Come on, I'll take you backstage." He motioned for Patterson to follow him toward the door on the left-hand side of the stage marked *staff only*.

Beyond the door was a concrete corridor as drab in appearance as the theater auditorium was opulent. They ascended a set of concrete steps and navigated another narrow corridor until they came to a black painted door inset with a small window. On the other side was the stage.

When they stepped into the wings, another man came hurrying forward. Patterson recognized him as the entertainment director, Fred Marelli. He shook her hand vigorously, then released it and turned back toward the stage where the band was thrashing through a number that she was sure only their most diehard fans would recognize.

"Okay, people," Marelli shouted above the melee, clapping his hands loudly with outstretched arms. "Looking good. Let's knock it on the head and take five."

The music petered out, and the band dispersed, setting down their instruments and heading toward the wings. Five of them shuffled out through the same door Patterson and Lund had entered by moments before, no doubt heading to their dressing rooms. The last man lingered, his nervous gaze alighting on the trio standing in the wings.

"You the FBI agent I was told about?" the musician asked. "Julie's sister?"

"That's right," Patterson replied, introducing herself. "You must be Trent Steiger."

"Yeah. I'm sorry about Julie. I had no idea that she'd gone missing."

"Thank you." Patterson stepped closer to Steiger and noticed that he was sweating profusely. She wondered if it was because of the stage lights or because he was nervous. Maybe it was a little of both. "I'm grateful that you agreed to talk to me."

"I had nothing to do with her going missing," Steiger said quickly. "Just so you know."

"I'm not saying that you did." Patterson glanced around. "Is there somewhere we can sit down?"

"Over here." Steiger led her to a raised platform at the back of the stage, upon which was a sprawling drum set. Steps on each side of the platform allowed access. Steiger sat on the bottom step and waited for Patterson to settle next to him. "You want to know about Santa Fe, I assume?"

"That's the last place I know my sister went before she disappeared." Patterson studied Trent Steiger's face. She looked into his eyes, wondering how many times Julie stared into those same dusty gray orbs. He was a good-looking man, she thought, and would have been even cuter sixteen years ago. She could see why Julie was attracted to him. On the other hand, those same eyes might have been the last thing Julie ever saw, for all she knew. "Want to tell me about it?"

"Sure. But I have to say, it was not my finest hour," Steiger replied. "We were dating for about a month when we got there. My cousin worked at this bar and got me a gig playing Saturday nights for a whole month. Amy's Roadhouse. I have no idea if it's still there."

"It is," Patterson said. "That's how I tracked you down."

Steiger nodded. "Anyway, we came up from Dallas after the band I was in played a festival there. It was a crappy gig, to tell the truth. The organizer was a real jerk. Typical lowlife promoter. Stiffed a bunch of people on their pay. After that, the band broke up. We went our separate ways."

"I know all this already," Patterson interrupted. "You went to Amarillo, then headed to Santa Fe alone with Julie."

"Yeah. That's right. We were both so broke. The first few nights we slept on my cousin's couch until I played my first gig and got paid. It still wasn't enough to get a hotel room or some other decent place to lay our heads, so Julie decided to bar tend. Figured she could make good tips, being so cute and all."

"You realize she wasn't twenty-one," Patterson said, not mentioning Stacy's driver's license because she wanted to see if Steiger's account matched what she already knew.

"That wasn't a problem. She had her friend's driver's license, and that girl was legal. I didn't think they looked much alike, but the bar manager of the roadhouse didn't seem to care so long as he'd paid lip service to verifying her age. I guess finding girls like Julie to lure in the cowboys and keep them drinking beer wasn't so easy. Not that she worked there long. I think she only did a couple of shifts."

"And why was that?" Patterson asked.

"Because I was an idiot. Thing is, I really liked her. Thought maybe she was the real deal. But then I screwed it all up. It was the second week playing the roadhouse. Some girl came up after the first set. She was all dolled up and probably drunk. She was all over me, saying how much she loved guitarists. At first, I pushed her away, but when I went out back to smoke a cigarette, she followed me. Things kind of got out of hand and . . ." Steiger shook his head as if he didn't want to remember what happened next. "Anyway, Julie came out back to bring me a beer. Thought I might be thirsty. She caught us in the alley. Not my finest moment. I tried to apologize, but she wasn't having any of it. We argued, and she took off. That was the last time I saw her."

"You didn't go after her?"

"I wanted to, but I had to play another two sets. By then we were staying in this hostel in the city. It was all we could afford. I was staying in a room with another guy, and she was sharing with two girls. I figured when I got back, she'd be there. But she wasn't." Steiger hung his head. He looked down gloomily at the floor. "I tried to find her, asked if anyone at the hostel knew where she'd gone, but they didn't. I even searched around the area for a while, hoping she was just walking the streets to clear her head. In the end, I went back to the hostel and waited, figuring she'd return in her own good time. She never did."

"That didn't worry you?" Patterson asked, incredulously.

"Yeah, of course it worried me. Like I said, I really liked Julie. But we hadn't been together that long. It wasn't like we were engaged or anything. I figured she probably hitched out of town and continued on her way alone, just like she was doing when we first met at the hotel in Oklahoma City. If I knew she was going to go missing, I would've gone to the police or something. Spent more time looking for her."

"Maybe you should have done that, anyway," Patterson said bitterly.

"Perhaps. I've thought about her on and off over the years, hoped I'd run into her again someday. You know, the one that got away. I guess that isn't going to happen."

"Probably not." Patterson kept her tone even despite the anger that roiled inside her. If Trent Steiger hadn't been a cheating asshole, her sister would probably still be alive. But now was not the time to call him out on it. There was one more thing she needed to know. Reaching into her pocket, she took out her phone and brought up a picture of Laura Beth Layton. One of the images she had downloaded from the NamUs database. She showed him the screen. "What about this girl? Have you ever seen her before?"

Steiger stared at the photo with narrowed eyes. Then he nodded. "Yeah. I know her. Or at least, I did back then." He looked almost wistful. "She was at the hostel. She shared a room with Julie."

FIFTY-NINE

CORBIN POPE SAT at the desk in his hotel room with the tools of his trade spread across it. Or at least, those he planned to use on Patterson Blake later that night.

With gloved hands, he picked up a syringe and filled it with five milligrams of clear liquid from a small brown bottle. Once injected, the sedative would be enough to make the FBI agent drowsy and susceptible to suggestion, but not a large enough dose to knock her out completely. The only tricky part was ensuring that she was sound asleep when he entered her room. The last thing he wanted was Patterson Blake fighting back before he could administer the drug.

Once the sedative took effect, he would try to get that note to explain her tragic end. A few words would do. Something along the lines of, *I can't live without Julie*. He still didn't think it was likely she would comply, even heavily drugged but it was worth a try. Then he would force enough pills down her throat to finish the job. After that, all that would be left was to stage the scene. Scatter some photos of Julie across the bed—the ones he had found in her bag—along with the remaining pills and pill bottle. And if the coroner went looking for signs of foul play, they wouldn't find anything they weren't expecting. The injection and the pills were both the same drug. A powerful sedative that was easily obtainable on the black market if you knew where to look. And as a federal law enforcement officer, Patterson Blake would have that knowledge. It would simply appear like she had gone to a drug dealer, got what she needed to achieve her goals, and checked out of her hotel the hard way.

Pope capped the syringe and placed it inside a protective white plastic case, then snapped it shut. Next, he checked the pill bottle, holding it up to examine the contents against the light. There were more than enough pills for his needs.

He added both the syringe case and the pill bottle to a dark green shoulder bag. Everything else he needed would already be in Patterson Blake's room. The photographs of Julie. The hotel stationary and cheap ballpoint pen upon which she would write the last words of her life.

Everything was set.

Now there was nothing to do but wait.

Pope pulled his gloves off and set them down on the desk next to the bag. He opened the minibar and withdrew a bottle of Springwater, drinking deeply. It was a splurge at eight dollars. He could buy a whole case of water at the convenience store down the street for about the same price. But that would mean showing his face in public, and Pope liked to keep a low profile when he was on an assignment. His only concession was a thousand dollars that he had quickly—and deliberately—lost on a blackjack table after his earlier excursion to Patterson Blake's room. Another five hundred had gone the same way playing video poker.

He had done this not because he enjoyed losing money, or even had a love of gambling, but to flesh out the alias of

Walter Davenport, the name under which he was checked into the hotel. He had also signed up for a players club card in the same false name to provide proof of his losses. Finally, he purchased a ticket for that night's performance in the Auditorium of the Stars. A show he had no intention of actually seeing. Because, while Pope hated leaving behind breadcrumbs that might document his activities or movements, an alias had to be more than just thin air. If something went wrong—which was unlikely but could not be ruled out—and the authorities started looking for a likely suspect in the FBI agent's death, Walter Davenport needed to look like every other slack-jawed light-dazzled tourist out for a good time, before returning to what Pope imagined would be a dreary life in Cleveland, Ohio.

And why Cleveland? Because that was where the driver's license Pope presented at check-in said he was from.

Smiling to himself, Pope went to the bed and laid on his back with his hands at his sides. Then he closed his eyes and took several deep, cleansing breaths. He would need all his wits for the upcoming task. That meant being rested and alert.

With the smile still on his lips, Pope let himself fall into a light and recuperative slumber, with thoughts of Patterson Blake's imminent death playing through his mind.

SIXTY

"WHAT DOES your sister's old roommate have to do with anything?" Steiger asked, still looking at the photo.

"She's dead," Patterson said. "Murdered around the same time my sister went missing. Someone strangled her and left her in a ditch near Amy's Roadhouse. She was a Jane Doe cold case until recently."

"Holy shit." Steiger's face had drained of color. "Are you serious?"

"You think I'd joke about something like that?" Patterson glared at the musician.

"I swear to God she was still alive the last time I saw her." A flicker of panic raced across Steiger's face. "I had nothing to do with Julie's disappearance, and I didn't touch that girl, either. I swear."

"It's okay. No one is accusing you of anything," Patterson said. The thought had crossed her mind that Trent Steiger might be a killer, especially since he admitted knowing Laura Beth Layton, at least in passing. Based solely on circumstance, he should be at the top of her list. One girl missing, and another dead, both around the time he was in Santa Fe. But until she had more than just suspicions, she wasn't going to start flinging accusations around, because then he would just clam up and she would never learn the truth. "What was the name of the hostel you were staying at with Julie?"

"Beats me. It was a decade and a half ago. I've stayed in hundreds of places since. Maybe even thousands. Life of a traveling musician."

"Do you remember where it was?" Patterson asked. If it was still there, maybe someone would remember Julie or Laura Beth Layton. Maybe they would remember Trent Steiger. It was a long shot, but it was all she had. "What street it was on?"

Steiger pressed his lips together, then shook his head slowly. "Never really paid much attention to that. My cousin used to pick us up on his way to work and bring us back at the end of the night."

"You had a van. Why didn't you drive yourself to the roadhouse?"

"Damn thing didn't run half the time. And it guzzled gas. Needed a new clutch. Couldn't afford to get it fixed right then, so I parked it up, and we rode with Trayton."

"You said Julie left before you the last night you saw her. That she stormed out early."

"That's right."

"How did she get back to the hostel?"

Steiger shrugged. "Beats me. Maybe she got a ride with someone who was heading back into town. The roadhouse was pretty much a locals bar, so everyone knew everyone else."

"Except Julie had only worked a few shifts."

"Yeah. On weekends, which were always packed. I'm sure

she met a ton of people. Any of them could have offered her a ride."

"But you didn't actually see her leave with anyone?"

"No. We were arguing and then she stormed off. I followed her back inside, but I was already late for my second set. I could see the woman who owned the place glaring at me, so I got up on stage and played. Figured she'd finish out her shift behind the bar and then we could talk. But when I went looking for her later, she was already gone. Trayton said she went back to the bar, then left. He tried to ask her what was going on, but she just told him she quit."

"Did you ask around?"

"Sure. Right after my second set. I mean, I didn't want her walking all the way back to the hostel in the dark. It was miles away. But no one knew if she'd gotten a ride back or not. I had one more set to play, so I got it done as quick as I could and got the hell out of there. Went back to the hostel. Laura Beth and the other girl she was rooming with were there. They refused to speak to me, so I guess she must've gone back there and told them what happened. They were pretty pissed. Called me some names that I'd rather not repeat and slammed the door in my face. Guess I deserved that."

"The other girl. Do you remember her name?"

Steiger was silent for a while. Then he nodded. "I think it was Shannon."

"Does she have a last name?"

Steiger thought on it for another long moment, then looked at Patterson apologetically. "I really don't remember. But now that I think about it, I'm sure her first name was Shannon."

"Thank you." Patterson consigned the name to memory.

"What about later? Did either of the girls talk to you once they'd calmed down?"

"Nope. Gave me the cold shoulder whenever I passed them in the hallway. I tried to ask about Julie a couple of times, but they just blanked me. In the end, I gave up. Like I said, I figured Julie must've moved on, continued on her trip. She was always talking about making her way to Los Angeles. I said we could do it together. It wasn't like I had anywhere to be. Amy's Roadhouse was just a way to make some money along the way. Easy work to get some gas money and repair the van. I actually made it out to LA about six months later and looked for her, but it's so big, and I didn't even know if that was where she'd gone in the end."

"How long did you end up staying in Santa Fe?"

"Another three weeks. I finished up the gigs at the roadhouse and moved on after I got the van repaired. Went to Flagstaff next and stayed a couple of months there."

"And Laura Beth Layton?"

"What about her?"

"Was she still at the hostel when you left?"

"Yeah. Both of them were. But even then, weeks later, they still weren't speaking to me."

Patterson caught movement from the corner of her eye. When she looked around, Marelli was striding toward them. The rest of the band were crossing the stage behind him and heading for their instruments.

"Okay, break time's over." Marelli stopped a few feet away from where Patterson and Steiger were sitting. "I hope you got everything you need, Special Agent Blake, because that's all the time I can give you right now. We have a lot to do before the curtain goes up."

"I'm good for now," Patterson replied. She stood up and

thanked Steiger. "If I have any more questions, I'll come back."

Steiger looked up at her. "When you find Julie, tell her I'm sorry for what happened back then. That is, if she's still . . ." He let the last word hang in the air, clearly not wanting to voice what they were both thinking.

"I'll tell her," Patterson promised. Then she turned toward Marelli. "There's one more thing you can do for me."

"Let me guess. A complimentary front row ticket to tonight's show and a VIP meet-n-greet afterward." Marelli laughed at his own sarcasm.

"No, but thanks for the offer," Patterson replied. "My request is a little more unusual. Do you have a costume department here at the auditorium?"

"Wouldn't be much of a theater if we didn't. It's behind the dressing rooms under the stage. Why?"

"There's an item I would like to borrow, just for a day, maybe two." Patterson told him. "A wig. I'm sure you must have some, this being Vegas and all."

He looked perplexed. "Sure. We have a whole closet full of them for the showgirls. Do I want to know what it's for?"

"Probably not. So, can I borrow one?"

Marelli sighed. "You'll just cause trouble until I say yes. Correct?"

Patterson grinned. "It's amazing how well you know me considering we've only just met."

"Come along, then." Marelli motioned for her to follow him. "I'll take you down there and you can pick one out. Just make sure to bring it back in one piece."

"I'll do my best." Patterson followed behind him.

Twenty minutes later, she was back in the auditorium with the wig in her hand.

As she hurried through the lobby and reentered the

casino, the band started playing the same song they were practicing when she entered. She could hear a guitar riff jangling behind the vocals, and wondered if it was Trent Steiger. The man who was either a cheating scumbag who had hurt her sister badly enough that she took off into the night never to be seen again, or a depraved killer who had taken the lives of both her sister and Laura Beth Layton. She just wasn't sure which.

SIXTY-ONE

PATTERSON PUSHED the wig under her jacket to hide it from prying eyes and strode across the casino floor toward the elevators.

She had learned a lot from Trent Steiger, assuming that what he said was true, and he wasn't the person responsible for her disappearance. Under other circumstances, she would have put the odds of that at about fifty-fifty, given his association with Laura Beth Layton. Yet he appeared genuinely surprised to hear that Julie had been missing for sixteen years, and it didn't look like an act. There were none of the usual tells she would expect to see if he was faking. He didn't speak faster or louder. His voice didn't rise in pitch or crack. He didn't cough or clear his throat repetitively to give himself time to think. He didn't close his eyes or look away when he answered her questions. His responses were not exaggerated. Either Trent Steiger was a great liar, or he really didn't know what had happened to Julie after they last saw each other that night in Amy's Roadhouse.

She had a new lead, too. Laura Beth Layton might be long

dead, but in all likelihood, the third roommate, Shannon, was not. If anyone knew where Julie had gone after her fight with Trent Steiger, it would be Shannon. But there was a problem. Steiger could not remember the name or address of the hostel they had stayed in back then. Likewise, he didn't know Shannon's last name. Without those things, she would be impossible to track down, assuming she was even still in the vicinity of Santa Fe.

But there was one person who might give her an answer. Trent Steiger's cousin, Treyton Cobb.

She glanced at her watch. It was 6:05 PM in Las Vegas and an hour ahead of that time in Santa Fe. Definitely not too late to make a call.

Patterson closed the gap to the elevators and waited among a throng of other hotel guests chatting excitedly among themselves and drinking frozen cocktails in plastic cups. When the elevator came, she pushed inside, ignoring a faint whiff of marijuana that battled for dominance with the alcohol breath of those around her.

She stepped out gratefully onto the seventh floor and hurried to her room. She dropped the wig on the bed, ready for when she would need it later, and went to the desk. Sitting down, she placed a call to Trent Steiger's cousin.

Treyton Cobb answered almost immediately.

"Special Agent Blake. Don't take this the wrong way, but I hoped not to hear from you again. Kind of makes a guy nervous when the FBI keeps calling."

"There's nothing to worry about, Mr. Cobb. I just spoke to Trent Steiger, and he gave me a lot of the information I needed, however he was vague on some of the details. I was hoping you could fill in the blanks."

"I can try. What is it that you want to know?"

"You used to pick him up on your way to work so you could ride together, correct?"

"Sure. I remember that. All three of us would pile into my car. Him, me, and Stacy."

"Julie," Patterson corrected him. "Her name was Julie."

"Sorry. She'll always be Stacy in my head."

"Don't worry about it," Patterson said, wondering why the name bothered her so much, especially when she had more important things to concern herself with. "Do you remember where you picked them up?"

"Sure. It was some hostel where backpackers and travelers used to stay."

"And the name of the hostel?" Patterson held her breath.

"Good question. It's been so long since I thought about that place." A long silence. Then Cobb spoke again. "I think it had something to do with sleeping or taking a break." There was another silence before Cobb gave a triumphant snort. "Rest-A-While. That was it. The Rest-A-While Hostel and Campground."

"You're sure about that?" Patterson asked.

"Sure as I can be."

"You know the road it was on? The address?"

"I don't know the address, but I can tell you where it was located because I drove there so much. Upper Canyon Road, near the corner of Cerro Gordo."

"Perfect," Patterson said. "I don't suppose you know if the hostel is still there?"

"Not a clue. But I do remember one thing. It was on the edge of town near the Santa Fe Canyon Preserve. There was a huge boulder at the entrance, and they painted a mural on it of an eagle soaring over a mountain peak. It was pretty cool. If it's still there, you can't miss the place."

"That's a great help." Patterson jotted all the information

down on a sheet of hotel stationery. "Just one more question. Did you ever meet a girl named Shannon at the hostel? She would have been about the same age as Julie. They were roommates."

"Can't say that I did. I never knew anyone at the hostel except Trent and Stac . . . sorry, Julie. Didn't really hang out there."

"I see." Patterson thanked Cobb and ended the call. She still didn't know Shannon's last name, but if the hostel was still there, she had a place to start looking for her. At least, if they had records going back that far.

After reading through her notes to make sure she hadn't missed anything, Patterson folded the piece of hotel stationery and slipped it into her bag, inside the folder along with everything else she had gathered on Julie since starting her investigation. Then she phoned Bauer and told him she was on her way up to fill him in on what she had, and had not, found out from Trent Steiger. A minute later, she was in the corridor and heading toward the elevators.

SIXTY-TWO

ARRIVING at Bauer's room on the eighth floor, Patterson knocked. A voice drifted from inside, telling her to come in. The door was unlocked. She stepped inside, turned, and engaged the deadbolt out of habit.

"Not very security conscious, are you?" she said, finding Bauer sitting in a chair on the far side of the room near the window with a paperback book in his hand. "And you read, too. I never knew that about you."

"The door was unlocked because you phoned and said you were coming up," Bauer replied. And as for the book, there isn't exactly much to do here so I needed to pass the time. And yes, I read."

"Not much to do?" Patterson snorted with laughter. "You realize this is Vegas, right?"

"And I'm not much of a gambler. Don't make enough money to fritter it away in a casino."

"There's more to Vegas than just gambling."

"What, like buying a ticket for that over the hill pop band that your witness is playing with?"

"I'm not sure they'd like to be called a *pop band*," Patterson said, bemused. "And I wasn't just talking about that. You could go wander the strip. Take in the sights. Or how about Fremont Street? There's the desert right on our doorstep, and even a nature preserve."

"That's not why I'm here. I need to stick close to you. And anyway, I'm happy with my book. But I appreciate the concern." Bauer slipped a piece of folded paper into the book to mark his place, and closed it, then laid it down on the nightstand next to the bed. "How did it go with Trent Steiger?"

"About as well as I thought it would. He and his cousin pretty much tell the same story. He got into a fight with Julie, and she stormed off. She left the bar and that was the last time he saw her."

"What was the fight about?"

"She caught him out behind the roadhouse, cheating on her with a groupie."

"Ouch. No wonder she was mad. Did he say where she went next?"

"No. Apparently she went back to the hostel where they were staying. She was there long enough to tell her roommates what had happened, but by the time he got home that night after playing two more sets in the bar, she was gone. For good this time. He never saw her again. After asking around at the hostel and spending some time searching the area, he gave up and just assumed that she continued on with her trip alone."

"Caring guy," Bauer said with obvious disgust. "It didn't occur to him that something might have happened?"

"Apparently not." *Or if it did*, Patterson thought, *he didn't care enough to do anything about it.* Because even though Steiger claimed that he really liked Julie, it wasn't enough to stop him cheating on her with a stranger in the same place they were both working.

"So where does that leave you?" Bauer asked.

"I have a first name for the third girl who was rooming with Julie at the hostel. Shannon. If I can find her, it might shed light not only on where my sister went, but on who killed Laura Beth Layton."

"That's a long shot with nothing but a first name."

"I know. But it's all I have. As soon as we're finished here, I'll fly back to Santa Fe and see if I can track down the hostel. Maybe they can give me a surname, or at least a place to start looking."

"That's a long shot. Even if the hostel is still in business, they would need to have registration records going back sixteen years."

"I know that." Patterson didn't need to be told how dire the situation was. Everything now hinged on finding a girl with only a first name who could be anywhere in the country all this time later. It wasn't impossible, but the odds weren't good. "Right now, I'm worried about a more immediate problem."

"The man you believe Newport sent after you."

"Yes." Patterson was sure the senator was behind whoever broke into her van at the airport. Why else would someone be following her? "He must be close to making his move. Did you scope out the hotel for possible entry and escape points on each floor?"

"I did. I also phoned the local field office and brought them up to speed on what's going on. We are in their territory, after all."

"And?"

"They were nice enough to let us borrow a couple of agents as backup, just in case. They'll be undercover in the public areas of the hotel, standing by for when and if we need them. They'll also be keeping an eye out for any suspicious activity, although I doubt they'll see anything."

Patterson groaned. "I should probably call the hotel's security director. I promised to keep him informed if there was an issue that might compromise hotel security. He would probably view a pair of undercover FBI agents roaming around the casino as falling into that category. Especially if Newport's man decides to make a move on the premises."

"Which I think is likely since he followed you here and won't want to risk losing you again. He's been surveilling you for at least a couple of days already. By now, he will have thought through all the variables, and decided on a plan of action. If he's a professional hitman, which I suspect he is if Newport is behind this, he won't wait longer than necessary," Bauer said. "But I'm one step ahead of you. I asked the SAC of the Vegas field office to reach out to Jason Lund and informed him of an operation on his premises unrelated to his boss or the operations of the casino."

"I bet that will go down well, especially since Jonathan already strong-armed him into cooperating with my investigation."

"I'm sure he won't cause problems. Especially once it's pointed out to him that an unrestrained shooter on the premises gunning for a member of federal law enforcement staying at his hotel will do more damage if left unchecked than allowing us to deal with the situation quietly and without alarming the other guests."

"We'd better hope we can pull that off. If not, I'll end up with a high-ranking senator *and* a Vegas mob boss out for my blood."

"We'll handle it," Bauer said with confidence. "In the

meantime, I suggest you go and get some rest. We have a long night ahead of us."

Patterson glanced at her watch. It was almost nine in the evening. The lights of the Strip pulsed like a man-made aurora borealis in the distance outside Bauer's hotel room window. "You know what to do?"

"I know what to do." Bauer made a shooing motion. "Now go."

SIXTY-THREE

AT TWO IN THE MORNING, Corbin Pope made his way through the hotel corridors toward the room previously occupied by Mr. and Mrs. McElroy until their incredibly fortunate upgrade to a suite earlier that day. A room now registered to the fictional Pat and Jack Carlton. He wore a bright Hawaiian shirt, and tan slacks.

Downstairs, on the ground floor, diehard gamblers still sat at the blackjack tables, roulette wheels, and slots. But the corridors of the seventh floor were empty save for Pope.

He reached the room and let himself in using the ghost key he had created earlier, then slipped on his gloves to make sure he left no fingerprints anywhere that could incriminate him later.

He carried a backpack slung over one shoulder, which he dropped on the bed. Crossing to the window, Pope looked out, taking in the Vegas skyline one last time. Soon, once he had dealt with Patterson Blake, he would speed through the night back toward Dallas. His bags were already packed. All he needed to do was collect them from his room two floors above and head for the parking lot. After that, he was home and free.

Turning away from the window, Pope went to the bed and opened the backpack. A minute later, the bright and gaudy Hawaiian shirt and slacks he wore to blend in with the other rubes in the casino were gone, replaced by black pants, shirt, and jacket. A pair of black sneakers and a baseball cap pulled low over his forehead completed the ensemble. Under the jacket—and the only reason he wore it—was a shoulder holster containing a Walther P22 semi-automatic pistol that he hoped he wouldn't need.

Now dressed to kill—literally—Pope went to the communicating door leading to the FBI agent's room, which was really a pair of doors that swung in opposite directions and could be locked from either side. Thanks to his excursion earlier when Patterson Blake was not in her room, the deadbolt on her side should not be engaged.

He opened his connecting door, then pressed an ear against the corresponding door that opened into the adjoining room and listened.

Silence.

Dropping to his knees, Pope pressed his face close to the minuscule gap between the door and the carpet. The room on the other side looked dark.

But he wasn't taking any chances. Climbing to his feet, Pope went to the bag on the bed one more time and took out what looked like a long phone charger cable. Except that instead of connecting to a wall plug, there was an endoscopic inspection camera at one end. He plugged the other end into his cell phone and opened the camera app, then returned to the door and dropped to his knees again. Slowly and carefully, he pushed the slim endoscopic camera under the door. The view on the other side appeared on the phone app as a gray-toned image, which meant the lights in the room were off. He was looking at the infrared spectrum.

Twisting the camera first in one direction, then in the other, Pope satisfied himself that no one was awake in the room. He could make out part of the bed from his vantage point, and a rising lump under the covers that corresponded to a sleeping person.

Withdrawing the camera, he coiled it back up, disconnected it, and returned it to the backpack. Now he withdrew the plastic syringe case containing the syringe he had prepared earlier. He opened it and withdrew the syringe, squirting just enough of the liquid to ensure that it was operational.

His hand rose to the gun under his jacket, fingers brushing the cool, smooth metal briefly. Another insurance against the unknown.

Then, leaving his phone on the bed and set to silent mode, he approached the connecting door and gripped the handle with a gloved hand. Turning it, he swung the door open just wide enough to pass through.

Just as he expected, Patterson Blake's room was swathed in darkness. Heavy curtains blocked any light that might seep in from the bright city beyond.

He stepped inside, his cushioned sneakers making no sound on the carpeted floor.

The FBI agent was in bed with the covers pulled up to her shoulders. She was facing away from him and hadn't stirred at his entrance.

A shiver of adrenaline rushed through him. This was the moment Pope savored the most. Those few brief seconds right before the kill, when he knew everything would come together perfectly and nothing could stop him. He imagined himself as a symphony conductor, bringing his orchestra to a thundering crescendo, or a renaissance painter laying down the last few confident brushstrokes on what he knew would be a masterpiece for the ages. Pope was an artist as much as any painter, actor, or musician. And he was about to complete another tour de force of supreme artistry and add Patterson Blake to the private gallery of death that lived within his head.

Crossing to the bed, he stood over the slumbering woman, syringe in hand. Reaching down, he took hold of the sheets and pulled them back, just enough to expose her neck, ready for the injection and all that would come after.

Then he stopped.

Something was wrong. Very wrong. He pulled the covers back with a quick yanking motion and swore under his breath, even as he took a step back. The hand carrying the syringe fell to his side. A swell of panic rose in him like an incoming tide. He had to get out of there, and quickly.

But before he could take a single step back toward the adjoining room, the sound of a door opening reached his ears. Moments later, a dark shape blocked his path, and he found himself staring down the barrel of a gun.

SIXTY-FOUR

THREE WEEKS BEFORE

HOW CARL HAD FOUND *her was anyone's guess, but Angel couldn't allow him to take her back to that farmhouse. Couldn't let him near Cherub ever again. She took a panicked step backwards, stumbling as her foot slipped off the curb, and almost fell. A frantic scream welled in her throat. She raised her arms instinctively to defend against the attack she knew was coming.*

"Whoa, there. Sorry." The man stopped and raised a calming hand. "Didn't mean to scare you."

The voice was not Carl's. And now that she could see him clearly under the light from a streetlamp, she realized the face wasn't, either. There was a passing resemblance, for sure, but the eyes were wrong, and his jawline was sharper. More defined.

Angel stared at the man, mouth agape. She tried to speak, but all that came out was a feeble croak.

"Are you okay, miss?" The man took a step toward her, concern creasing his brow.

"I . . . I'm fine," Angel lied. She couldn't stop shaking. The

277

terror refused to yield. It's not him, not Carl, she repeated silently to herself, over and over. But those first few moments, when it had been Carl looming out of the darkness played like a looping horror movie inside her head.

"You don't look fine."

"Please, just leave me alone," Angel stammered. *Then she found her legs and fled back to the bus, sprinted down the aisle, and dropped back into the seat next to her sleeping daughter. Ignoring the startled look from the woman across the aisle, Angel buried her face in her hands and tried to breathe. She stayed that way for several minutes, ignoring the other passengers as they retook their seats.*

Soon, she heard the swoosh of the door closing at the front of the bus, felt a tremble run through the vehicle as the driver pressed his foot on the accelerator and pulled away from the curb.

"Mommy?" *Cherub was awake.*

Angel put her hands down, lifted her head. "Yes, honey?"

"Were you crying?"

"No." *Angel shook her head.* "Just resting."

"You look sad." *Cherub put her hand out, rested it on Angel's arm.* "Do you miss home?"

Angel shook her head a second time. That farmhouse was the last place she would ever miss. If she never saw it again, it would be too soon.

An image of Ma, lying on the kitchen floor, flitted through her mind. Was the old woman still there where she dropped, slowly rotting from the inside out, or had Carl found her? That thought made Angel smile in a brief moment of schadenfreude. Carl walking in and finding her. Discovering the cruel bitch was dead and his family were missing all at the same time. It would send him into a fury, she was sure. He would want to kill Angel, choke the life out of her. He'd come close a few times before, but always checked himself before going too far. Once, he'd done it in front of their daughter as she looked on with tears streaming down her face. He was a monster. But it didn't matter. He was never going to find them. Not in a million years. She would make sure of that.

The incident outside the bus had scared her. For a second, she had thought that Carl must have supernatural powers. Some paranormal ability to appear out of nowhere ready to drag her and Cherub back to hell. But he didn't. He was just a pathetic loner with anger issues and a cruel streak five miles deep. He was also just a bulk-standard, everyday normal human being. Well, hardly normal, but certainly not possessed of any unearthly powers or divine knowledge. He would have no idea where she and Cherub had gone and no way to find them.

Angel finally relaxed. She pulled her daughter close and put an arm around her. Cherub sighed softly and rested against her mother. Angel looked down at her, watched as her daughter drifted back to sleep, then she closed her eyes and let thoughts of their new life in San Diego, a life free of terror, fill her head.

SIXTY-FIVE

PATTERSON STOOD in the darkness and waited, her gun aimed at the bathroom door, ready to defend herself if anyone came through it.

From somewhere in the room beyond, she heard a barely perceptible stir of air as a door was quietly opened.

She held her breath. Timing was everything. Step out too early, and she would come face-to-face with the man sent to kill her before she had the upper hand. Step out too late, and he might discover her ruse and flee. She counted off the seconds in her head, the breath still captive in her lungs, as she listened for any sound that might provide a clue to the whereabouts of the intruder in the room beyond. At the same time, she played through a movie in her head, imagining him crossing the room and approaching the bed.

When she received no auditory confirmation of the intruder's location—the man sent to kill her was obviously a consummate professional able to move with the silence of a cat stalking his prey—she moved toward the door, taking only a second to withdraw the phone from her pocket and hit send on a pre-prepared text to Marcus Bauer that simply read 'it's happening'.

At the door, she hesitated for the briefest of moments and gathered her wits. Then she pulled the door open, stepped out, and turned in a quick and fluid movement.

The intruder was standing over the bed, covers drawn back to reveal three pillows arranged in the vague shape of a person. The wig she had borrowed from the hotel theater's costume department earlier in the day set askew on the top pillow. It wasn't a great representation of her actual hair, but good enough to fool a person wandering around in the dark who wasn't expecting anything else. People saw what they wanted to see, and that included hired killers.

"Don't move," she barked, even as the intruder turned to face her with a look of alarm. "Drop the syringe right now and place your hands on top of your head."

The intruder hesitated, then gave a slight nod and started to raise his hands.

The room was still dark.

Patterson reached for a light switch on the wall near the bathroom door, never taking her eyes off the man who had come to kill her. But as her fingers fumbled for the switch, the figure in front of her stopped raising his hands, and instead lunged sideways across the bed in a lightning-fast movement, while reaching under his jacket at the same time.

Patterson had been prepared for the intruder to lunge at her in a frantic bid to escape, but not to go in the opposite direction. Her finger tensed on the trigger as she swung the gun to the right in an attempt to reacquire her target.

But the intruder, blessed with the element of surprise, had already withdrawn his weapon and sent a wildly aimed bullet hurtling in her direction even as he tumbled over the bed and dropped down out of sight on the other side.

Patterson leaped backwards behind the bathroom wall even as the bullet sailed past her and impacted the opposite wall near the adjoining door. Her ears should have been ringing, but they weren't. The intruder obviously had a suppressor screwed to the barrel of his gun, making it unlikely that anyone outside the room had heard the shot.

But they didn't need to. Bauer had been waiting out of sight in the vending area further along the corridor and would surely be racing toward her even now. She wondered why he was taking so long, then realized that the entire encounter had occurred over a span of no more than ten seconds. She realized something else, too. She was vulnerable in the small corridor next to the bathroom. All the intruder had to do was fire toward the wall, which was surely made of flimsy materials since it was designed to enclose a bathroom and not provide cover in a gunfight.

Her own bead on the intruder was worse. He was behind the king-sized bed, forcing her to fire through the mattress at an oblique angle, which would significantly slow down the bullet and hamper her ability to score a hit.

As if to confirm her fear, a volley of three rapid shots smacked into the wall next to her in quick succession, puncturing the drywall and sending it flying in all directions. One bullet exited the wall inches from her head, sending Patterson scrabbling further back into the bathroom doorway where she hoped the wooden surround would offer at least a little more protection.

The silence after the shots felt like forever, the seconds ticking away at a crawl. Patterson steeled herself to step back out into the corridor. Finally return fire, even if all it did was pin the intruder down long enough for Bauer to arrive.

But before she could move, she sensed a shift in the shadows on the wall beyond the bathroom. Someone was moving. Making for the door. The intruder was up and trying to escape before she could gather her wits. She took a step further back into the bathroom, unwilling to provide an easy target for her assailant. She raised her gun from the low ready position, holding it at arms-length with both hands. The intruder would have to pass by the bathroom in order to escape. When he did, she would take her shot.

Except that the man in the bedroom must have anticipated just such a scenario. Instead of appearing in the doorway, another tight cluster of shots punched through the wall, causing her to twist quickly sideways and drop to her knees out of the line of fire. In the process, she lost her aim.

In the next instant, a figure filled the bathroom doorway, gun pointed right at her. She would never be able to bring her own gun back up and take the shot before the intruder put a bullet through her skull.

Time came to a halt.

Patterson closed her eyes against what she knew was about to come. She could almost sense the shooter's finger flexing on the trigger of his pistol. A thought of Julie filled her head, her older sister smiling and saying it was okay. At least they would finally be together.

Then, just as she had made peace with dying, the sound of a door opening brought her back to reality.

It was Bauer. She knew as much by the startled exclamation he uttered upon seeing the intruder standing mere feet away with gun drawn, aiming into the bathroom.

The gunman was equally startled.

He wavered, turning toward the hotel room door for a split second. That was all Patterson needed. She brought the gun up and fired.

The bullet hit her adversary in the chest, sending him staggering backward. She jumped up and pressed her advantage, rushing to the bathroom door ready to take a second shot.

But there was no need.

The gunman was on the floor with Bauer, weapon drawn, standing over him.

There was no blood, which surprised Patterson until she saw the hole in the man's black shirt and another equally black material below. A ballistic vest. The man groaned and clutched his chest. The vest might have stopped her bullet, but almost certainly cracked his ribs. Not that she had any sympathy.

The intruder's gun lay a few feet away. Patterson stepped around him and kicked it further out of reach, then turned toward Bauer just as two more figures entered the room, guns drawn. The FBI agents provided by the Las Vegas field office. Bauer must have notified them of the situation.

As they approached the gunman and dragged him to his feet, Patterson crossed to the bed and sat down.

Bauer holstered his gun and observed the pillows and wig that had fooled the man sent by Senator Newport to kill her. "I guess your crazy plan worked."

"Almost didn't." Patterson had come within a hair's breadth of losing her life, and she knew it. Strangely, a small part of her was sad. When that gun was pointed at her head, when she knew the last seconds of her life were ticking away, she had felt closer to Julie than at any other time in the last sixteen years. All it needed was one squeeze of the gunman's trigger, and her long search would have been at an end. She would have finally been reunited with her sister.

"You okay there, partner?" Bauer asked, sitting on the bed next to her.

"I will be," Patterson replied, shaking off the maudlin thoughts. She looked around at the destruction. The shattered drywall and bullet holes. "But I think I'll need another room for the rest of the night."

"You won't be getting your security deposit back," Bauer said. "That's for sure."

"Yeah." Patterson laid back and stared up at the ceiling. "Thanks for saving my life, Marcus . . . Again."

Bauer laid down next to her. "You're welcome. Just don't make it a habit."

SIXTY-SIX

IT WAS THE NEXT MORNING. There was nothing left to do in Las Vegas. Patterson booked an afternoon flight back to Santa Fe, with a layover in Phoenix.

She suspected that Jason Lund, head of security at the Prospector's Paradise, was pleased to see her go. He had shown up at the damaged hotel room minutes after the fun was over, along with two of the hotel's security guards. He was less than pleased to see the state of the room and discover that a hired killer had been stalking her on the premises. At first, she thought he was going to throw her out onto the street along with Bauer and anyone else involved in the incident, but he had relented once it was pointed out that his cooperation with the FBI would not go unnoticed. She changed rooms—this time to one of the few without an adjoining door—and slept for the next six hours.

The man Senator Newport had sent to kill her received less salubrious accommodations. He was cooling his heels in a downtown police cell where he would stay until her superiors at the FBI figured out what to do with him. At the very least, the man was in for days if not weeks of grueling interrogation as they tried to get to the bottom of his identity and that of the people he worked for. Not that she expected him to give them much beyond what they had already found in his personal possessions. Several fake identities, an NSA grade laptop, and a burner phone containing phone numbers that she was sure would turn out to be more burner phones. No one in their right mind would call a man like that from a phone that could be traced back to them.

As for Bauer, he had decided to take some well-earned vacation time and stay in Vegas for a few days more, despite his earlier misgivings about Sin City. But he wouldn't be alone. Phoebe had used up the last of her own vacation days and was flying out to be with him. Patterson was glad she wouldn't still be there when Bauer's girlfriend arrived. Although in fairness, she had avoided getting Bauer shot, stabbed, or made an accessory to murder on this particular occasion. She hoped that the next time they crossed paths, Phoebe would remember that.

After spending the morning taking in the Strip and trying to stay out of trouble, Patterson headed for the airport. After taking her seat on the plane, she sent a text message to Bauer, reminding him that his per diem could be spent playing the slots, and added a winking smiley face just for good measure.

As the plane pushed back from the gate, she turned her phone off and put it into her pocket. Five hours later, as the sun was setting over the Sangre de Cristo Mountain Range, she drove back into Santa Fe and headed straight for the RV lot at Amy's Roadhouse.

She was eager to follow up on the information provided by Trent Steiger and his cousin, and almost drove straight out to the location of the hostel where Julie and Steiger had stayed sixteen years before. But she was exhausted, and it would be dark by the time she got there. Better to wait until the next morning.

Instead, she walked across to the roadhouse and sat at the bar with a beer and a bacon cheeseburger, neither of which lasted long. Returning to the van, she flopped down on the bed, closed her eyes, and fell into a troubled sleep full of shadowy hitmen chasing her through dark and narrow streets, while somewhere far away, her sister screamed for mercy.

SIXTY-SEVEN

AT NINE O'CLOCK THE next morning, Patterson drove to the intersection of Upper Canyon Road and Cerro Gordo where she hoped the Rest-A-While Hostel and Campground would still be in business. But upon arriving, she found no sign of the hostel. What she did find was the boulder Trayton Cobb had told her about. The one with the mural of the eagle soaring over a mountain top.

It had faded from years of harsh sun beating down upon it, and the paint had flaked away in several places to reveal the bare stone beneath, but there was no mistaking that she was in the right place.

Next to the boulder was an entrance with a pair of open gates flanked by two stone pillars. A metal sign arching between them read: Picacho Peak Summer Camp. It didn't take much to deduce that this was the previous home of the hostel and campground where her sister and Trent Steiger had stayed all those years ago.

Sitting there in the van, looking up at that sign, she was overcome by a deep sense of loss. This was the only lead she had left. With the hostel gone and nothing but a first name with which to locate the third roommate, her search for Julie had effectively reached a dead end. Her only hope now was that someone currently working at the summer camp remembered the previous owners and could tell her where they were now.

It was a long shot.

Even more of a longshot, assuming she could even track the hostel's owners down, was that they still had the reservation records going back to the early two-thousands.

It was such a remote possibility that Patterson almost turned around and drove back in the other direction, but she was there, so she might as well ask, if only to eliminate what little hope remained.

She pulled through the gates and started up a long and winding dirt driveway that ended in a roughly marked out parking lot surrounded by low hills and scrubland dotted with cottonwood trees and sagebrush. Beyond the parking lot was a timber two-story building that she assumed had once housed the hostel. Beyond this, she could see small cabins dotted throughout the landscape, and a fire pit with horizontal logs laid around it for seating.

The parking lot was almost empty, and Patterson pulled close to the building. When she approached the front doors, she found them locked. A sign affixed to the wall next to the doors gave parents bringing their children to camp a number to call if no one was available to check them in. With no other recourse, Patterson phoned the number.

The woman who picked up appeared mildly surprised that anyone was calling, and even more surprised when Patterson identified herself as an FBI agent, but told her she would be right down.

Patterson hung up and waited.

A couple of minutes later, a woman in her late fifties with graying hair and a tanned, rugged face appeared on the other side of the door. She unlocked it and stepped aside for Patterson to enter.

"Judy Devlin," the woman said after Patterson introduced herself. "How can I help you, Special Agent Blake?"

"I'm following up on a lead related to a sixteen-year-old cold case," Patterson said, stepping inside and looking around. She was in a large lobby with a tiled floor and cathedral ceiling. A semicircular check-in desk occupied one wall. On the opposite wall were large panels showing scenes from the summer camp. Happy children sitting around a campfire at night holding mugs of what looked like cocoa. Teenagers canoeing on a large lake. More kids playing soccer. It looked like an institutionalized version of the fishing trips her father had taken the teenaged Patterson and Julie on back before everything fell apart. "I was looking for the Rest-A-While Hostel but found this summer camp instead."

"The hostel closed ten years ago," Judy said. "There were too many problems with drugs and alcohol. Unsavory types that couldn't afford a hotel. That's when we turned it into the summer camp."

"Oh." Ten years. Patterson's heart fell. That felt like too long for anyone to have any information from back then or tell her where the prior owners had gone. But she'd come this far. "I don't suppose you have information on the owners of the hostel. It's important that I speak to them."

"Well now, that would be me and my husband. I can't imagine we can be of any help, but we'll do our best. What is it you want to know?"

Patterson could hardly believe her luck. The hostel might have closed long ago, but instead of selling, the owners had turned it into a summer camp for teens. Still, she didn't want to get her hopes up. "My sister Julie and her boyfriend stayed here sixteen years ago. She shared a room with two other girls. Julie vanished around the time she was here, and one of those two girls was murdered not long after. I'm trying to track down the third occupant of that room. She might have pertinent information that can help find my sister and possibly solve a homicide."

"Wow. How horrible." Judy looked shocked. She clasped her hands together. "But if you're hoping I can tell you about someone who stayed here over a decade and a half ago, you're going to be disappointed. Thousands of young men and women came and went when this place was a hostel. Most of them only stayed a few days, maybe a week. I can't remember the names of half the kids staying at the summer camp right now, let alone a random girl from so long ago."

"You don't have any records from back then?" Patterson said, her previous hope deflating. "Like registration cards or a guest book?"

"I'm sorry." Judy shook her head. "Anything we had from back then is long gone. It doesn't look like I can be of any help."

"How about I tell you the names of the three girls, and maybe that will jog your memory?" Patterson wasn't willing to give up yet. She had come so far and now it looked like her journey was at an end, but she might as well follow the line of questioning to its logical conclusion.

Judy shrugged. "Sure. But I don't think it will do any good."

Patterson reeled off the three names, and also Stacy's name, which Julie was using to work at the bar since she wasn't yet twenty-one. She studied Judy's face, looking for any hint of recognition, but when she finished, all she got was a blank expression and another apology.

"I understand." Patterson tried to keep the disappointment from her reply. She thanked the woman for her time and turned to leave, but then another voice spoke up.

"I remember them. Stacy, Laura, and Shannon."

Patterson turned to see a woman in her early thirties standing in a doorway behind Judy. She bore a striking resemblance to the older woman, except that her features were more refined and her hair jet black.

"You knew my sister?" Patterson's hopes surged anew.

"Yes." The woman nodded. "I knew both of them. We were friends. I also remember what happened the night Stacy left."

SIXTY-EIGHT

"TELL me how you know my sister and Laura Beth Layton," Patterson asked, focusing her attention on the younger of the two women sitting across the desk from her. All three were now in Judy's office. The younger woman, it turned out, was Judy's daughter, Heather, who would have been sixteen years old back when Julie stayed at the hostel. She had lived on the premises all her life and now worked under her mother as assistant camp director.

"I knew a lot of the girls that came through back then," Heather said. "I spent most of my free time here at the camp, although it was still the hostel at that point, of course. I didn't have a lot of friends at school, but I was quite happy to socialize with all the interesting people that stayed here. I remember a lot of them, but I especially remember Stacy and Laura because they both left so suddenly and never came back."

"Stacy wasn't my sister's real name," Patterson told her. "It was Julie."

"I know. She told me all about her friend's license, and

how she was using it because she was underage and couldn't legally work in Amy's Roadhouse under her own name. She even told me how she got ahold of it. Getting robbed, and her friend leaving her alone. Seems like a pretty shitty thing to do, if you ask me."

"And the third girl?" Patterson asked. "Shannon?"

Heather nodded. "I didn't know Shannon very well. She was kind of standoffish. She spent a lot of time on her own. Wasn't that friendly with the rest of us. Laura and Julie were nice, though."

"You said you remember them so well because they both left suddenly. Can you tell me about that?"

"Sure." Heather nodded. "Julie was the first to leave. She only stayed for about ten days, even though she and her boyfriend were supposed to be here for a month. I guess she caught him cheating. She came back in a hell of a state one Saturday night, crying and angry. I remember that the three of us sat in her room. Me, Laura, and Julie, drinking a bottle of cheap vodka that Laura had smuggled in, and commiserating with her."

Judy gave her daughter a sharp look. "You were drinking? You were only sixteen and still in school. No wonder you liked hanging out with the guests."

"For heaven's sake. Lighten up," Heather snapped. "It was a long time ago and I'm a grown woman. What are you going to do, send me to my room and ground me retrospectively?"

"You don't need to talk to me like that. I was just—"

"I know what you were doing. This isn't the time." Heather focused her attention back on Patterson. "Like I was saying, we were in the room drinking and talking about how crappy men are. Julie was getting pretty drunk. After a while, she asked if she could use a phone. Said she wanted to make a call. It was pretty late at night and there was no one around, so I snuck her into the office to use the landline in there."

Judy gave her daughter another withering look, which Heather ignored.

"Do you know who she was calling?" Patterson asked.

"No. She never said."

"You didn't hear the call?"

Heather shook her head. "I showed her the phone and left. Went back to the room so she could have some privacy. I assumed she was going to call her family, or maybe someone she met at the bar to come get her. She was pretty miserable and said she didn't want to be here anymore. Couldn't stand to see her boyfriend when he came home from the bar. He was a musician."

"I know that already," Patterson said. "He was playing gigs at Amy's Roadhouse."

"That's right. He was pretty good, too. Played a few songs here at the hostel when we were all hanging out the first week before Julie left. I thought he was kind of cute. I guess he was really just a jerk."

"What happened after the phone call?"

"She came back to the room and had some more vodka. Not long after that, a pickup truck showed up with some guy behind the wheel. She said he was a friend. She went out to talk to him, then she climbed in, and they took off before we knew what was going on."

"You didn't try to stop her?" Patterson asked.

"I was sixteen, and I'd known her for less than two weeks. What was I going to do?"

"Did you recognize the man driving the truck?"

Again, Heather shook her head. "No. I'd never seen him before. Although I only got a quick glimpse of his face when he climbed out to greet her."

"And?"

"He was older. Probably mid-twenties. A white guy with short cropped dark hair and a goatee. The truck was either blue or black, but it was dark and hard to tell. That's all I can remember."

"Did she come back?" Patterson had a feeling she knew the answer but had to ask.

"No. That's the last time I saw her. We figured she would come back, because she left her bag behind with her clothes and everything in it."

"You didn't think that was odd?"

"Maybe. But we figured the guy must have been a friend or something and she was staying with him to avoid her boyfriend. After a few days, I began to wonder if she'd just carried on with her trip alone or gone back home to wherever she lived. She really seemed like she didn't want to stick around here. She was so humiliated."

"Did you tell anyone what happened?"

"No." Heather looked ashamed. "I was afraid of getting into trouble. We both were, because we were drinking, which was a no-no at the hostel. Plus, I would have been in so much trouble if my parents found out."

Judy shot her another disapproving look.

"What happened to the bag?" Patterson asked. "Her belongings?"

"I hid them in my room and kept them for a couple of months. By then, her boyfriend had moved on and she hadn't returned, so Laura and I decided to split the stuff she left behind. There were some good clothes in there."

"Laura Beth Layton was still here that long after my sister left?"

"Yes. She stayed for about three months in all. It was longer than most of our guests stuck around."

"How did she pay to stay here that long?" Patterson asked, realizing that Laura Beth Layton's extended stay at the hostel probably ruled out Trent Steiger as a suspect in her murder. She was still there for at least a month after he went on his way. But it didn't preclude the man in the truck who picked up Julie. If he was a local, he might have killed her sister, then laid low for a while before committing his next murder.

"Mom let her work for a free bed."

"Oh, I think I remember her now. Pretty girl, with long brown hair?" Judy said. "I gave her odd jobs around the hostel. I sometimes did that for some of our residents when it was obvious that they needed a place to stay and didn't have the money to pay for it."

"That was very nice of you," Patterson said before turning her attention back to Heather. "Do you remember the clothes of my sister's that she took?"

Heather thought for a moment. "Not really. I remember there was a pretty nice pair of Levi's and some T-shirts. I let her take most of the stuff because she looked like she needed it. She didn't have much of her own, except a high school sweatshirt she said her boyfriend had given her and a few other pieces of ratty clothing. I never asked, but I kind of figured that she'd been sleeping rough before coming to us."

"I see." That explained the driver's license. It had been in the pocket of Stacy's Levi's when Julie found it, and she probably put it back there after using it to get the job at Amy's Roadhouse. No doubt she intended to return the jeans and license to her friend when she got back to Chicago, which never happened.

"When you were talking to my mother, you told her a girl was murdered." There was a tinge of apprehension in

Heather's voice. "Since you said Julie is missing, I assume you're talking about Laura Beth Layton?"

"That's right," Patterson replied. "Her body was found in a ditch down the road from Amy's Roadhouse the spring after Trent and Julie worked there. She was a Jane Doe until just a few days ago. The cops couldn't identify her."

"But now they have."

"Yes." Patterson nodded. "We matched an item of clothing found with the body to a missing teenager from Oregon. She left her home after a fight with her parents. She'd run away a few times before, but this time she never came back."

"And she ended up here, in Santa Fe," Heather said. "And someone murdered her."

"That's what we believe. The identification isn't a hundred percent conclusive yet. We're waiting on DNA results, but we're almost certain it's her."

"Was she . . ." Heather's question trailed off.

"We can't tell if she was raped, if that's what you're asking," Patterson replied. "I would like to know what you remember about the time between my sister leaving the hostel and Laura Beth Layton's departure."

"Not much. We hung out sometimes, but by then she started seeing this guy. He was a couple of years older than her. A real loser. Lived in a trailer outside of town."

"He was a local?"

"Yes. He worked for a construction company that was putting up a second building, so we had more rooms to rent. I don't exactly know how they met, but she started seeing him more and more. Eventually, she told us she was moving out."

"To live with this guy?" Patterson asked.

"That's the impression I got, although she never told me in so many words. I didn't like him. Thought he was creepy."

"How often did you see her after she moved out?"

"Only once. She came back a couple of days later and we hung out for a few hours. After that, I never saw her again, even though she hadn't mentioned leaving town or anything."

Patterson had a bad feeling. Was this the same man who had picked up her sister the night she discovered Trent Steiger cheating on her? "Did this construction worker drive a pickup truck?"

"I don't remember."

"That's okay." There was one more question Patterson had to ask, and she prayed that Heather's response would be different. "Do you remember anything about him, like maybe his name?"

"I know his name," Heather said. "He must've lost the construction job, because about eighteen months later, he showed up as a janitor at my school. I guess he recognized me as Laura's friend from when she was staying here, because he made a point of talking to me. He came up to me several more times over the next few months. At first it was just innocent, but then he started hitting on me. You know, flirting and stuff. About a week before graduation, he invited me to a party at the trailer park where he lived. I said no, of course. I knew what he wanted."

"You never asked him about Laura Beth Layton?"

"I did. He said she hung around at his place for a couple of months, then one morning he got up and she was gone. Said she left a note saying it was time to move on."

"You never told me any of this," Judy said, staring at her daughter.

"Why would I? Guys used to hit on me all the time. He was just one more creep."

Judy's face had turned to stone. "Laura went to live with that man, and it was the last anyone heard of her. Now you say he claimed that she just up and left, moved on somewhere else? That doesn't make sense. Sounds more like he killed her to me."

"It does sound like that . . . now," Heather was ashen. "Guess I had a lucky escape."

Patterson was thinking the same thing. "What was this guy's name?"

"Brody Quaid."

"You know if he still lives in town?"

"I have no idea." Heather looked at Patterson, her eyes heavy with concern. "You don't really think he killed her, do you?"

"That's what I intend to find out," Patterson replied. *And if he had anything to do with my sister's disappearance*, she thought. Because right now, Brody Quaid was all she had left in her hunt for Julie.

SIXTY-NINE

BRODY QUAID LIVED in the same double-wide trailer that he'd occupied years before when Laura Beth Layton had gotten herself mixed up with him. It sat a couple of miles out of town in a dusty trailer park full of decrepit-looking housing that a person could be forgiven for thinking was abandoned if it wasn't for the obvious signs of habitation thereabouts. Like the kids' bicycles laying sideways where they fell next to trailers with cracked open doors, older model cars with sun-bleached paint sitting along the sides of what passed as a road, and laundry hanging from makeshift lines strung between two trees.

Patterson sat in the passenger seat of Detective Anderson's unmarked car and studied her surroundings with a mixture of repulsion and sadness. They were just miles away from million-dollar homes, and yet this miserable plot of land surely housed some of the county's poorest residents.

The trailer they were looking for sat near the back of the park overlooking a vast swath of empty scrubland that rose toward a low hill dotted with pinyon trees.

When they pulled up out front, Patterson thought the trailer might be unoccupied, because she saw no vehicles parked out front. But as they climbed out and approached the door, a curtain twitched and for a brief moment, she caught sight of a face peering out. Before they could even knock, the door opened just wide enough for the man inside to get a look at them.

"What do you want?" he asked, eyes narrowed with suspicion. "Who are you?"

"This here is Special Agent Patterson Blake from the FBI," Detective Anderson said before introducing himself. "Are you Brody Quaid?"

"What of it?"

"I'll take that as a yes," Anderson said. We'd like to have a little chat about a cold case we're investigating. Would you mind if we come in?"

Quaid observed them for a moment, then opened the door wider and jerked his head to the side to indicate they should enter.

They climbed the steps and entered.

The air inside the cabin was laced with a faint aroma of sweat mixed with the musty odor of old furniture. The trailer probably dated to the 1970s and the decor inside looked like it hadn't changed much since. A table next to the small kitchenette was littered with beer cans. More cans sat next to a threadbare orange sofa with a large hole in one cushion that exposed the foam cushioning beneath. An ashtray sitting on a side table next to the sofa held the last remnants of what looked like a joint.

"You want to tell me why you're standing in my house?" Quaid said without bothering to hide his contempt. "What's all this talk about a cold case?"

Patterson reached into her pocket and took out a photo of

Laura Beth Layton. She held it up in front of Quaid's face. "You recognize this young woman?"

A slight smile lifted one side of Quaid's mouth to expose yellow teeth. "She's pretty hot. Got cute eyes. But I can't say I've seen her before."

"You're sure about that?"

"Sure as I can be. If that's all you wanted to ask me, it looks like you've had a wasted trip out here."

"Think hard, Mr. Quaid," Anderson said. "Because we have an eyewitness who claims that you dated this young woman sixteen years ago."

Patterson stepped closer to the man, ignoring the stale body odor that wafted off him. "So I will ask you again, do you know this woman?"

Quaid squinted and leaned closer to the photograph. Then he nodded. "You know what, now that I look closer, I think I did date her back in the day. Only for a few weeks, though. Then she up and left on me. Haven't seen her since. Don't even remember her name anymore. Not like I can remember every girl who shared my bed."

"Right, because you're such a Casanova," Anderson said, looking around at the trailer's filthy interior without bothering to hide his disgust. "Her name was Laura Beth Layton, and she's dead."

"Well now, I'm so sorry to hear that. Maybe I'll pay my respects and send some flowers. You must tell me the date of the funeral."

"She's been dead for sixteen years. Her body was found in a ditch near Amy's Roadhouse on the other side of town." Anderson clenched and unclenched his fist. "She was murdered. We only identified the remains a few days ago."

"And so far as we know, you're the last person to have

seen her alive," Patterson said. "Want to tell us what happened between the two of you?"

"I didn't kill no one." The defiance in Quaid's voice had notched down a tone. Now he sounded positively nervous. "She stayed here a few days. We had a good time, if you know what I mean, then she left. I never saw her again. And you can't prove otherwise."

"You're right, we can't prove who killed her . . . At least, not just yet," Anderson replied. "But it won't take long to close in on her killer now that we have an identity for our Jane Doe and know where she was and who she was with in the days prior to her death. Forensics has come a long way in the last two decades, Mr. Quaid. Even now they're examining the body, checking to see if any foreign fibers are present. If any DNA transfer occurred. You know what DNA transfer is, Mr. Quaid?"

"Nope. Why would I?"

"Right." Anderson nodded slowly. "How about I educate you. DNA transfer is the exchange of DNA between objects or people. So, for example, if we found a stray hair on clothing the victim was wearing when she died, and we could match that hair to another individual, it would be evidence that those two people were together around the time of her death. Likewise, with any foreign skin cells under her fingernails that got there when she was fighting off her killer."

"And then there's fingerprinting," Patterson said. "They can lift fingerprints from almost anything these days, even if it's been, for the sake of argument, sitting inside a bag in a ditch exposed to the elements for months, almost two decades ago. Now, they might not get any prints off of the clothing in that bag, but the driver's license that was in there would be another matter."

Quaid glanced between Patterson and the detective, as if trying to gauge whether they really could pull foreign DNA and fingerprints from a body that old. Then, before either of them could react, he shoved Patterson aside, sending her staggering backwards, and bolted out the door.

SEVENTY

"SHIT." Detective Anderson made a grab for Quaid, but his fingers found only empty air as the man leapt from the trailer steps, landed on the dusty ground beyond, and ran full pelt toward the scrubland behind the building.

"Guess we have our answer," Patterson said, regaining her feet and sprinting past the detective and out the door.

Quaid was already hopping a low fence that separated the trailer park from the wilderness beyond. By the time Patterson got there, with the detective hard on her heel, he was already on the other side and fleeing toward the distant low-lying hills, weaving around the sagebrush in a frantic bid to escape.

"Where the hell does he think he's going?" Anderson gasped as he sprinted alongside Patterson. "There's nothing out here but dirt and rattlers."

"Great. I hate snakes," Patterson said. She could feel the afternoon heat sapping her strength already. Her breath was coming in short gasps.

"Don't worry about it. They'll hear us and hightail it away long before we see them."

"Really?" Patterson risked a glance sideways, then looked forward again for fear of tripping.

"Probably not. I just thought it would make you feel better."

"That's so considerate of you." Patterson would have laughed if the situation weren't so serious.

Up ahead, Quaid was still barreling along, arms pumping at his sides like some sort of Olympic sprinter. But then, just as he was pulling ahead, he came to a skidding halt, arms flailing in the air to keep his balance.

At first, Patterson didn't understand what the problem was. But as they drew closer, she saw a slightly darker band of grit and dust against the lighter landscape beyond. The sagebrush, which had been consistent until that point, was no longer visible, either. When they did reappear, the bushes were smaller. Distant.

The reason, she realized, was a sharp ridgeline cutting across their path. And there must have been a considerable drop on the other side because Quaid wasn't attempting to jump to the lower ground. Instead, he changed direction and took off parallel to the ridge.

Detective Anderson must have been waiting to see where Quaid would go next. Now he peeled off from Patterson, motioning for her to keep going straight and cut off Quaid's retreat while he took the path that would place him directly in front the fleeing man. At least, if he could get there in time.

Then Quaid helped him out. His foot caught on a gnarly root and he tumbled forward, hitting the ground and rolling in a cloud of dust. By the time he regained his feet, it was over. Patterson had positioned herself behind him on the ridgeline and closed in on him from the rear. Anderson took a more direct route, making sure he couldn't run forward or back in the direction from which he'd come.

That didn't stop Quaid from trying.

Realizing he was cut off, he did exactly that. He turned and sprinted back toward the trailer park.

Except there was nowhere to go.

As Patterson veered toward him, Anderson dug his heels in and turned, then launched himself through the air like a linebacker going after a running back. He reached his arms out, wrapped them around Quaid's waist as the smaller man tried to speed past, and both of them crashed sideways to the ground with Anderson on top.

Patterson arrived a moment later, drawing her gun, and covered Quaid while Detective Anderson climbed to his feet and dusted himself off.

Less than a minute later, Quaid was lying on his front, hands behind his back, with a pair of cuffs on his wrists.

As Anderson pulled him upright, Patterson said, "That was some kind of move you just pulled. You get this job fresh out of the NFL or something?"

The detective grinned. "I played some ball in my youth."

"Let me guess. Defense."

"What gave it away?" Anderson gave Quaid a shove, and together the three of them started back toward the trailer park.

Patterson holstered her gun, shielded her eyes against the sun's glare, and followed behind. She was sure Quaid was a killer, if only because innocent men didn't run. Now she just needed to find out if he had killed one girl or two.

SEVENTY-ONE

"HE DIDN'T KILL YOUR SISTER." Detective Anderson spoke the words standing in a starkly lit hallway outside an interview room in the Santa Fe Police Department's headquarters. It was late evening, and Brody Quaid had spent the last five hours being questioned.

Realizing he was unlikely to talk his way out of the situation, he had become surprisingly chatty, telling the two cops interviewing him—Detective Anderson and a female detective by the name of Linda Ostrom—all about what had happened sixteen years ago, and how Laura Beth Layton ended up dead.

Patterson watched every moment from a room down the hall, sitting in front of a large monitor that displayed the feed from a closed-circuit camera in the interrogation room.

Quaid had told them how he met Laura when he was doing construction work at the Rest-A-While Hostel and Campground, confirming what Heather had said earlier. She and Quaid had hit it off and were soon seeing each other.

After a while, he asked her to move in with him and she agreed.

They spent the next couple of months living in the trailer, but it was hardly domestic bliss. They started fighting. Quaid lost his construction job and was unemployed. Money was tight and the electric got cut off more than once. Then he came home with a guy he'd met at a local dive bar, told Laura that the guy would pay them a hundred bucks to sleep with her. She almost did it. Went into the bedroom with him. But once they were on the bed, she couldn't do it. Started crying. The guy left without paying.

At this point in the interview, Quaid fell silent, dropping his eyes to the floor and refusing to say anything else for almost an hour. Eventually, though, the detectives cajoled him into continuing.

What he told them next sent a shiver of disgust up Patterson's spine. After the guy departed, Quaid went into the bedroom, where Laura was pulling her clothes back on, still crying. He was incensed, told her it was their last chance to get money before the utilities were cut off yet again. That they were going to starve, and it was all her fault. All she had to do was lay there for ten minutes, let the guy finish his business, and their problem would have been solved. At least in the short term.

When she told him she didn't want to sleep with men for money, Quaid hit her. When she fought back, slapping his face, he hit her again. And he didn't stop until she sank to her knees, unable to defend herself anymore, and begged him to stop.

But he didn't.

Caught up in his rage, Quaid put his hands around her neck and started squeezing. He squeezed until she stopped fighting back. Then he pushed her away from him and left the bedroom. Went back into the cramped space that served as a living room and put the TV on.

An hour later, after his rage had subsided, and he realized she hadn't come out of the bedroom, he went back in to look.

Laura Beth Layton was dead.

Quaid claimed that he hadn't meant to kill her, just put her in her place. Teach her a lesson for defying him. He wanted to make sure that the next time he brought someone back to the trailer, she would go through with it and sleep with the guy.

Panicking, he bundled her up, still only partially dressed, and put her in the trunk of his car, then drove her out past the roadhouse, where he dumped her, and the meagre belongings she had with her, in a ditch. He wasn't thinking straight. All he wanted to do was get rid of her.

By the next morning he realized that once she was found, it wouldn't take long to identify her, and then the cops would be on his doorstep. He thought about fleeing but had no money to even put gas in his car, so he waited, sure he would end up in jail charged with murder.

Except that didn't happen.

By the time the body was discovered many months later, Laura Beth Layton was too badly decomposed to make an id. Likewise, there was nothing in the backpack found with her to provide a clue regarding her identity except an Illinois driver's license that was substantially water damaged. Only the letters of a first name were readable. An S and a T. Even the photo on the license wasn't much help, since they didn't have a face left to compare it to. Just a skull. So, Laura Beth Layton became a Jane Doe cold case, and Brody Quaid carried on with his life thinking he had gotten away with murder. At least, until Patterson came snooping around and recognized Stacy's license and her sister's favorite tee, triggering the events that led right back to him.

But as for her sister, Quaid swore that he had never even met Julie. He also claimed that he was driving an older model Ford Taurus back then, not a pickup truck.

Which was how Patterson ended up standing in a corridor outside an interrogation room and listening to Detective Anderson dash her hopes of ever finding out what happened to Julie.

"We checked with the DMV. Brody Quaid was telling the truth. He had a Ford Taurus back then. In fact, he's never even owned a pickup truck," the detective said.

"Maybe he borrowed one," Patterson replied desperately, unwilling to watch the last strands of her search for Julie evaporate. She was out of leads. Santa Fe was a dead end. Julie could have gone anywhere after she climbed into that truck with the mystery man. There was no trail left to follow. If Quaid was telling the truth and had never met Julie, then Patterson's search was over.

"You heard the man," Detective Anderson said. "Laura Beth Layton was a crime of passion. Or at least, one of anger. He didn't set out to murder her. He isn't a cold-blooded killer, just some random sleazeball who let his temper get the better of him and went too far. There was no premeditation. Even the way he dumped the body was haphazard. He should have been caught sixteen years ago, but he got lucky. Do you really believe that he went to the trouble of borrowing a truck just to drive your sister off and kill her?"

"No." Patterson knew Anderson was right. For Quaid to have been involved in her sister's disappearance, he would have needed to be a cold and calculating predator planning his killings in advance and meticulously covering his tracks. Nothing about Quaid indicated anything other than a lowlife with a short fuse. Laura Beth Layton's death, tragic as it was, had no connection to her sister. Even the items of Julie's clothing ended up in that ditch by circumstance, and not because a serial killer had mixed up the possessions of two victims. Laura and Heather had split Julie's things between them when they realized she wasn't coming back. Maybe they should have gone to the police instead, but they didn't. It was just a case of two naïve teenagers making bad decisions. Even Laura's death was because of a bad decision. She should never had moved in with Quaid. She should have seen him for what he was. Bad news. Maybe Julie should have thought the same of whoever was behind the wheel of the pickup truck. But that was the problem with teenagers. They were apt to make bad decisions. In this case, those decisions had cost the life of one girl, and probably Julie, too.

There was nothing more she could learn from Brody Quaid. Thanking the detective, Patterson left the police headquarters and returned to her van, then she drove back to the RV lot at Amy's Roadhouse, because she could think of nowhere else to go. It was gone nine. Maybe tomorrow things would be better, but right now, Patterson felt hopeless. She had let Julie down, and now her sister was destined to be lost forever.

SEVENTY-TWO

FIVE DAYS BEFORE

ANGEL AND CHERUB *had been in San Diego for a couple of weeks, and only now was she beginning to relax. Carl had surely returned to the farmhouse and found Ma dead in the kitchen, but he had no way of locating her. At least, that was what she told herself.*

For all she knew, Ma's car was still in the long-term parking at the airport in Phoenix. Or maybe Carl had gotten a call about it and took possession of the vehicle. Angel didn't know how long a car could sit in a place like that before someone took notice of it, but she suspected it was a while. Either way, he had no way of knowing where she had gone after ditching the car. She suspected that he had found his stash of money gone, providing enough funds for her and Cherub to fly somewhere, but he would also know that you needed identification to fly. Something Angel hadn't been in possession of for a very long time.

That might lead him to conclude that she had taken a Greyhound bus from the station near the airport—thankfully she didn't need ID for a bus ticket—but he would not be able to determine her destination. Busses left for all sorts of places, and she had picked randomly based on when the next one was departing, not because of any affinity for a particular place.

After arriving in San Diego, she had found a cheap hotel in a less than perfect area of town. One of those weekly places that catered to people one step away from homeless. Even better, it would accept cash, it was cheap, and they didn't ask questions, unlike the fancier hotels downtown, or an apartment complex. They didn't even bother asking for a driver's license or some other form of ID. Which was good because Angel didn't have one.

After that, she had laid low, fearing Carl would somehow find her even though she knew it was unlikely. When several days passed uneventfully, Angel started to think about her future. She couldn't stay inside the hotel room forever, a prisoner of her own paranoia. And the money she took from the farmhouse, while enough to keep her going in the short term, would not last forever. One thing was obvious. She needed a job if she and Cherub were going to survive long-term.

But it was not that simple. The matter of identification would surely come up at any job interview, even for crappy employment like flipping burgers or stocking shelves. She couldn't provide a social security number. And not because she didn't have one, but because she couldn't remember it. And she wouldn't have used it even if she could because that would mean providing her real name and trying to account for the long lapse in her employment history. Or lack of one altogether. Angel had never held a full time job. Then there were other hurdles. Like providing references, or a phone number, because she didn't even have access to a phone. Which left only one option. She would need to find the kind of employment that didn't require those things. The kind of jobs that illegal immigrants took. And there were plenty of illegal immigrants in San Diego. After all, Tijuana was right across the border, and provided a steady stream of such people who found their way into the country despite the Border Patrol's best efforts.

But there was one problem she couldn't surmount. Cherub. The kid could hardly be left alone while she went to work, and she knew nobody able and willing to watch her for that long. Her only hope on that score was the occupant of the next room. A waif-thin woman named Gloria with straggly blonde hair and a pimple strewn face who looked like she might at one time have been an addict. The two had struck up a conversation a few days before, and Gloria, who appeared to be as averse to leaving the hotel as Angel, had offered to keep an eye on Cherub if she needed to run out for provisions or take care of some other short errand. Angel wondered if the woman was running from her own demon. If so, there was opportunity. Maybe, just maybe, the offer could eventually be expanded to a longer time frame. But in the short term, Angel had decided to take Gloria up on her offer and leave Cherub with her while she left the hotel for the first time since on her own. The only other times she had left were a couple of short trips to the convenience store on the corner and she had taken Cherub. She didn't want to take her for this, though.

"Where are you going, mommy?" Cherub asked when Angel knocked on Gloria's door.

"Nowhere you need to worry about, sweetie," Angel replied. During the weeks staying at the hotel, she had started thinking about Carl, and the threats he had made to keep her in line for so many years. And not just threats to the safety of herself and Cherub, but also her family.

"You ever try to leave me . . . you ever tell them where you are . . . and I'll kill them," he would say. "I know where they live. I know all about them."

That might have been an idle threat—one of many he'd made over the years—but it was enough to ensure she remained docile. Now though, since running from dead Ma and the farmhouse, she worried that Carl might actually do it. At the same time, she *couldn't go back home and tell them about the danger they were in. He would expect that, he would be watching. Then her family would be dead for sure, and she would end up back at the farmhouse.*

But she could warn them.

And now, after two weeks of hiding, she had finally gotten up the courage to do it. Which was why, when Gloria's door opened, she left Cherub with a stranger for the first time in her life and headed for the post office two blocks away.

SEVENTY-THREE

PATTERSON WAS AWAKENED by the sound of her phone ringing. She groaned and rolled over. Weak sunlight was poking in through a gap in the blinds next to her bed. From somewhere outside the van, she heard the rumble of an engine as one of the other RVs in the lot prepared to leave.

The phone was still ringing, the sound shrill and insistent.

She fumbled around for it, her hand closing over the handset even as the last remnants of the dream she was having before it woke her dissipated like a spider's gossamer threads in the wind. A dream about Julie riding off into the unknown in a black pickup truck. A truck with a demonic figure behind the wheel who cackled and laughed even as her sister screamed for help.

"Hello?" She pulled the phone to her ear after picking up the call. Her eyes were so bleary she couldn't read the name on the screen. It wasn't even seven yet. Too early for anyone to be calling.

"Peanut?" It was her father. There was a note of stress in his voice.

Patterson sat up in the bed, suddenly wide awake. "What's happened? Is something wrong?"

"Peanut," her father repeated. "There's another one."

"Another one what?"

"A postcard."

"You found another postcard?" Patterson swung her legs off the bed and stood up. A brief flare of hope ignited within her. Maybe it would contain some clue regarding where Julie had gone after Santa Fe.

"I didn't find another postcard. It came in the mail a few minutes ago," her father said. There was a long pause. When he spoke again, his voice trembled like he was crying. "It's from Julie. Your sister is still alive."

READY FOR MORE PATTERSON BLAKE?

The conclusion of the Patterson Blake FBI Mystery Thriller series.

I Will Find Her

Julie has never been so close.

As danger closes in around her, Patterson Blake reaches the end of her journey and finally learns the fate of her sister, Julie. But forces out of her control are bent on stopping her . . . at any cost.

Pre-order now

ABOUT THE AUTHORS

A. M. Strong is the pen name of supernatural action and adventure fiction author Anthony M. Strong.

Sonya Sargent grew up in Vermont and is an avid reader when she isn't working on books of her own. They divide their time between Florida's sunny Space Coast and a tranquil island in Maine.

Find out more about the authors at
AMStrongAuthor.com